COLD HAND IN MINE

COLD HAND IN MINE

Strange Stories

by

ROBERT AICKMAN

CHARLES SCRIBNER'S SONS
NEW YORK

For

MARY GEORGE

and

ANN PYM

who lent me a beautiful apartment

without which this book

could in no wise

have taken

form

In the end it is the mystery that lasts and not the explanation.
—SACHEVERELL SITWELL
"For Want of the Golden City"

CONTENTS

1

THE SWORDS

Corazón malherido
Por cinco espadas

FEDERICO GARCIA LORCA

My first experience?

My first experience was far more of a test than anything that has ever happened to me since in that line. Not more agreeable, but certainly more testing. I have noticed several times that it is to beginners that strange things happen, and often, I think, to beginners only. When you know about a thing, there's just nothing to it. This kind of thing included—anyway, in most cases. After the first six women, say, or seven, or eight, the rest come much of a muchness.

I was a beginner all right; raw as a spring onion. What's more, I was a real mother's boy: scared stiff of life, and crass ignorant. Not that I want to sound disrespectful to my old mother. She's as good as they come, and I still hit it off better with her than with most other females.

She had a brother, my Uncle Elias. I should have said that we're all supposed to be descended from one of the big pottery families, but I don't know how true it is. My gran had little bits of pot to prove it, but it's always hard to be sure. After my dad was killed in an accident, my mother asked my Uncle Elias to take me into his business. He was a grocery salesman in a moderate way—and nothing but cheap lines. He said I must first learn the ropes by going out on the road. My mother was thoroughly upset because of my dad having died in a smash, and because she thought I was bound to be in moral danger, but there was nothing she could do about it, and on the road I went.

It was true enough about the moral danger, but I was too simple and too scared to involve myself. As far as I could, I steered clear even of the other chaps I met who were on the road with me. I was pretty certain they would be bad influences, and I was always bound to be the baby of the party anyway. I was dead rotten at selling and I was utterly lonely—not just in a manner of speaking, but truly lonely. I hated the life but Uncle Elias had promised to see me all right and I couldn't think of what else to do. I stuck it on the road for more than two years, and then I heard of my present job with the building society—read about it, actually, in the local paper—so that I was able to tell Uncle Elias what he could do with his cheap groceries.

For most of the time we stopped in small hotels—some of them weren't bad either, both the room and the grub—but in a few towns there were special lodgings known to Uncle Elias, where I and Uncle Elias's regular traveller, a sad chap called Bantock, were ordered by Uncle Elias to go. To this day I don't know exactly why. At the time I was quite sure that there was some kickback for my uncle in it, which was the obvious thing to suppose, but I've come since to wonder if the old girls who kept the lodgings might not have been my uncle's fancy women in the more or less distant past. At least once, I got as far as asking Bantock about it, but he merely said he didn't know what the answer was. There was very little that Bantock admitted to knowing about anything beyond the current prices of soapflakes and Scotch. He had been 42 years on the road for my uncle when one day he dropped dead of a thrombosis in Rochdale. Mrs Bantock, at least, had been one of my uncle's women off and on for years. That was something everyone knew.

These women who kept the lodgings certainly behaved as if what I've said was true. You've never seen or heard such dives. Noises all night so that it was impossible to sleep properly, and often half-dressed tarts beating on your door and screaming that they'd been swindled or strangled. Some of the travellers even brought in boys, which is something I have never been able to understand. You read about it and hear about it, and I've often seen it happen, as I say, but I still don't understand it. And there was I in the middle of it all, pure and unspotted. The woman who kept the place often cheeked me for it. I don't know how old Bantock got on. I never found myself in one of these places at the same time as he was there. But the funny part was that my mother thought I was extra safe in one of these special lodgings, because they were all particularly guaranteed by her brother, who made Bantock and me go to them for our own good.

Of course it was only on some of the nights on the road. But always it was when I was quite alone. I noticed that at the time when Bantock was providing me with a few introductions and openings, they were always in towns where we could stay in commercial hotels. All the same, Bantock had to go to these special places when the need arose, just as much as I did, even though he never would talk about them.

One of the towns where there was a place on Uncle Elias's list was Wolverhampton. I fetched up there for the first time, after I had been on the job for perhaps four or five months. It was by no means my first of these lodgings, but for that very reason my heart sank all the more as I set eyes on the place and was let in by the usual bleary-eyed cow in curlers and a dirty overall.

There was absolutely nothing to do. Nowhere even to sit and watch the telly. All you could think of was to go out and get drunk, or bring someone in with you from the pictures. Neither idea appealed very much to me, and I found myself just wandering about the town. It must have been late spring or early summer, because it was pleasantly warm, though not too hot, and still only dusk when I had finished my tea, which I had to find in a café, because the lodging did not even provide tea.

I was strolling about the streets of Wolverhampton, with all the girls giggling at me, or so it seemed, when I came upon a sort of small fair. Not knowing the town at all, I had drifted into the rundown area up by the old canal. The main streets were quite wide, but they had been laid out for daytime traffic to the different works and railway yards, and were now quiet and empty, except for the occasional lorry and the boys and girls playing around at some of the corners. The narrow streets running off contained lines of small houses, but a lot of the houses were empty, with windows broken or boarded up, and holes in the roof. I should have turned back, but for the sound made by the fair; not pop songs on the amplifiers, and not the pounding of the old steam organs, but more a sort of high tinkling, which somehow fitted in with the warm evening and the rosy twilight. I couldn't at first make out what the noise was, but I had nothing else to do, very much not, and I looked around the empty back streets, until I could find what was going on.

It proved to be a very small fair indeed; just half a dozen stalls,

where a few kids were throwing rings or shooting off toy rifles, two or
three covered booths, and, in the middle, one very small roundabout.
It was this that made the tinkling music. The roundabout *looked*
pretty too; with snow-queen and icing sugar effects in the centre, and
different coloured sleighs going round, each just big enough for two,
and each, as I remember, with a coloured light high up at the peak.
And in the middle was a very pretty, blonde girl dressed as some kind
of pierrette. Anyway she seemed very pretty at that time to me. Her
job was to collect the money from the people riding in the sleighs, but
the trouble was that there weren't any. Not a single one. There
weren't many people about at all, and inevitably the girl caught my
eye. I felt I looked a Charley as I had no one to ride with, and I just
turned away. I shouldn't have dared to ask the girl herself to ride with
me, and I imagine she wouldn't have been allowed to in any case. Unless, perhaps, it was her roundabout.

The fair had been set up on a plot of land which was empty simply
because the houses which had stood on it had been demolished or just
fallen down. Tall, blank factory walls towered up on two sides of it,
and the ground was so rough and uneven that it was like walking on
lumpy rocks at the seaside. There was nothing in the least permanent
about the fair. It was very much here today and gone tomorrow. I
should not have wondered if it had had no real business to have set
up there at all. I doubted very much if it had come to any kind of
agreement for the use of the land. I thought at once that the life must
be a hard one for those who owned the fair. You could see why fairs
like that have so largely died out from what things used to be in my
gran's day, who was always talking about the wonderful fairs and cir-
cuses when she was a girl. Such customers as there were, were almost
all mere kids, even though kids do have most of the money nowadays.
These kids were doing a lot of their spending at a tiny stall where
a drab-looking woman was selling ice-cream and toffee-apples. I
thought it would have been much simpler and more profitable to concentrate on that, and enter the catering business rather than trying to
provide entertainment for people who prefer to get it in their houses.
But very probably I was in a gloomy frame of mind that evening. The
fair was pretty and old-fashioned, but no one could say it cheered you
up.

The girl on the roundabout could still see me, and I was sure was
looking at me reproachfully—and probably contemptuously as well.
With that layout, she was in the middle of things and impossible to
get away from. I should just have mooched off, especially since the

people running the different stalls were all beginning to shout at me, as pretty well the only full adult in sight, when, going round, I saw a booth in more or less the farthest corner, where the high factory walls made an angle. It was a square tent of very dirty red and white striped canvas, and over the crumpled entrance flap was a rough-edged, dark painted, horizontal board, with written on it in faint gold capital letters THE SWORDS. That was all there was. Night was coming on fast, but there was no light outside the tent and none shining through from inside. You might have thought it was a store of some kind.

For some reason, I put out my hand and touched the hanging flap. I am sure I should never have dared actually to draw it aside and peep in. But a touch was enough. The flap was pulled back at once, and a young man stood there, sloping his head to one side so as to draw me in. I could see at once that some kind of show was going on. I did not really want to watch it, but felt that I should look a complete imbecile if I just ran away across the fairground, small though it was.

"Two bob," said the young man, dropping the dirty flap, and sticking out his other hand, which was equally dirty. He wore a green sweater, mended but still with holes, grimy grey trousers, and grimier sandshoes. Sheer dirt was so much my first impression of the place that I might well have fled after all, had I felt it possible. I had not noticed this kind of griminess about the rest of the fair.

Running away, however, wasn't on. There were so few people inside. Dotted about the bare, bumpy ground, with bricks and broken glass sticking out from the hard earth, were 20 or 30 wooden chairs, none of them seeming to match, most of them broken or defective in one way or another, all of them chipped and off-colour. Scattered among these hard chairs was an audience of seven. I know it was seven, because I had no difficulty in counting, and because soon it mattered. I made the eighth. All of them were in single units and all were men: this time men and not boys. I think that I was the youngest among them, by quite a long way.

And the show was something I have never seen or heard of since. Nor even read of. Not exactly.

There was a sort of low platform of dark and discoloured wood up against the back of the tent—probably right on to the factory walls outside. There was a burly chap standing on it, giving the spiel, in a pretty rough delivery. He had tight yellow curls, the colour of cheap lemonade but turning grey, and a big red face, with a splay nose, and very dark red lips. He also had small eyes and ears. The ears didn't seem exactly opposite one another, if you know what I mean. He wasn't much to look at, though I felt he was very strong, and could probably have taken on all of us in the tent single-handed and come out well on top. I couldn't decide how old he was—either then or later. (Yes, I did see him again—twice.) I should imagine he was nearing 50, and he didn't look in particularly good condition, but it seemed as though he had just been made with more thew and muscle than most people are. He was dressed like the youth at the door, except that the sweater of the chap on the platform was not green but dark blue, as if he were a seaman, or perhaps acting one. He wore the same dirty grey trousers and sandshoes as the other man. You might almost have thought the place was some kind of boxing booth.

But it wasn't. On the chap's left (and straight ahead of where I sat at the edge of things and in the back row) a girl lay sprawled out facing us in an upright canvas chair, as faded and battered as everything else in the outfit. She was dressed up like a French chorus, in a tight and shiny black thing, cut low, and black fishnet stockings, and those shiny black shoes with super high heels that many men go for in such a big way. But the total effect was not particularly sexy, all the same. The different bits of costume had all seen better days, like everything else, and the girl herself looked more sick than spicy. Under other conditions, I thought to begin with, she might have been pretty enough, but she had made herself up with green powder, actually choosing it apparently, or having it chosen for her, and her hair, done in a tight bun, like a ballet dancer's, was not so much mousy as plain colourless. On top of all this, she was lying over the chair, rather than sitting in it, just as if she was feeling faint or about to be ill. Certainly she was doing nothing at all to lead the chaps on. Not that I myself should have wanted to be led. Or so I thought at the start.

And in front of her, at the angle of the platform, was this pile of swords. They were stacked criss-cross, like cheese-straws, on top of a low stool, square and black, the sort of thing they make in Sedgeley and Wednesfield and sell as Japanese, though this specimen was quite plain and undecorated, even though more than a bit chipped. There must have been 30 or 40 swords, as the pile had four corners to it, where the hilts of the swords were set diagonally above one another. It struck me later that perhaps there was one sword for each seat, in case there was ever a full house in the tent.

If I had not seen the notice outside, I might not have realized they *were* swords, or not at first. There was nothing gleaming about them, and nothing decorative. The blades were a dull grey, and the hilts were made of some black stuff, possibly even plastic. They looked thoroughly mass-produced and industrial, and I could not think where they might have been got. They were not fencing foils but something much solider, and the demand for real swords nowadays must be mainly ceremonial, and less and less even of that. Possibly these swords came from suppliers for the stage, though I doubt that too. Anyway, they were thoroughly dingy swords, no credit at all to the regiment.

I do not know how long the show had been going on before I arrived, or if the man in the seaman's sweater had offered any explanations. Almost the first thing I heard was him saying, "And now, gentlemen, which of you is going to be the first?"

There was no movement or response of any kind. Of course there never is.

"Come *on*," said the seaman, not very politely. I felt that he was so accustomed to the backwardness of his audiences that he was no longer prepared to pander to it. He did not strike me as a man of many words, even though speaking appeared to be his job. He had a strong accent, which I took to be Black Country, though I wasn't in a position properly to be sure at that time of my life, and being myself a Londoner.

Nothing happened.

"What you think you've paid your money for?" cried the seaman, more truculent, I thought, than sarcastic.

"You tell us," said one of the men on the chairs. He happened to be the man nearest to me, though in front of me.

It was not a very clever thing to say, and the seaman turned it to account.

"You," he shouted, sticking out his thick, red forefinger at the man who had cheeked him. "Come along up. We've got to start somewhere."

The man did not move. I became frightened by my own nearness to him. I might be picked on next, and I did not even know what was expected of me, if I responded.

The situation was saved by the appearance of a volunteer. At the other side of the tent, a man stood up and said, "I'll do it."

The only light in the tent came from a single Tilley lamp hissing away (none too safely, I thought) from the crosspiece of the roof, but the volunteer looked to me exactly like everyone else.

"At last," said the seaman, still rather rudely. "Come on then."

The volunteer stumbled across the rough ground, stepped on to my side of the small platform, and stood right in front of the girl. The girl seemed to make no movement. Her head was thrown so far back that, as she was some distance in front of me, I could not see her eyes at all clearly. I could not even be certain whether they were open or closed.

"Pick up a sword," said the seaman sharply.

The volunteer did so, in a rather gingerly way. It looked like the first time he had ever had his hand on such a thing, and, of course, I never had either. The volunteer stood there with the sword in his hand, looking an utter fool. His skin looked grey by the light of the Tilley, he was very thin, and his hair was failing badly.

The seaman seemed to let him stand there for quite a while, as if out of devilry, or perhaps resentment at the way he had to make a living. To me the atmosphere in the dirty tent seemed full of tension and unpleasantness, but the other men in the audience were still lying about on their hard chairs looking merely bored.

After quite a while, the seaman, who had been facing the audience, and speaking to the volunteer out of the corner of his mouth, half-turned on his heel, and still not looking right at the volunteer, snapped out: "What are you waiting for? There are others to come, though we could do with more."

At this, another member of the audience began to whistle "Why are we waiting?" I felt he was getting at the seaman or showman, or whatever he should be called, rather than at the volunteer.

"Go on," shouted the seaman, almost in the tone of a drill instructor. "Stick it in."

And then it happened, this extraordinary thing.

The volunteer seemed to me to tremble for a moment, and then plunged the sword right into the girl on the chair. As he was standing between me and her, I could not see where the sword entered, but I could see that the man seemed to press it right in, because almost the whole length of it seemed to disappear. What I could have no doubt about at all was the noise the sword made. A curious thing was that we are so used to at least the idea of people being stuck through with swords, that, even though, naturally, I had never before seen anything of the kind, I had no doubt at all of what the man had done. The noise of the sword tearing through the flesh was only what I should have expected. But it was quite distinct even above the hissing of the Tilley. And quite long drawn out too. And horrible.

I could sense the other men in the audience gathering themselves together on the instant and suddenly coming to life. I could still see little of what precisely had happened.

"Pull it out," said the seaman, quite casually, but as if speaking to a moron. He was still only half-turned towards the volunteer, and still looking straight in front of him. He was not looking at anything; just holding himself in control while getting through a familiar routine.

The volunteer pulled out the sword. I could again hear that unmistakable sound.

The volunteer still stood facing the girl, but with the tip of the sword resting on the platform. I could see no blood. Of course I thought I had made some complete misinterpretation, been fooled like a kid. Obviously it was some kind of conjuring.

"Kiss her if you want to," said the seaman. "It's included in what you've paid."

And the man did, even though I could only see his back. With the sword drooping from his hand, he leaned forwards and downwards. I think it was a slow and loving kiss, not a smacking and public kiss, because this time I could hear nothing.

The seaman gave the volunteer all the time in the world for it, and, for some odd reason, there was no whistling or catcalling from the rest of us; but in the end, the volunteer slowly straightened up.

"Please put back the sword," said the seaman, sarcastically polite.

The volunteer carefully returned it to the heap, going to some trouble to make it lie as before.

I could now see the girl. She was sitting up. Her hands were pressed together against her left side, where, presumably, the sword had gone in. But there was still no sign of blood, though it was hard to be certain in the bad light. And the strangest thing was that she now looked not only happy, with her eyes very wide open and a little smile on her lips, but, in spite of that green powder, beautiful too, which I was far from having thought in the first place.

The volunteer passed between the girl and me in order to get back to his seat. Even though the tent was almost empty, he returned to his original place religiously. I got a slightly better look at him. He still looked just like everyone else.

"Next," said the seaman, again like a sergeant numbering off.

This time there was no hanging back. Three men rose to their feet immediately, and the seaman had to make a choice.

"You then," he said, jabbing out his thick finger towards the centre of the tent.

The man picked was elderly, bald, plump, respectable-looking, and wearing a dark suit. He might have been a retired railway foreman or electricity inspector. He had a slight limp, probably taken in the way of his work.

The course of events was very much the same, but the second comer was readier and in less need of prompting, including about the kiss. His kiss was as slow and quiet as the first man's had been: paternal perhaps. When the elderly man stepped away, I saw that the girl was holding her two hands against the centre of her stomach. It made me squirm to look.

And then came the third man. When he went back to his seat, the girl's hands were to her throat.

The fourth man, on the face of it a rougher type, with a cloth cap (which, while on the platform, he never took off) and a sports jacket as filthy and worn out as the tent, apparently drove the sword into the girl's left thigh, straight through the fishnet stocking. When he stepped off the platform, she was clasping her leg, but looking so pleased that you'd have thought a great favour had been done her. And still I could see no blood.

I did not really know whether or not I wanted to see more of the details. Raw as I was, it would have been difficult for me to decide.

I didn't have to decide, because I dared not shift in any case to a seat with a better view. I considered that a move like that would quite probably result in my being the next man the seaman called up. And one thing I knew for certain was that whatever exactly was being done, I was not going to be one who did it. Whether it was conjuring, or something different that I knew nothing about, I was not going to get involved.

And, of course, if I stayed, my turn must be coming close in any case.

Still, the fifth man called was not me. He was a tall, lanky, perfectly black Negro. I had not especially spotted him as such before. He appeared to drive the sword in with all the force you might expect of a black man, even though he was so slight, then threw it on the floor of the platform with a clatter, which no one else had done before him, and actually drew the girl to her feet when kissing her. When he stepped back, his foot struck the sword. He paused for a second, gazing at the girl, then carefully put the sword back on the heap.

The girl was still standing, and it passed across my mind that the Negro might try to kiss her again. But he didn't. He went quietly back to his place. Behind the scenes of it all, there appeared to be some rules, which all the other men knew about. They behaved almost as though they came quite often to the show, if a show was what it was.

Sinking down once more into her dilapidated canvas chair, the girl kept her eyes fixed on mine. I could not even tell what colour her eyes were, but the fact of the matter is that they turned my heart right over. I was so simple and inexperienced that nothing like that had ever happened to me before in my whole life. The incredible green powder made no difference. Nothing that had just been happening made any difference. I wanted that girl more than I had ever wanted anything. And I don't mean I just wanted her body. That comes later in life. I wanted to love her and tousle her and all the other, better things we want before the time comes when we know that however much we want them, we're not going to get them.

But, in justice to myself, I must say that I did not want to take my place in a queue for her.

That was about the last thing I wanted. And it was one chance in three that I should be next to be called. I drew a deep breath and managed to scuttle out. I can't pretend it was difficult. I was sitting near the back of the tent, as I've said, and no one tried to stop me. The lad at the entrance merely gaped at me like a fish. No doubt he was quite accustomed to the occasional patron leaving early. I fancied that the bruiser on the platform was in the act of turning to me at the very instant I got up, but I knew it was probably imagination on my part. I don't think he spoke, nor did any of the other men react. Most men at shows of that kind prefer to behave as if they were invisible. I did get mixed up in the greasy tent flap, and the lad in the green sweater did nothing to help, but that was all. I streaked across the fairground, still almost deserted, and still with the roundabout tinkling away, all for nothing, but very prettily. I tore back to my nasty bedroom, and locked myself in.

On and off, there was the usual fuss and schemozzle in the house, and right through the hours of darkness. I know, because I couldn't sleep. I couldn't have slept that night if I'd been lying between damask sheets in the Hilton Hotel. The girl on the platform had got deep under my skin, green face and all: the girl and the show too, of course. I think I can truly say that what I experienced that night altered my whole angle on life, and it had nothing to do with the rows that broke out in the other bedrooms, or the cackling and bashing on the staircase, or the constant pulling the plug, which must have been the noisiest in the Midlands, especially as it took six or seven pulls or more for each flush. That night I really grasped the fact that most of the time we have no notion of what we really want, or we lose sight of it. And the even more important fact that what we really want just doesn't fit in with life as a whole, or very seldom. Most folk learn slowly, and never altogether learn at all. I seemed to learn all at once.

Or perhaps not quite, because there was very much more to come.

The next morning I had calls to make, but well before the time arrived for the first of them I had sneaked back to that tiny, battered, little fairground. I even skipped breakfast, but breakfast in Uncle Elias's special lodging was very poor anyway, though a surprising number turned up for it each day. You wondered where so many had been hiding away all night. I don't know what I expected to find at the fair. Perhaps I wasn't sure I should find the fair there at all.

But I did. In full daylight, it looked smaller, sadder, and more utterly hopeless for making a living even than the night before. The weather was absolutely beautiful, and so many of the houses in the immediate area were empty, to say nothing of the factories, that there were very few people around. The fair itself was completely empty, which took me by surprise. I had expected some sort of gypsy scene and had failed to realize that there was nowhere on the lot for even gypsies to sleep. The people who worked the fair must have gone to bed at home, like the rest of the world. The plot of land was surrounded by a wire-mesh fence, put up by the owner to keep out tramps and meth-drinkers, but by now the fence wasn't up to much, as you would expect, and, after looking round, I had no difficulty in scrambling through a hole in it, which the lads of the village had carved out for fun and from having nothing better to do. I walked over to the dingy booth in the far corner, and tried to lift the flap.

It proved to have been tied up at several places and apparently from the inside. I could not see how the person doing the tying had got out of the tent when he had finished, but that was the sort of trick of the trade you would expect of fairground folk. I found it impossible to see inside the tent at all without using my pocketknife, which I should have hesitated to do at the best of times, but while I was fiddling around, I heard a voice just behind me.

"What's up with you?"

There was a very small, old man standing at my back. I had certainly not heard him come up, even though the ground was so rough and lumpy. He was hardly more than a dwarf, he was as brown as a horse-chestnut or very nearly, and there was not a hair on his head.

"I wondered what was inside," I said feebly.

"A great big python, two miles long, that don't even pay its rent," said the little man.

"How's that?" I asked. "Hasn't it a following?"

"Old-fashioned," said the little man. "Old-fashioned and out of date. Doesn't appeal to the women. The women don't like the big snakes. But the women have the money these times, *and* the power and the glory too." He changed his tone. "You're trespassing."

"Sorry, old man," I said. "I couldn't hold myself back on a lovely morning like this."

"I'm the watchman," said the little man. "I used to have snakes too. Little ones, dozens and dozens of them. All over me, and every one more poisonous than the next. Eyes darting, tongues flicking, scales shimmering: then *in*, right home, then back, then in again, then back. Still in the end, it wasn't a go. There's a time and a span for all things. But I like to keep around. So now I'm the watchman. While the job lasts. While anything lasts. Move on then. Move on."

I hesitated.

"This big snake you talk of," I began, "this python——"

But he interrupted quite shrilly.

"There's no more to be said. Not to the likes of you, any road. Off the ground you go, and sharply. Or I'll call the police constable. He and I work hand in glove. I take care to keep it that way. You may not have heard that trespass is a breach of the peace. Stay here and you'll be sorry for the rest of your life."

The little man was actually squaring up to me, even thought the top of his brown skull (not shiny, by the way, but matt and patchy, as if he had some trouble with it) rose hardly above my waist. Clearly, he was daft.

As I had every kind of reason for going, I went. I did not even ask the little man about the times of performances that evening, or if there were any. Inside myself, I had no idea whether I should be back, even if there were performances, as there probably were.

I set about my calls. I'd had no sleep, and, since last night's tea, no food, and my head was spinning like a top, but I won't say I did my business any worse than usual. I probably felt at the time that I did, but now I doubt it. Private troubles, I have since noticed, make very little difference to the way most of us meet the outside world, and as for food and sleep, they don't matter at all until weeks and months have passed.

I pushed on then, more or less in the customary way (though, in my case, the customary way, at that job, wasn't up to very much at the best of times), and all the while mulling over and around what had happened to me, until the time came for dinner. I had planned to eat in the café where I had eaten the night before, but I found myself in a different part of the city, which, of course, I didn't know at all, and, feeling rather faint and queer, fell instead into the first place there was.

And there, in the middle of the floor, believe it or not, sitting at a Formica-topped table, was my girl with the green powder, and, beside her, the seaman or showman, looking more than ever like a run-down boxer.

I had not seriously expected ever to set eyes on the girl again. It was not, I thought, the kind of thing that happens. At the very most I might have gone again to the queer show, but I don't think I really would have done, when I came to think out what it involved.

The girl had wiped off the green powder, and was wearing a black coat and skirt and a white blouse, a costume you might perhaps have thought rather too old for her, and the same fishnet stockings. The man was dressed exactly as he had been the night before, except that he wore heavy boots instead of dirty sandshoes, heavy and mud-caked, as if he had been walking through fields.

Although it was the dinner-hour, the place was almost empty, with a dozen unoccupied tables, and these two sitting in the centre. I must almost have passed out.

But I wasn't really given time. The man in the jersey recognized me at once. He stood up and beckoned to me with his thick arm. "Come and join us." The girl had stood up too.

There was nothing else I could do but what he said.

The man actually drew back a chair for me (they were all painted in different, bright colours, and had been reseated in new leatherette), and even the girl waited until I had sat down before sitting down her-self.

"Sorry you missed the end of last night's show," said the man.

"I had to get back to my lodgings, I suddenly realized." I made it up quite swiftly. "I'm new to the town," I added.

"It can be difficult when you're new," said the man. "What'll you have?"

He spoke as if we were on licensed premises, but it was pretty obvious we weren't, and I hesitated.

"Tea or coffee?"

"Tea, please," I said.

"Another tea, Berth," called out the man. I saw that the two of them were both drinking coffee, but I didn't like the look of it, any more than I usually do.

"I'd like something to eat as well," I said, when the waitress brought the tea. "Thank you very much," I said to the man.

"Sandwiches: York ham, salt beef, or luncheon meat. Pies. Sausage rolls," said the waitress. She had a very bad stye on her left lower eyelid.

"I'll have a pie," I said, and, in due course, she brought one, with some salad on the plate, and the bottle of sauce. I really required something hot, but there it was.

"Come again tonight," said the man.

"I'm not sure I'll be able to."

I was finding it difficult even to drink my tea properly, as my hands were shaking so badly, and I couldn't think how I should cope with a cold pie.

"Come on the house, if you like. As you missed your turn last night."

The girl, who had so far left the talking to the other, smiled at me very sweetly and personally, as if there was something quite particular between us. Her white blouse was open very low, so that I saw more than I really should, even though things are quite different today from what they once were. Even without the green powder, she was a very pale girl, and her body looked as if it might be even whiter than her face, almost as white as her blouse. Also I could now see the colour of her eyes. They were green. Somehow I had known it all along.

"In any case," went on the man, "it won't make much difference with business like it is now."

The girl glanced at him as if she were surprised at his letting out something private, then looked at me again and said, "Do come." She said it in the friendliest, meltingest way, as if she really cared. What's more, she seemed to have some kind of foreign accent, which made her even more fascinating, if that were possible. She took a small sip of coffee.

"It's only that I might have another engagement that I couldn't get out of. I don't know right now."

"We mustn't make you break another engagement," said the girl, in her foreign accent, but sounding as if she meant just the opposite.

I managed a bit more candour. "I might get out of my engagement," I said, "but the truth is, if you don't mind my saying so, that I didn't greatly care for some of the others in the audience last night."

"I don't blame you," said the man very dryly, and rather to my relief, as you can imagine. "What would you say to a private show? A show just for you?" He spoke quite quietly, suggesting it as if it had been the most normal thing in the world, or as if I had been Charles Clore.

I was so taken by surprise that I blurted out, "What! Just me in the tent?"

"In your own home, I meant," said the man, still absolutely casually, and taking a noisy pull on his pink earthenware cup. As the man spoke, the girl shot a quick, devastating glance. It was exactly as if she softened everything inside me to water. And, absurdly enough, it was then that my silly pie arrived, with the bit of green salad, and the sauce. I had been a fool to ask for anything at all to eat, however much I might have needed it in theory.

"With or without the swords," continued the man, lighting a cheap-looking cigarette. "Madonna has been trained to do anything else you want. Anything you may happen to think of." The girl was gazing into her teacup.

I dared to speak directly to her. "Is your name really Madonna? It's nice."

"No," she said, speaking rather low. "Not really. It's my working name." She turned her head for a moment, and again our eyes met.

"There's no harm in it. We're not Catholics," said the man, "though Madonna was once."

"I like it," I said. I was wondering what to do about the pie. I could not possibly eat.

"Of course a private show would cost a bit more than two bob," said the man. "But it would be all to yourself, and, under those conditions, Madonna will do anything you feel like." I noticed that he was speaking just as he had spoken in the tent: looking not at me or at anyone else, but straight ahead into the distance, and as if he were repeating words he had used again and again and was fed up with but compelled to make use of.

I was about to tell him I had no money, which was more or less the case, but didn't.

"When could it be?" I said.

"Tonight, if you like," said the man. "Immediately after the regular show, and that won't be very late, as we don't do a ten or eleven o'clock house at a date like this. Madonna could be with you at a quarter to ten, easy. And she wouldn't necessarily have to hurry away either, not when there's no late-night matinée. There'd be time for her to do a lot of her novelties if you'd care to see them. Items from her repertoire, as we call them. Got a good place for it, by the way? Madonna doesn't need much. Just a room with a lock on the door to keep out the non-paying patrons, and somewhere to wash her hands."

"Yes," I said. "As a matter of fact, the place I'm stopping at should be quite suitable, though I wish it was brighter, and a bit quieter too."

Madonna flashed another of her indescribably sweet glances at me. "I shan't mind," she said softly.

I wrote down the address on the corner of a paper I had found on my seat, and tore it off.

"Shall we call it ten pounds?" said the man, turning to look at me with his small eyes. "I usually ask twenty and sometimes fifty, but this is Wolverhampton not the Costa Brava, and you belong to the refined type."

"What makes you say that?" I asked; mainly in order to gain time for thinking what I could do about the money.

"I could tell by where you sat last night. At pretty well every show there's someone who picks that seat. It's a special seat for the refined types. I've learnt better now than to call them up, because it's not what they want. They're too refined to be called up, and I respect them for it. They often leave before the end, as you did. But I'm glad to have them in at any time. They raise the standard. Besides, they're the ones who are often interested in a private show, as you are, and willing to pay for it. I have to watch the business of the thing too."

"I haven't got ten pounds ready in spare cash," I said, "but I expect I can find it, even if I have to fiddle it."

"It's what you often have to do in this world," said the man. "Leastways if you like nice things."

"You've still got most of the day," said the girl, smiling encouragingly.

"Have another cup of tea?" said the man.

"No thanks very much."

"Sure?"

"Sure."

"Then we must move. We've an afternoon show, though it'll probably be only for a few kids. I'll tell Madonna to save herself as much as she can until the private affair tonight."

As they were going through the door on to the street, the girl looked back to throw me a glance over her shoulder, warm and secret. But when she was moving about, her clothes looked much too big for her, the skirt too long, the jacket and blouse too loose and droopy, as if they were not really her clothes at all. On top of everything else, I felt sorry for her. Whatever the explanation of last night, her life could not be an easy one.

They'd both been too polite to mention my pie. I stuffed it into my attaché case, of course without the salad, paid for it, and dragged off to my next call, which proved to be right across the town once more.

I didn't have to do anything dishonest to get the money.

It was hardly to be expected that my mind would be much on my work that afternoon, but I stuck to it as best I could, feeling that my life was getting into deep waters and that I had better keep land of some kind within sight, while it was still possible. It was as well that I did continue on my proper round of calls, because at one of the shops my immediate problem was solved for me without my having to lift a finger. The owner of the shop was a nice old gentleman with white hair, named Mr Edis, who seemed to take to me immediately I went through the door. He said at one point that I made a change from old Bantock with his attacks of asthma (I don't think I've so far mentioned Bantock's asthma, but I knew all about it), and that I seemed a good lad, with a light in my eyes. Those were his words, and I'm not likely to make a mistake about them just yet, seeing what he went on to. He asked me if I had anything to do that evening. Rather pleased with myself, because it was not an answer I should have been able to make often before, not if I had been speaking the truth, I told him Yes, I had a date with a girl.

"Do you mean with a Wolverhampton girl?" asked Mr Edis.

"Yes. I've only met her since I've been in the town." I shouldn't have admitted that to most people, but there was something about Mr Edis that led me on and made me want to justify his good opinion of me.

"What's she like?" asked Mr Edis, half closing his eyes, so that I could see the red all round the edges of them.

"Gorgeous." It was the sort of thing people said, and my real feelings couldn't possibly have been put into words.

"Got enough small change to treat her properly?"

I had to think quickly, being taken so much by surprise, but Mr Edis went on before I had time to speak.

"So that you can cuddle her as you want?"

I could see that he was getting more and more excited.

"Well, Mr Edis," I said, "as a matter of fact, not quite enough. I'm still a beginner in my job, as you know."

I thought I might get a pound out of him, and quite likely only as a loan, the Midlands people being what we all know they are.

But on the instant he produced a whole fiver. He flapped it in front of my nose like a kipper.

"It's yours on one condition."

"I'll fit in if I can, Mr Edis."

"Come back tomorrow morning after my wife's gone out—she works as a traffic warden, and can't hardly get enough of it—come back here and tell me all about what happens."

I didn't care for the idea at all, but I supposed that I could make up some lies, or even break my word and not go back at all, and I didn't seem to have much alternative.

"Why, of course, Mr Edis. Nothing to it."

He handed over the fiver at once.

"Good boy," he said. "Get what you're paying for out of her, and think of me while you're doing it, though I don't expect you will."

As for the other five pounds, I could probably manage to wangle it out of what I had, by scraping a bit over the next week or two, and cooking the cash book a trifle if necessary, as we all do. Anyway, and being the age I was, I hated all this talk about money. I hated the talk about it much more than I hated the job of having to find it. I did not see Madonna in that sort of way at all, and I should have despised myself if I had. Nor, to judge by how she spoke, did it seem the way in which she saw me. I could not really think of any other way in which she would be likely to see me, but I settled that one by trying not to think about the question at all.

My Uncle Elias's special lodging in Wolverhampton was not the kind of place where visitors just rang the bell and waited to be admitted by the footman. You had to know the form a bit, if you were to get in at all, not being a resident, and still more if, once inside, you were going to find the exact person you were looking for. At about half past nine I thought it best to start lounging around in the street outside. Not right on top of the house door, because that might have led to misunderstanding and trouble of some kind, but moving up and down the street, keeping both eyes open and an ear cocked for the patter of tiny feet on the pavement. It was almost dark, of course, but not quite. There weren't many people about but that was partly because it was raining gently, as it does in the Midlands: a soft, slow rain that you can hardly see, but extra wetting, or so it always feels. I am quite sure I should have taken up my position earlier if it hadn't been for the rain. Needless to say, I was like a cat on hot bricks. I had managed to get the pie inside me between calls during the afternoon. I struggled through it on a bench just as the rain was beginning. And at about half past six I'd had a cup of tea and some beans in the café I'd been to the night before. I didn't want any of it. I just felt that I ought to eat something in view of what lay ahead of me. Though, of course,

I had precious little idea of what that was. When it's truly your first experience, you haven't; no matter how much you've been told and managed to pick up. I'd have been in a bad state if it had been any woman that was supposed to be coming, let alone my lovely Madonna.

And there she was, on the dot, or even a little early. She was dressed in the same clothes as she had worn that morning. Too big for her and too old for her; and she had no umbrella and no raincoat and no hat.

"You'll be wet," I said.

She didn't speak, but her eyes looked, I fancied, as if she were glad to see me. If she had set out in that green powder of hers, it had all washed off.

I thought she might be carrying something, but she wasn't, not even a handbag.

"Come in," I said.

Those staying in the house were lent a key (with a deposit to pay on it), and, thank God, we got through the hall and up the stairs without meeting anyone, or hearing anything out of the way, even though my room was at the top of the building.

She sat down on my bed and looked at the door. After what had been said, I knew what to do and turned the key. It came quite naturally. It was the sort of place where you turned the key as a matter of course. I took off my raincoat and let it lie in a corner. I had not turned on the light. I was not proud of my room.

"You must be soaked through," I said. The distance from the fairground was not all that great, but the rain was of the specially wetting kind, as I've remarked.

She got up and took off her outsize black jacket. She stood there holding it until I took it and hung it on the door. I can't say it actually dripped, but it was saturated, and I could see a wet patch on the eiderdown where she had been sitting. She had still not spoken a word. I had to admit that there seemed to have been no call for her to do so.

The rain had soaked through to her white blouse. Even with almost no light in the room I could see that. The shoulders were sodden and clinging to her, one more than the other. Without the jacket, the blouse looked quainter than ever. Not only was it loose and shapeless, but it had sleeves that were so long as to droop down beyond her hands when her jacket was off. In my mind I had a glimpse of the sort of woman the blouse was made for, big and stout, not my type at all.

"Better take that off too," I said, though I don't now know how I got the words out. I imagine that instinct looks after you even the first time, provided it is given a chance. Madonna did give me a chance, or I felt that she did. Life was sweeter for a minute or two than I had ever thought possible.

Without a word, she took off her blouse and I hung it over the back of the single bedroom chair.

I had seen in the café that under it she had been wearing something black, but I had not realized until now that it was the same tight, shiny sheath that she wore in the show, and that made her look so French.

She took off her wet skirt. The best I could do was to drape it over the seat of the chair. And there she was, super high heels and all. She looked ready to go on stage right away, but that I found rather disappointing.

She stood waiting, as if for me to tell her what to do.

I could see that the black sheath was soaking wet, anyway in patches, but this time I didn't dare to suggest that she take it off.

At last Madonna opened her mouth. "What would you like me to begin with?"

Her voice was so beautiful, and the question she asked so tempting, that something got hold of me and, before I could stop myself, I had put my arms round her. I had never done anything like it before in my whole life, whatever I might have felt.

She made no movement, so that I supposed at once I had done the wrong thing. After all, it was scarcely surprising, considering how inexperienced I was.

But I thought too that something else was wrong. As I say, I wasn't exactly accustomed to the feel of a half-naked woman, and I myself was still more or less fully dressed, but all the same I thought at once that the feel of her was disappointing. It came as a bit of a shock. Quite a bad one, in fact. As often, when facts replace fancies. Suddenly it had all become rather like a nightmare.

I stepped back.

"I'm sorry," I said.

She smiled in her same sweet way. "I don't mind," she said.

It was nice of her, but I no longer felt quite the same about her. You know how, at the best, a tiny thing can make all the difference in your feeling about a woman, and I was far from sure that this thing was tiny at all. What I was wondering was whether I wasn't proving not to be properly equipped for life. I had been called backward before now, and perhaps here was the reason.

Then I realized that it might all be something to do with the act she put on, the swords. She might be some kind of freak, or possibly the man in the blue jersey did something funny to her, hypnotized her, in some way.

"Tell me what you'd like," she said, looking down at the scruffy bit of rug on the floor.

I was a fool, I thought, and merely showing my ignorance.

"Take that thing off," I replied. "It's wet. Get into bed. You'll be warmer there."

I began taking off my own clothes.

She did what I said, squirmed out of the black sheath, took her feet gently out of the sexy shoes, rolled off her long stockings. Before me for a moment was my first woman, even though I could hardly see her. I was still unable to face the idea of love by that single, dim electric light, which only made the draggled room look more draggled.

Obediently, Madonna climbed into my bed and I joined her there as quickly as I could.

Obediently, she did everything I asked, just as the man in the blue sweater had promised. To me she still felt queer and disappointing—flabby might almost be the word—and certainly quite different from what I had always fancied a woman's body would feel like if ever I found myself close enough to it. But she gave me my first experience none the less, the thing we're concerned with now. I will say one thing for her: from first to last she never spoke an unnecessary word. It's not always like that, of course.

But everything had gone wrong. For example, we had not even started by kissing. I had been cram full of romantic ideas about Madonna, but I felt that she was not being much help in that direction, for all her sweet and beautiful smiles and her soft voice and the gentle things she said. She was making herself almost too available, and not bringing out the best in me. It was as if I had simply acquired new information, however important, but without any exertion of my feelings. You often feel like that, of course, about one thing or another, but it seemed dreadful to feel it about this particular thing, especially when I had felt so differently about it only a little while before.

"Come on," I said to her. "Wake up."

It wasn't fair, but I was bitterly disappointed, and all the more because I couldn't properly make out why. I only felt that everything in my life might be at stake.

She moaned a little.

I heaved up from on top of her in the bed and threw back the bed-clothes behind me. She lay there flat in front of me, all grey—anyway in the dim twilight. Even her hair was colourless, in fact pretty well invisible.

I did what I suppose was rather a wretched thing. I caught hold of her left arm by putting both my hands round her wrist, and tried to lug her up towards me, so that I could feel her thrown against me, and could cover her neck and front with kisses, if only she would make me want to. I suppose I might under any circumstances have hurt her by dragging at her like that, and that I shouldn't have done it. Still no one could have said it was very terrible. It was quite a usual sort of thing to do, I should say.

But what actually happened was very terrible indeed. So simple and so terrible that people won't always believe me. I gave this great, bad-tempered, disappointed pull at Madonna. She came up towards me and then fell back again with a sort of wail. I was still holding on to her hand and wrist with my two hands, and it took me quite some time to realize what had happened. What had happened was that I had pulled her left hand and wrist right off.

On the instant, she twisted out of the bed and began to wriggle back into her clothes. I was aware that even in the almost nonexistent light she was somehow managing to move very swiftly. I had a fright-ful sensation of her beating round in my room with only one hand, and wondered in terror how she could possibly manage. All the time, she was weeping to herself, or wailing might be the word. The noise she made was very soft, so soft that but for what was happening, I might have thought it was inside my own head.

I got my feet on to the floor with the notion of turning on the light. The only switch was of course by the door. I had the idea that with some light on the scene, there might be certain explanations. But I found that I couldn't get to the switch. In the first place, I couldn't bear the thought of touching Madonna, even accidentally. In the sec-ond place, I discovered that my legs would go no farther. I was too ut-terly scared to move at all. Scared, repelled, and that mixed-up some-thing else connected with disappointed sex for which there is no exact word.

So I just sat there, on the edge of the bed, while Madonna got back into her things, crying all the while, in that awful, heart-breaking way which I shall never forget. Not that it went on for long. As I've said,

Madonna was amazingly quick. I couldn't think of anything to say or do. Especially with so little time for it.

When she had put on her clothes, she made a single appallingly significant snatch in my direction, caught something up, almost as if she, at least, could see in the dark. Then she had unlocked the door and bolted.

She had left the door flapping open off the dark landing (we had time-switches, of course), and I could hear her pat-patting down the staircase, and so easily and quietly through the front door that you might have thought she lived in the place. It was still a little too early for the regulars to be much in evidence.

What I felt now was physically sick. But I had the use of my legs once more. I got off the bed, shut and locked the door, and turned on the light.

There was nothing in particular to be seen. Nothing but my own clothes lying about, my sodden-looking raincoat in the corner, and the upheaved bed. The bed looked as if some huge monster had risen through it, but nowhere in the room was there blood. It was all just like the swords.

As I thought about it, and about what I had done, I suddenly vomited. They were not rooms with hot and cold running water, and I half-filled the old-fashioned washbowl, with its faded flowers at the bottom and big thumbnail chippings round the rim, before I had finished.

I lay down on the crumpled bed, too fagged to empty the basin, to put out the light, even to draw something over me, though I was still naked and the night getting colder.

I heard the usual sounds beginning on the stairs and in the other rooms. Then, there was an unexpected, businesslike rapping at my own door.

It was not the sort of house where it was much use first asking who was there. I got to my feet again, this time frozen stiff, and, not having a dressing-gown with me, put on my wet raincoat, as I had to put on something and get the door open, or there would be more knocking, and then complaints, which could be most unpleasant.

It was the chap in the blue sweater; the seaman or showman or whatever he was. Somehow I had known it might be.

I can't have looked up to much, as I stood there shaking, in only the wet raincoat, especially as all the time you could hear people yelling and beating it up generally in the other rooms. And of course I hadn't the slightest idea what line the chap might choose to take.

I needn't have worried. Not at least about that.

"Show pass off all right?" was all he asked; and looking straight into the distance as if he were on his platform, not at anyone or anything in particular, but sounding quite friendly notwithstanding, provided everyone responded in the right kind of way.

"I think so," I replied.

I daresay I didn't appear very cordial, but he seemed not to mind much.

"In that case, could I have the fee? I'm sorry to disturb your beauty sleep, but we're moving on early."

I had not known in what way I should be expected to pay, so had carefully got the ten pounds into a pile, Mr Edis's fiver and five single pounds of my own, and put it into the corner of a drawer, before I had gone out into the rain to meet Madonna.

I gave it to him.

"Thanks," he said, counting it, and putting it into his trousers pocket. I noticed that even his trousers seemed to be seaman's trousers, now that I could see them close to, with him standing just in front of me. "Everything all right then?"

"I think so," I said again. I was taking care not to commit myself too far in any direction I could think of.

I saw that now he was looking at me, his small eyes deep-sunk.

At that exact moment, there was a wild shriek from one of the floors below. It was about the loudest human cry I had heard until then, even in one of those lodgings.

But the man took no notice.

"All right then," he said.

For some reason, he hesitated a moment, then he held out his hand. I took it. He was very strong, but there was nothing else remarkable about his hand.

"We'll meet again," he said. "Don't worry."

Then he turned away and pressed the black time-switch for the staircase light. I did not stop to watch him go. I was sick and freezing.

And so far, despite what he said, our paths have not recrossed.

2

THE REAL ROAD TO THE CHURCH

BUT WAS THAT the true meaning? *Le vrai chemin de l'église?* The overtones of symbolism and conversion seemed clear enough, but Rosa
still rather wondered whether the significance of the phrase was not
wholly topographical. One could so easily read far too much into the
traditional usages of simple people.

Probably all that was meant was the simplest and directest route
(and perhaps the ancientest); the alternative to the new (but no
longer very new) and metalled main road that wound along the bor-
ders of properties, instead of creeping through them. Though by now,
Rosa reflected, all roads had begun to barge through once again, and
no longer went courteously around and about. Very much so: *that,* she
thought, was symbolic, if anything was. Of everything: of the changed
world outside and also of her own questionable place in it. But when
one began to think in that way, all things become symbolic of all other
things. Not that that was in itself untrue: though it was only *one*
truth, of course. And when one *admitted* that there were many truths
existing concurrently, upon which of them could one possibly be
thought to stand firm—let alone, to rest? Almost certainly, the simple
people who used that phrase, gave no thought at all to its meaning. It
was a convention only, as are the left hand side and the right. Conven-
tions are, indeed, all that shield us from the shivering void, though
often they do so but poorly and desperately.

As a matter of fact, Rosa was shivering now as she stood in the living-room of La Wide (if living-room it could yet be called) and
thought about the tone in which Mrs Du Quesne, her newly found
home help with the aristocratic name, had spoken. Nor was it only
Mrs Du Quesne's name that seemed to echo breeding. Rosa had read

many books during those years she spent abroad; read them mainly, as it had since seemed to her, while waiting for men to keep some appointment or other; and Mrs Du Quesne had brought back Tess of the D'Urbervilles to her, though Mrs Du Quesne was far, far older than Tess had been permitted to be.

Rosa's convent French, though presumably reinforced during the year or two she had lived in Paris (but always with men who were English), was of little avail in understanding the island tongue: not so much a patois, she gathered, as a hybrid, a speech half-Latin and half-Norse. At one period, Rosa had lived in Stockholm with an actual Swede (far and away the worst year of her life—or more than a year: it had all ended in her breakdown), but the language of Sweden (and never would she forget the pitch of it) seemed to have nothing whatever in common with the language of Mrs Du Quesne and her friends. If Mrs Du Quesne had not mixed in equal parts of very clear English, Rosa could hardly have employed her. There were not many left who spoke the local tongue at all; but that was a factor which strongly inclined Rosa to employ, and thus, perhaps, aid, those who did. Any resulting difficulty or sacrifice she fervently justified to herself.

Rosa was fairly well aware that it was the more oracular remarks which Mrs Du Quesne and her friends left in their natal hybrid, nor could by any reasonable persuasion be induced to anglicize. She suspected, indeed, that just now she herself had gone somewhat beyond persuasion that was reasonable. She was sure she had begun to croak, when her gullet had suddenly dried around what had been her voice; and that she had pounded several times upon the Du Quesne kitchen table (except that neither table nor kitchen were the words they all used). When it came to the choice, no doubt important in its way, between one three-letter washing powder and another, Mrs Du Quesne spoke plain advertisers' English; but her warnings, or at least admonitions, deeper and more personal to Rosa and her place of abode, were as masked as the gurglings of any ancient oracle. And everyone else in the kitchen that was called something else kept quiet when Mrs Du Quesne said these plainly important things. Probably those sitting around at Delphi fell silent in like circumstances.

And there could be no doubt at all about La Wide having been unoccupied for years and years before she, Rosa, had bought it. The very first thing she had thought when she had set eyes on it had been, It must be haunted, but it had not so far in her occupancy seemed to be so, and the first twelvemonth was almost over, albeit a casual visitor might not have thought it from the state of the rooms.

The fact that the little structure had been so cheap as to be within Rosa's means had also made her suspect that trouble went with it. She had not been so unsophisticated as not to think of that. But during the year she had realized that on this point the answer might lie elsewhere.

The explanation, she had come to suspect, lay in the present social categorization of the island population. First, there were the few immensely old families, who dwelt in crumbling châteaux, within weedy moats. Second, there were the tax refugees from the British mainland: sad, very loud-voiced people in once-fashionable clothes, who seemed not to have houses at all, but to reside always in not quite compatible bars and restaurants, never truly drunk, never truly sober. Third, there was the great residential majority: the prosperous growers, their suppliers and agents. These lived in new or rehabilitated bungalows or houses, frantically competitive, each with all the others. Finally, there were the few real natives or aboriginals; and they had so diminished in number under the weight of all the others, or of the times in general, that they no longer needed more than a proportion of the cots and crofts built for them, mostly in the solidest, most enduring stone. The first three groups would not have considered La Wide, and the fourth had no need of it. The end of the tomato boom was said to be imminent, but in that event, those who trimmed and watered it would migrate not to La Wide but more probably to the Antipodes.

Moreover, La Wide was to be reached only by a bumpy and neglected track running uphill between hedges: difficult for a baby carriage, impossible for a saloon car. It was, in fact, this track that had initiated the dark talk from Mrs Du Quesne and her group; Rosa having expressed concern about the difficulty Mrs Du Quesne might find in making her way during the season of winter wet that once more lay ahead. (Rosa had arrived the previous October, but then, and right through that winter, there had been no Mrs Du Quesne in her life.)

Rosa, still shivering, sank upon a chair by the small fireplace as she thought about what had been said; though, as far as she was concerned, but slenderly understood. I am far too sensitive, she thought, for the five hundredth or one thousandth time; though words had never been necessary to frame the thought. She was in such distress (surely, this time, without full justification) that she might have gone on to think I am mad, and thus derive some faint, familiar comfort from the implication of non-responsibility for what happened to her and of escape, but instead was struck by the idea that, in this case, the word "sensitive" might require to be applied in a new meaning.

Dennis, fifteen years ago, had said at first that he thought she might be "a sensitive", and indeed claimed that it was one reason why he was "interested in her". He always professed a special concern with such things, and could certainly talk without end about them, though perhaps without much meaning either. He had, however, quite soon found an Indo-Chinese girl who was far more of a sensitive, and was believed, in so far as you could believe anything about Dennis, to have started living with her instead. Already, Dennis had explained to Rosa that being "*a* sensitive" had nothing at all to do with being "sensitive" in the ordinary meaning of the word. Rosa had thought this just as well in all the circumstances, and had summoned resolution to exclude all notion of herself owning any special psychic status. She had hardly thought about it again until now. If I *am* sensitive in that way, she thought, then the Du Quesne lot may have sensed it. Whenever she visited Mrs Du Quesne's abode, which she had found herself doing surprisingly frequently, she discovered a small crowd of kindred and affinity mumbling their confused lingo in the non-kitchen. "The Du Quesne lot" were fast becoming an over-wise chorus in the background of her own life: and perhaps edging towards the front of it.

Though it was already the end of October, there was no fire in the grate. This was partly because it was so difficult to get coal. Apparently the tomato-houses required almost all that was imported. The previous winter, Rosa had frozen for as long as eight or nine weeks before she had obtained a supply by making one of her scenes in the merchant's office. She had then received a whole ton, almost immediately, carried by a pair of youths in half-hundredweight sacks all the way up her lumpy lane from the road: which made her wonder whether coal was really so short, after all. Quite probably it was one of the many necessities only to be procured by such as she through resort to degrading devices. Rosa was unsure whether she did not prefer to endure the cold. Then she reasoned with herself that winter had of course not even begun, and that even autumn was less than half gone. She rose, went through to the back room, her bedroom and boudoir, removed her sweater, glanced in the looking-glass at the reflection of her bust, as she always did, and put on a thicker, chunkier sweater. The room was rather sad and dark, because the single window was close to the bank of earth which rose behind almost perpendicularly. Probably the room had been intended for "the children", while Father and Mother slept in the room adjoining, which was now Rosa's unfinished living-room; and all had lived their waking lives in the remaining room, into which the outer door led, and which had now become Rosa's kitchen and scullery only. Rosa entered this kitchen and scullery, and started to slice up materials for a meal.

But that day it was her first meal her mother could possibly have called "real", and it had the effect, with the coffee that followed it, of concentrating Rosa's perceptions. Mrs Du Quesne had left her with much to be surmised, but the facts, or rather the claims, were clear, even though the overtones and explanations might not be.

It had begun when Mrs Du Quesne, in a friendly way, had been answering one of the others who had apparently enquired for details as to where Rosa resided. "Ah," the other woman had blurted out, "it is there that they change the porters." Patois or hybrid the tongue might be, but Rosa could understand that much. "What porters?" she had enquired, her mind full of French railway stations. There had been a pause and a silence, and then something evasive had been said, though doubtless kindly meant. "No," Rosa had cried, the scent of mischief full in her nostrils. "I want to know. Please tell me." Mrs Du Quesne then said something much firmer, and perhaps in a less kindly tone; and soon Rosa was beginning to lose control, in the way she now regretted. So, in the end, Mrs Du Quesne did tell some of it, out of resentment or out of necessity. Mrs Du Quesne explained certain aspects of the matter, while the others inserted quiet or excited comments in their vernacular.

All over the island, Mrs Du Quesne had said, all over the island when one knew, were these paths: *"les vrais chemins de l'église"*. It was the way one went to one's church—when one knew. Several other things were said that Rosa had not comprehended. There was another pause and then the nub of the matter was hinted at: by these paths one also went to one's grave. Along these paths one's body was borne; and not only did such a path find its way past La Wide, so that each time the burden must pass within inches of Rosa's front door, but La Wide was also one of the places where, as she had heard already, "they changed the porters". Great significance seemed to be attached to that. And everyone made it clear that to make one's last journey by any other route was most inappropriate. Words were used to describe the consequences which, though few, were impressive, so awed and reluctant was their utterance, so charged the silence that followed them. Rosa had no precise idea what these words meant, but they had made those dead who were unquiet, almost visible and tangible in Mrs Du Quesne's homestead.

"But," Rosa had, in the end, cried out, "but I have never heard *any-*

thing." She thought that at this point she had actually clutched at Mrs Du Quesne's sleeve.

"No," Mrs Du Quesne had replied, very simply and memorably. "Until now you hadn't the knowledge." And everyone was again silent after she had spoken.

Rosa could not see how that could possibly make any difference. Either these dreary cortèges went past, in which case she would have surely seen at least one of them in a whole year; or they did not, and she had somehow missed the whole point.

"And whatever happens," said Mrs Du Quesne rather loudly, "if you *do* hear, don't look." Everyone continued silent; not one of them even nodding.

And what was more, she had learned nothing further. There had been some more talk, either in the difficult tongue, or else merely silly. Soon, Rosa had stalked out.

Now she looked around at the half-completed repainting and the miscellany of furniture brought from her room in London. It had been costly to move, of course, but it was certainly not true that it would have been cheaper to buy new furniture on the island. New furniture might have been more agreeable and more appropriate, but it would finally have emptied Rosa's financial store. As for the painting, she had set about doing it herself for the same reason, and because she thought it would give her something to do before she started looking for a thing that was better, but had been surprised by the physical effort involved, and, some time ago, had desisted until she had more strength. By now, she had ceased to notice the result for most of the time, though at this moment she did notice it. Properly, as she well knew, she could not afford even Mrs Du Quesne, but truly she could not do *everything*, and Mrs Du Quesne also provided a certain company—cheerful and confident company for much of the time. Besides, Mrs Du Quesne cost very little.

That, indeed, was why it had been possible to employ her, when a woman requiring the open market rate would have been out of the question; but at this moment it struck Rosa for the first time that Mrs Du Quesne's cheapness was like the cheapness of the house: slightly unnatural. Unaccustomed cheapness is something that takes much explanation in the world around us. It occurred to Rosa that perhaps she, Rosa, was beginning to regret having come at all, and that all these new difficulties and apprehensions were, as Dennis used to say, "projections". Nothing had been more familiar to Rosa than the sensation of early regret for almost every step she had ever taken; but this time she had thought that she had evaded the demon, even though perhaps by also managing to evade herself, for nearly a whole year. Where just now Rosa had undoubtedly been frightened, the notion that her external alarums had emanated, as so often, from inside her, left her merely depressed.

She looked at her reflection, though only in the glass of the sitting-room window. The light was just right for the purpose, and even the grime helped to define her image. Certainly it was all the definition she wanted. She had always found life to move by contraries, usually petty ones, though sometimes not; and, as often before when she had been depressed, now found herself surprised that she looked as well as she did. She had long ago learned that it was when she had been feeling more confident that the sight of her appearance came always as something of a shock. Life evens things up or down; in small matters and in large (even though Rosa would have hesitated to distinguish between the two). Now she felt quite pleased. Her figure was still noticeably good, or at least well proportioned; and the thick, chunky sweater was in her right style. Even her face was still pretty, she thought, beneath the grey hair. At least she had the decency to keep her grey hair short: but then there had been a man who positively liked, and chose, short grey hair—though that, for better or for worse, had been when her own hair was neither, but carroty and rather long. Still, long grey hair always looked greasy and witch-like; and at once she thought anew of Mrs Du Quesne, though Mrs Du Quesne's hair was not grey at all, but quite black. And my skin is amazingly good for my age, Rosa thought to herself. (She had long ago made a decision to defer *talking* to herself for as long as she could.) She attempted a smile, though she knew it could only be a bitter one, at least for the most part. But it proved to be not so much a bitter smile, as a timid and frightened smile. She was smiling like a shaky adolescent. And then the image in the dirty window lost shape and identity. Rosa turned away, once more depressed.

She took down her coat from one of the pegs at the back of the door on to the lane and set out for a walk. It was a respectable and even an expensive coat. Rosa still spent far more on clothes than on "the home"—or, indeed, on anything else that was in the least optional. And they were ladylike, conventional clothes that she picked, though simpler than the convention, because she had taste. Though her adult life had so far divided into two phases, neither of them especially ladylike, she had felt from first to last that her appearance must always show what she *really* was. And now that she had entered upon a third phase, this limbo at La Wide, she divined that her appearance was almost all she was left with. It was something that need never fail her while she had two pennies to rub together, and had mercifully little to do with the quite independent aspect of her naked body, provided that she did not allow her grey hair to grow long and greasy, or her hands to go too far in the direction of, say, Mrs Du Quesne's hands. With determination, she would be able to do something with her appearance until the last day came . . . She twisted her mind away from the thought of the morning's conversation.

Rosa was winding her way along the cliff path, high and narrow above the autumnal billows (they are as grey as hair, thought Rosa); steeply up and vertiginously down, both billows and path. Rosa walked not fast but steadily: the cliff path ran for many miles, and was exceedingly wild and beautiful, recalling what the cliff paths of England were, the coastguard paths, well within living memory. The ascents and descents, beyond either the powers or the will of the ordinary visitor, meant little to Rosa; but then the beauty and the wildness meant little to her either, and the windblown cliff flora, the jagged, streaky geology, nothing at all. All these different things entered her awareness only vaguely. Almost every day, she went slowly on and on, in her good clothes; passing others, persons from the car parks behind, and men with guns, without acknowledgement of any kind, without one half-step aside, assuredly without a smile. "She looks just like a ghost," the women said, not understanding that she might conceivably have been one. "Didn't she look pale?" enquired other women rhetorically of their bored husbands. Rosa was one whom the weather affected little. "She looks like a mad-woman," the bored husbands would sometimes reply. "Perhaps she's searching for something," a girl might interpose more sympathetically. And the crushing answer would come: "Most likely searching for her wits".

Rosa had thus walked for miles along the cliff path almost each day during all but a year, but now she soon began to feel tired and settled herself on a rough bench. She sat staring out to sea for possibly half an hour; letting the heavy waves erode her misery and break up her despair. Then a figure in black appeared on the path in the opposite direction to that from which she had come. A tall elderly man struggled forward against the wind. As he drew near, Rosa saw that he was in clerical dress, without an overcoat, and with his big black hat in his hand. His white hair was sparse and windblown. He stopped in front of Rosa and she looked up. Her first thought was: a sensitive face.

"Good afternoon," said the man. "I believe you are Mrs Hughes."

"Yes," said Rosa. "I am."

"You have bought the little house at the place where they change the porters? At least I assume that you have bought it."

"Yes," said Rosa. "I admit it."

"You are seeking peace?"

"Aren't we all?" The cheap words had sprung to her lips on some volition of their own.

"Yes, Mrs Hughes. Indeed, we all are. Indeed."

Rosa said nothing. She felt that any words she could find would be likewise unworthy of her; would show her in an unjust light. It was a long time since she had conversed with any "educated person".

"Perhaps I might sit beside you for a moment?"

Rosa nodded and, as one does, drew the skirt of her coat more closely to her.

"And what was your life before you came here? If you care to speak of it, of course."

"For the last eight years, I was a secretary. Then the manager sent for me and told me I was past being a secretary with *that* company, but that he had arranged for me to be transferred to the handling side. I said No."

"I am sure you were wise," said the man. "And what happened to you before the last eight years?" Both of them were staring straight ahead across the pulsing, empty sea.

"Before that I was seeing more of life."

"Did you prefer that?"

"No," replied Rosa. "I disliked both times," and, when he said nothing, she spoke again. "Who are *you*?"

"I am the curate in charge of your parish. I too am retired, but I come here every autumn in order to permit your rector to rest. He is very elderly, even more so than I am, and, alas very infirm indeed, as I expect you know."

"No," said Rosa, once more defiant, as always when confronted with any kind of official demand. "I don't go to church."

"Possibly not," said the man. "But then you have no need to."

"I wonder how you know," said Rosa, cheaper than ever, and misunderstanding.

"You already live in a holy place."

"What's that?" asked Rosa, her heart in a sudden vice.

"I myself should not dare to live there."

"Tell me," said Rosa, with all the stolidity she could muster. "What exactly is there that I should be afraid of?"

"It is not a matter of anything to fear in the usual sense. It is a spiritual matter."

"As how? I don't know about such things."

"Oh," he said. "Where were you educated?"

"In a convent," she replied, more quietly. "But I've long ago forgotten everything I was taught."

He replied in a murmur, as if to himself. "I can hear the beating of your heart."

But having said that, he said nothing more, while Rosa sat waiting, almost peacefully, for whatever might befall.

"I come here daily," he said in the end. "I like to contemplate the immensity. There is a lack of immensity in the world. Do you find that also?"

"Yes," said Rosa. "I suppose I do. But I don't look very much for it. I don't look very much for anything."

"It is perhaps odd," he continued, "that we have not met until now. I believe that you too walk along the cliff."

"Yes," said Rosa. "And I may have passed you without noticing. I do that often."

"I think I should have noticed *you*," he said, as if seriously thinking about it.

Rosa noticed that upon the grey sea was now the beginning of a black shadow.

"This," she remarked, "is when my mother would have said 'The days are drawing in'."

"Yes," he replied. "Soon we shall have to light the lamp before tea-time."

A sea bird descended from the blackening clouds, screaming and searching.

"You haven't told me," said Rosa. "This thing about changing the porters. People seem to keep talking about it. It sounds rather pointless to me. And, anyway, it doesn't happen. I've been there nearly a year and it hasn't happened yet, as far as I know."

"Perhaps you have not known what to look for and to listen for. The porters are changed very quietly. No one speaks. No one grumbles. Surely you have not been given the impression that they go by shouting, like a trade union march?"

"I have to admit," said Rosa, taking the plunge, "that I never heard about it at all until this morning, and then only from my char, if that is what I should call her. She said the great thing was if I *did* hear anything, not to look for what it was."

"It is a disturbing sight for those unaccustomed to death and the hereafter: which is most of the world around us, as I need hardly say. I think that you are one, Mrs Hughes, who could not only listen and look, but kneel and touch with impunity."

"Do I really want to?" asked Rosa, turning to him completely for the first time.

"Oh, yes, indeed, Mrs Hughes," he replied. "To kneel and to touch are the proper practices of the pilgrim. That must be one of the things you have temporarily forgotten."

"As with saints and relics and so forth?"

He smiled at her for the first time.

"But what should I get out of it?" She blushed. "No, I don't quite mean that. What I mean is why me? Why should I be supposed to do it more than another?"

"Because, Mrs Hughes, your whole life has been a quest for perfection. You have always been concerned only with perfection, and as in this world there is no perfection, you are sad. Sadness can be a very special—shall I say, concession?"

"I am sure the nuns used to tell us it was a sin."

"As with so many things, it depends upon what kind of sadness it is."

"Do you know," said Rosa impulsively, "I'm not sure that you haven't changed my entire afternoon!"

"Where you now live," he replied, "there was for centuries a shrine with an image; and before that, probably on the very same spot, another image, very different and yet in important ways just the same; and, before that—who knows?—perhaps the goddess herself, *in propria persona*, if you will permit the words. Needless to say, no one could behold the goddess herself in her grove and continue to live. That is possible only when the divine is provisionally mediated into man."

"For a clergyman you seem to take stock in an awful lot of different gods."

"There is only one."

"Yes," she said. "I see that too. At least I do now. You seem to make me understand things that I never understood before. And yet you don't say anything that's in the least new."

"Daily life is entirely a matter of the pattern men and women impose upon it: of style, as the artist calls it. And the character of that pattern is very important, as day follows day. None the less, reality lies far behind, and is unchangeable: is ritual, in fact. It was of reality, I suspect, that your charwoman was speaking—perhaps gossiping. Reality is often dangerous, so she was cautioning you to avoid it."

"And you?"

"I advise you to advance towards it. When you hear the faint sounds I spoke of, throw open your door and see what there is to see. Fall upon your knees and stretch out your hand, as I said. And of course be prepared for a big change; something indescribable, unpredictable."

"I have no idea what you are talking about," said Rosa slowly.

"Few have. My general reputation in the parish is that of a complete visionary. I am said to go around upsetting people. Not that many care one way or the other." On the instant, he rose to his feet. "But now I must return to them. I am very glad indeed to have met you, Mrs Hughes." As he could not lift his hat, he waved it vaguely around. She had a few seconds in which to examine his full face closely.

"I understand almost nothing you have said," Rosa repeated. "And yet you have made me feel much better. Thank you."

She would have gone after him along the cliff path, had he proposed it, but he did not. He merely bowed slightly and strode rapidly away. For a minute or so in the dusk, she could see his long black shape flickering and capering like a scrap of burned paper blown along by the wind, but soon he was no longer visible.

A heavy raindrop fell upon the back of her left hand. She looked up. The sky was now really black, with a blackness that was not entirely of the oncoming night. There was nothing to do but make the best speed possible homewards. But though she scuttled along more swiftly than for a long time, she failed to glimpse the shape ahead of the man who had been speaking to her. The visibility was so poor as to make the rough path almost dangerous; and when Rosa at last re-entered La Wide, her good clothes and she herself were saturated more completely than ever before in her life, save perhaps once, that day in the Bois de Vincennes, of all places, with Dennis. People looked down their noses at the Bois de Vincennes, but when the rain began, it had proved astonishingly wild and shelterless. Then Rosa recalled that she was wrong. The man with whom she had shared a soaking had not been Dennis but Michael: vile, bloody, deceitful, dear old Mike.

There was no electricity at La Wide. For lighting she depended upon lamps, exactly as her new acquaintance had said; and the oil supply for them had been another of the wearing nuisances which she hoped that Mrs Du Quesne would be able to deal with better than she had. At least, she, Rosa, would not have to listen to the supplier's patronizing comments upon her backward and impoverished existence. But now, before lighting a lamp, she stripped off all her clothes in the almost total darkness and flung them about the floor.

Dennis, Michael, Oskar, Ted, Tom, Frank, Gwyn, and Elvington: those were some of the names, and what comic names they were! Rosa ignited a pair of lamps, then lined the men up in her mind. It was possibly the first time ever that she had deliberately done so, and, perhaps for that reason, some of the names had no proper faces, and certain other faces that she saw, peering and intruding from the darker areas, had no names. And after those days, during her years of respectable and responsible business life, there had been virtually no men at all; assuredly none with power over her. She took out an unused bath towel and rubbed herself vigorously. Then she put on another sweater and a pair of trousers, which she seldom wore; and over them her thick winter dressing gown. All these things felt pleasantly new, one after the other. The dressing gown she had had cleaned during the summer, so that it smelt impersonally of chemicals. The file of men had soon vanished; without even being dismissed. It was as if on their own they had marched away into life's battle and failed to return.

What had happened to them: to them as individuals? It was another thought upon which Rosa had seldom dwelt. In almost every case, her final and consuming idea had been simply to get away, and to drag her sagging heart away also. She had sought to avoid all thought of the man's continuing existence. And then when another man had appeared, it had been even more important not to reflect much upon the past. All she could now recollect was that Elvington, poor weak American boy, had destroyed himself with the contents of a killing bottle, though not on her account, but whole years later; and that big, fat Oskar had been actually killed, Scandinavian-style, in a fight, and a fight that was at least partly about her. Afterwards she had collapsed completely, very completely; and had had to be fetched back to England "under sedation" (and as cheaply as possible) by her half-sister, Judith. Frank was supposed to have perished in a car smash outside Bolton, where he had, at rather long last, found a job of some kind. It was her room-mate, Agnes, who had told her that, and professed herself willing to swear to it; but one could not rely upon Agnes even when she probably *wished* to speak the truth. Agnes had also said that Frank had been married only a week before the accident . . . All the rest of them were quite possibly still alive. Rosa won-

dered how many of them would reach Heaven, and how many of their
respective women, and what would happen to them all then. She was
still not seeing them standing in a line, as they had been doing, ten,
twenty, or thirty minutes ago. Rosa had often noticed that such inner
visions come upon one apparently unsolicited; soon vanish; and can
by no effort be recaptured. She uncrossed her legs and said out loud:
"We control nothing of importance that happens to us."

She realized that she had not yet rubbed her hair, except to prevent
it actually dripping upon her dry clothes. The new towel was soaking
wet and quite unsuitable. She took out another new towel, leaving but
one more on the pile. Seated on a hard chair, she rubbed away at her
head, feeling active and effective. Then she had to consider what to
do with two wringing wet towels, and several very humid garments. It
really was not cold enough to justify the lighting of a fire. Rosa felt so
full of vigour that she almost regretted this. She settled for ranging
the wet objects upon strings which she stretched round the room. Fortunately, several pegs and hooks had been left behind in odd places,
to which the strings could be tied; but the total effect was unconvincing, and more than a little eerie. There were new shadows, some of
them vast; and intermittent small shiftings and flappings. I feel
penned in by wet vampire bats, thought Rosa; but, as a matter of fact,
the feeling was far more alarming than that, and far less specific.

"This is my hour of trial," said Rosa. "It is like nothing that has
gone before." She realized that she was disregarding her strong re-
solve not to soliloquize out loud before she positively could not help
herself. Perhaps, she thought, but did not say, this is where I *cannot*
help myself. She closed her eyes, to shut out the big, frightening bats.
She crossed her arms over her bosom, placing a hand upon each opposite shoulder. She started to breathe very deeply and regularly: formally terminating the period of short gasps and panting that had attended her scrambling rush for home, and the self-pummelings and
retchings that had necessarily followed. Soon she found that her
crossed arms weighed upon her lungs, so that, while mysteriously glad
that she had passed through that position, she fell away, letting her
hands fade in her lap.

There were clocks, one of which struck the hours and the half-
hours; there was a cricket, which, so late in the year, activated itself
for astonishingly long periods; there were the two lamps, in which the
oil burned evenly away.

"This is amounting to a wake," said Rosa to herself, as the clock
suddenly struck ten. "Not to mention a fast."

Her limbs had become a little stiff, but she was surprised that things were not far worse. She had felt herself to be slightly exalted ever since her conversation on the cliffs, and this unreasonable restlessness seemed to confirm it.

All the same, she moved to a more comfortable chair. "Why ever not?" she enquired vaguely, and once more aloud. She noticed that the rain had stopped. Perhaps it had stopped hours ago.

The room seemed peculiarly warm. "Perhaps delusions are setting in." Rosa had read about explorers marooned on icefloes who dreamed of the Savoy Grill. Ted had once worked as a waiter in a place like that, as she was unlikely to forget—though, as a waiter, Ted was understood to be rather good. Rosa cast off her dressing gown.

The clock struck half past ten, eleven, and half past eleven. Rosa was now half-asleep for much of the time. She had abandoned all idea of special preparation for what lay ahead. She lay empty and resigned.

Some time after that, the flame in both lamps began to flicker and waver. Rosa had filled the lamps herself and knew well that they held enough oil to last through two nights and more. But she rose to her feet very conventionally, in order to make an inspection. Immediately, the two lamps went out. The flame in both seemed to vanish at exactly the same moment, as if by pre-arrangement.

Rosa realized that, in the dark, her brow was covered with moisture. She was uncertain whether this was fear, or a medical consequence of her previous soaking, or simply the temperature of the room. Certainly the room was quite unaccountably hot.

Then Rosa became aware that behind the patterned curtains she had drawn across the two windows before throwing off her clothes, was now a gleam that seemed more than the contrast between the blackness of the room and the perhaps slightly more luminous night outside. Moreover, it was as if the gleam were moving. The faint light was strengthening, as, presumably, it moved towards her.

So far she had heard nothing but the ticking of the clock; and now she ceased to hear even that. She had not noted the clock's last tick. She simply realized that it was ticking no longer.

"Oh God," said Rosa, "please protect me." She had not chosen either the words or the voice. She had, in fact, no idea where they had come from. She sank, not upon her knees, but in a heap on the floor, burying her face between her legs, and holding her hands over her ears. She seemed to squat, in desperate discomfort, for an appreciable time. In an earlier year, she had known something like that hopeless, inhuman posture when she had been so badly seasick—and on more than one occasion—in the Baltic.

Then there was a faint fluttering knock, not necessarily at the outer door. Rosa could not tell where it came from. It might have been made by a small creature which had been entrapped in the room with her.

It seemed worse not to know than to know. Rosa unwound herself. She looked and listened.

There was still not much to hear, but the light had grown strong enough for the shapes she had hung from strings to be dimly and strangely visible. Another new development was, however, that these distorted forms seemed no longer to be entirely within the room, but to continue outside it, as if she could see faintly through the wall. The weak light, moreover, was wanly pink and wanly blue, in a way that not even the pattern of the curtains could entirely account for.

Punching at the wet objects that touched her face and head, Rosa ran for the outer door. Though it too seemed to have become faintly transparent, it opened quite normally. Rosa was in flight, and in flight that was unorganized and demented. No longer was she capable of resignation or acquiescence, let alone of meeting events with anything more positive. But at the doorway, she managed to stop herself. She stood there for a moment, gasping and staring.

She had half expected that the light would be very bright. After all, there had been evidence that it might be.

In fact, however, it was quite faint; only half as bright again, perhaps, as it had been inside the room. Remote might have been the word for the quality of it; even though the source, or seeming source, was almost under Rosa's nose; *le vrai chemin de l'église* not being at all wide. The light came from candles, but, mysteriously, it still manifested that wan pinkness and pale blueness that Rosa had already discerned. "Inexplicable," said Rosa softly, "inexplicable."

It was hard even to guess how many of these candles there were, each giving barely more than the light of a tiny taper, though visibly far sturdier than that. The candles were in the hands of men; and inside the irregular ring the men made, were other men, without candles: the bearers (Rosa rejected the word "porters"), now in process of being changed. And at the centre of all was that which was being borne: of itself, apparently, not without luminosity.

After Rosa had opened the door, very far from quietly, owing to the clumsiness of her fear, the men on that side of the ring, whether the light-bearers or the burden-bearers, had slowly and gravely moved aside, so that a wide way lay open before her.

Already she was part of it all, and had no refuge. She went delicately and timidly out, stepping like a girl.

And what she saw lying before her, though gilded and decked and perfumed and beflowered as any saint, was the twin, the image, the double of herself. Not even of herself when a girl or of herself when a hag, but, she had no doubt about it, of herself as she was now. On the instant she sank to her knees beside the litter and diffidently touched the hand that lay there, which at once responded with a gentle clasp.

"Who am I?" whispered Rosa. "And who are you?"

"I am your soul," replied a remote voice she did not know.

"But," cried Rosa, "where then are you going?"

"To the church. Where else should a soul go?"

"Shall I see you no more?"

"One day."

"When will that be?"

"I do not know."

"And until then?"

"Live. Forget and live."

"How can I forget? How can anyone? How can anyone *forget?*"

Here Rosa glanced upwards and around her; and the idea passed through her mind that these silent men, all somehow ministering, it was to be supposed, to her soul, might be those same men for whom earlier that evening she had sometimes found names and sometimes found recollections only.

Whatever the truth of that, Rosa's last question found no answer. The new bearers were assuming their task. (Who, Rosa wondered, in that case—if that case were conceivable—could *they* be?) With hands and arms, they had already drawn Rosa away; and now they were raising the litter on to their shoulders. The entire faintly lighted throng were moving on towards the hilltop, where the church had replaced the temple, where the temple had been surrogate for the goddess personally in the grove.

"Farewell." Rosa never knew whether she had actually spoken that word.

Remarkably soon, the rough lane was silent, with all life stilled, and starlessly dark. But Rosa saw through the curtained windows that the lamps inside her living-room burned as usual; and when, not too hurriedly, she went to look and listen, the clock was ticking, and implying that the time was only ten minutes after midnight.

It was no occasion for giving further thought to the problem of the wet clothes. That could wait for the morning, when Rosa would be packing anyway, with a view to returning to London, at least as a first move. It was impossible to know where she would go thereafter.

3

NIEMANDSWASSER

SHORTLY AFTER 3 A.M., when the September air was thinly strewn with drizzle, the young Prince Albrecht von Allendorf, known as Elmo to his associates, because of the fire which to them emanated from him, entered the *Tiergarten* from the Liechtensteinallee, leaping over the locked gate; then found his way to the shore of the big lake to his left; and there, in the total darkness, made to shoot himself.

For upwards of an hour he had strode and stumbled, not always by the most direct route, for he was unused to making the journey on foot, northwards from Schöneberg, where within the small, low room in which the two of them were in the long habit of meeting, Elvira Schwalbe still lay across the big bed in her chemise. She was neither happy to be rid of Elmo, this time surely for ever, nor unhappy to have lost him; certainly not dead, which, considering the apparent intensity of Elmo's feelings, was perhaps surprising, but not fully alive either. The principal upshot of it all was a near-paralysis of will and feeling. Thus she was very, very cold, but for many hours made no movement of any kind. Not until the middle of that afternoon did she gather herself together. Then she spent a considerable time making her hair even more beautiful, put on her taffeta dress with the wide grey and white stripes (very wide), locked up the magic apartment for ever and a day, and proceeded round the corner to the *Konditorei*, where she ate more cakes than she would normally have done, and drank more coffee, and even concluded with a concoction of hot eggs, having found herself still hungry. Happy, happy Elvira, renewed, strengthened, and made lovelier than ever by just a little suffering; happy to leave us with the wide world once more spread freely before her from which to pick and choose! *So endet alles.* Later, at a suitable moment, she threw the key of the room into the Spree.

Elmo, the young prince, was perhaps young only by comparison; in that he had four elder brothers, all of whom had always seemed old beyond their years. All were in the army, and all were doing well in their careers, by no means only because of their excellent connections. When not on the parade ground or manoeuvres, they were at lectures and courses, or even reading military books. All were married to ladies of precise social equilibrium, and all had children, in no case only one, and in every case with boys predominating. Despite the demands of service, there was usually at least one son at Allendorf to support their elderly father in what for most of the year were the daily pleasures of chase and gun. Thus too they in turn learnt to rule; especially, of course, the eldest.

The Hereditary Prince of Allendorf had managed to escape mediatization and still exercised a surprising degree of authority over his moderately-sized patriarchy; neither so small as to be something of a joke, nor so large as to negate the personal touch. The survival of so much individual authority in a changed world was not unconnected with the fact that almost all his subjects loved him; and that in turn was because he was an excellent ruler, carefully reared to it from birth, and completely unselfconscious in his procedures. The few who were dissatisfied made tracks for Berlin in any case. It would be absurd to set about the making of trouble in Allendorf.

The Hereditary Prince had long been a widower (Elmo could hardly remember his mother), but he was well looked after by the Countess Sophie-Anna, long a widow herself, a distant cousin (and her late husband had been another cousin), and still quite attractive, including in some cases to those younger than herself. She resided in a large, rococo house, just across the Schlossplatz. When she had first arrived, the elder boys had been doubtful, but Elmo, aged ten, and very tired of masterful matrons (and not yet called Elmo), had fallen for her completely, and could hardly be kept out of her abode, where, among other things, and when opportunity offered, he stole away and, in awe and wonder, went repeatedly through the soft dresses and perfumed underclothes in her bedroom presses and closets. Things were much less formal and ordered than in the Schloss, and no one here ever thought to say him nay in anything. None the less, Schloss Allendorf itself was a beautiful and romantic structure, fantastic as a dream; and the Hereditary Prince took care that the aged, the apparently sempiternal Emperor was as often as practicable his guest.

As well as the Allendorfpalast in Berlin, quite near to where Elmo now sat in darkness, the family properties included, confusingly, a second, and much older, Schloss Allendorf, this time on the shores of Lake Constance, the Bodensee. No senior member of the family had seemingly found the time to go there since the present Hereditary Prince, when a quite small child, had spent a week there with his father. This apparently universal family indifference to the place was normal enough behaviour, but, in the present instance, it happens that there was a specific reason for it: some particular thing (of which details were never disclosed) had happened when the quite small child had visited the Schloss, which had had the effect of his never either being taken there again, or himself wanting to go there when he had become his own master. His attitude influenced those around him, his family and others, without, probably, a word being ever clearly spoken. Probably few of those affected were accustomed to showing much enterprise in such matters as visiting remote family properties in any case. There were elderly dependables to look after the place, year in and year out, and that sufficed.

Elmo alone formed a habit of going there, incognito, or as near to that as could be managed. He had been drawn in the first place by the knowledge that it was from this semi-ruinous lakeside congeries that his family, which was a family to be proud of, had come to importance at the beginning. The family were too closely knit for his elder brothers ever to be actually unkind to him, but, undeniably, there were differences, and Elmo found it particularly felicitous that at almost any time he could withdraw from father and brothers and the wives and children of brothers, to a spot where there was no element of betrayal or disloyalty, and which was of such wondrous beauty also.

If, when the moon is shining and near the full, you scull over, alone, or with some single quietly beloved and beautiful person, from Konstanz, past the Staad peninsula with its lighthouse, to Meersburg, you will experience a peace and acceptance of all things that the wider oceans of the world cannot offer. For some of the time, the scale seems to be maritime, with land, at such an hour, almost out of sight, even beneath the moon; but all the while you are conscious that the smooth and silky water is not saline but the current of the great Rhine, newly released from the Alps. And, of course, there is the clear air; the Bodensee being set at 400 metres above the restless sea. Every ripple is poetry and every zephyr a tender release.

Naturally, Elmo, as well as his brothers, was in the army; but in his case more ornamentally, as was still possible, though becoming less so. In the course of his service, he had met Viktor, whose position in the world was perfectly accommodable to his own (Viktor's father commanded the guard in one of the kingdoms); and in Viktor for the first time he had found a friend who actually enhanced (instead of slightly spoiling and diminishing) the experience of boating on the lake, more often than not at night. Viktor, who was olive-skinned and black-haired, sometimes dressed as a girl for this purpose, and it was as if Elmo had mysteriously, albeit but momentarily, acquired the sister he had so much lacked.

One night or early morning when the circumstances were such, there was an odd episode. Viktor was trailing his hand in the water while Elmo worked intermittently at the sculls. It was hard to tell where exactly they were on the lake. This is always one of the most delightful things on the Bodensee, in that the agreeable uncertainty contains little element of actual risk: soon one always sees land *somewhere,* sometimes all too soon. But that night or early morning, a risk did emerge, unexpectedly, devastatingly, and literally; because the hand that the relaxed Viktor was gently trailing through the water was, with all quiet around, suddenly bitten half away. He lost his fourth and fifth fingers altogether, and, even when the doctors had finished, was left without a portion of his hand—and, worse still, of his right hand, with which he wrote his verses and fingered the strings of his guitar. Furthermore, the experience had a marked emotional effect also: one proof of which was that Elmo and Viktor quarrelled.

Even so, Viktor, who had resigned his commission (he was offered a job of consequence in an army office, but declined it—as henceforth he was to decline most things); Viktor, then, seemed to commit himself to sitting in solitude and without occupation, each day and every day, on the Bodensee shore. He was not always in the same spot, was indeed seldom to be found in the same spot on two consecutive days; but always he was in the locality, for the most part as near to the fringe of the lake itself as possible, though often half hidden away in a coppice or in the lee of a fisherman's hut. Everyone knew that he had taken up a lodging with an elderly couple who lived in a respectable homestead three miles away from Schloss Allendorf, and that he took all his meals alone, as he did not wish people to see him eat, owing to his maimed right hand, the hand in which one holds the knife.

Elmo, who had not felt himself responsible in any way for their quarrel, though in a manner understanding that it was unavoidable, was concerned as to how Viktor would fare during the coming autumn and winter, the accident having happened on a sultry night in August, and the Bodensee being often an inclement region during at least half the year. One of the doctors with whom Elmo spoke expressed the medical view that the entity which had inflicted the terrible injury had also infected the entire physiology of the victim with some bacillus, perhaps unknown, which had in a measure unbalanced his judgement. On the evidence, this seemed very likely.

As to the entity itself, opinions inevitably differed. Among the unsophisticated, reference was made to the monster known to have inhabited the deepest depths of the lake from earliest time, and to have been actually seen by Carolus Magnus, and both seen and interviewed by Paracelsus. The more general and representative view was that Viktor's injury had been done by a freshwater shark. It was just the sort of random tearing that a shark goes in for, said those who had met sharks in the East and places like that.

There would have been a far greater popular sensation had Viktor been a more popular and acceptable figure, or had he lived more according to his rank, instead of, like Elmo, as far as possible incognito. The nicer people even felt that Viktor would not *want* to be the centre of a major and long-enduring sensation. Even so, in many quarters at that part of the lakeside, the children were provided with a list of precise prohibitions. Perhaps in consequence, there seemed to occur no record of any child being attacked as Viktor had been attacked. Sooner than might have been expected, there was little trace of what had happened to Viktor, other than Viktor himself, who continued forlornly to haunt the shores of the lake, even, as Elmo had apprehended, on many days during the cold of winter.

Viktor's strange way of life inspired the great poetess who resided in one of the best situated of the lakeside castles to write a symbolic poem, though not all who know and love the poem, are informed about how it came to be written, or would believe if told.

Elmo no longer felt the same about Schloss Allendorf, and went back to Berlin and his regiment almost with relief. But he then met Elvira at a place where the younger officers mingled with aspirant actresses, singers, and (especially) dancers, after the fall of the curtain.

Elvira was a dancer, though she danced less often and regularly after she passed within Elmo's protection. Beneath Elvira's spell, Elmo nearly forgot about Viktor and a dozen others. He was deeply in love with her, and seemingly more and more so as the years passed. He never doubted either that she felt the same about him or that it would go on for ever, even though in the nature of things he could never marry her. He was surrounded by such relationships, even among older people; and in some cases a relationship of the kind had seemed to endure, even though persons who knew nothing about it claimed in a general way that duration was always impossible. As for practicalities, Elmo, being one to whom only the ideal was entirely existent, sincerely believed it to suffice that he had money, where Elvira had little or none, and even less in the way of prospects. Moreover, Elvira was not a dancer in a Paris boîte, but in a minor opera house. There was an inspirational force within Elmo of which the sensitive soon became aware, and which had led to his *Spottname* or nickname. Even in a tight corner on a battlefield, he might conceivably have accomplished more than any of his robuster, better-trained relations, and sacrificed fewer lives.

However, when the setting was a tight corner by the large lake in the *Tiergarten*, all decision was virtually taken out of his hands, though not immediately. Elmo, who thought that by now he knew himself through and through, had never doubted his capacity to destroy himself on the instant in the terrible circumstances that had descended upon him at once so conclusively and so unexpectedly; nor did he lack the means.

Never for one instant, by day or by night, had he lacked the means, since, on his fourteenth birthday, his distant cousin, Sophie-Anna, had given him her own, small, delicately lacquered pistol, and bidden him always thereafter to have it with him. She was wearing a lilac dress with a pattern of large, vague, white roses for the family celebration of which he was the centre. "A woman should always have money," she had said in her boudoir before they went down. "A man should always have—this." It was perhaps because of the circumstances in which he had received the pretty pistol that Elmo had never, as yet, once discharged it, though he took care that one of his men regularly maintained and oiled it; but he had been given plenty of practice at the range with weapons of a generally similar kind. Elmo knew how to shoot straight and on the instant and to kill.

But he found that it was difficult to kill himself in the almost total darkness. He was astonished that the effulgence of the city lights, albeit renowned, should make so little impression upon the heart of the *Tiergarten*. The trees must be far denser than he had ever supposed; and a lake does imply either a moon or a storm. Probably the truth was that Elmo had succumbed to the same near-paralysis of will and feeling as was at that moment depriving Elvira even of the purpose to keep herself warm, and which, with supposed mercifulness, always supervenes at the end of a great love before the months and years of loss and deprivation set in. Sometimes this almost total numbness lasts for as long as 48 hours. But for Elmo it was the darkness that seemed to be the trouble. It was like trying to act decisively in limbo.

Then Elmo actually began to shiver. Partly, he realized, it was the first of the dawn at which hour so many pass that even the insensitive, if in an open space at the centre of a large city, are aware of their passing.

There was a strange, faint, even light descended upon the water, acceptable, perhaps, as the last of evening, but infinitely perturbing as the first of day. All with hearts must shiver to see it and close their minds to thought.

But there was a figure in the lake, or above it: if in it, then not of it. It was a beautiful woman; it was a woman more beautiful than any man could have conceived or imagined as possible. She was white and naked, and she had large eyes, like the eyes of the Blessed Virgin, and a wide red mouth, which smiled.

Elmo knew at once that he had fallen asleep from cold and wretchedness and that this was a dream, devised for his further torment. Because all that the vision had done was to reinstate the thought and recollection of Elvira in full brutality; unbearably to invigorate sentiments lately numbed into brief abeyance. "Curse you, curse you," groaned Elmo; and, as he cursed, the little pistol in his hand was discharged by him for the first time. It was unfortunate, too, that, dream or no dream, his hand was still shaking as much as if he were fully awake at that hour; indeed his entire arm. The vision had faded or vanished anyway, and it was hard to say where the bullet had lodged. There were still occasional duels in the *Tiergarten*, and small holes were sometimes found in trees. As for the vision, it had probably lingered for less than a second, much as if it had been an apparition of the Virgin indeed. And the pistol was of the lady's kind that contains only one bullet.

Elmo recalled a simple truth that had, as it happened, been uttered in his case, by the mistress of the ballet at Elvira's minor opera house, the lady who saw to it that the girls were properly dressed and equipped, punctual, and diligent, though naturally she did not herself devise any of the works in which they danced: "We do not die merely because we want to," this woman had said in Elmo's hearing. In the faint and frightening light of a new dawn, the big trees stood around watching his every gesture, absorbing his every breath. No other mode of death was possible for a soldier and a prince. With another curse, Elmo threw the pistol into the lake.

Even in this respect, what happened seemed mysteriously significant. That same day the pistol was seen gleaming upwards through the water by a park attendant. He recovered it with the long rake provided for such incidents, and, because the pistol bore on its butt the name of the Countess Sophie-Anna, it was respectfully returned to her by the superintendent, whose staff spent much time in wrapping it with sufficient care for the post. This time the Countess retained it. She merely sent Elmo a short letter. Elmo had, in fact, lost his chance with the Countess, who from now on regarded him with indifference. But the Countess addressed her little letter to the family residence in the capital (she was fully in Elmo's confidence about Elvira); with the result that Elmo never received it, as he had left Berlin by an evening train on the day of his disintegration in the *Tiergarten*.

Elmo realized that he was dead anyway. Elvira had killed him, life had killed him, the passing years had killed him: whichever it was. There was no need for a weapon, or for action of any kind on his part. When the heart is dead, all is dead, though the victim may not fully realize it for a long time. Elmo had realized when he had thrown away the pistol; and the Countess's action in contemptuously depriving him of any second chance was superfluous.

Elmo went to the Bodensee, because there seemed to be nowhere else where he could so easily be alone, indeed settle himself in a solitude. Before leaving Berlin, he had telegraphed the major-domo (in truth only a senior peasant, elevated, at the most, to caretaker) to arrange for the carriage to meet him at Stuttgart. He reached that other Schloss Allendorf by ten o'clock the next morning, feeling very hungry. Both with sleep and with appetite, unhappiness sometimes augments and sometimes destroys. It was eight years since he had been there.

For a year, he confined himself to the semi-ruinous buildings and to the neglected park stretching vaguely away behind them. He never once went down to the lake, lest he be observed. The park was at least walled, and it would have been a serious matter with the Hereditary Prince if the wall had been permitted to crumble at any point. Elmo never allowed as much as the light of a candle in any of his rooms unless the shutters had first been closed and the long, dusty curtains drawn tight. He gave orders that his arrival was to be mentioned nowhere, and that all letters (if there were to be any) were to be cast away unopened.

He read Thomas à Kempis and Jakob Böhme in copies from the castle library; of which the pages were spotted and flaky, and from which the leathery covers parted in his hands, revealing pallid, wormy activities within. Every now and then he inscribed thoughts of his own on the blank pages of an old folio. It was a book on magic. There were printed words and diagrams only in the first half of the volume. The remaining pages had been left blank for the purchaser or inheritor to add reports of his or her own, but no one seemed so far to have done so. Elmo found, as have many, that the death of the heart corrupted the pen into writing a farrago of horrors and insanities, not necessarily the less true for their seeming extravagance, but inaccessible for the most part to the prudent. Thus another autumn followed another summer, and then another cold, damp winter drew near.

Elmo discovered that even the imminence of spring, the worst quarter of the year for the sensitive, the period of most suicides, the season of greatest sadness, no longer disturbed him, or not that he was aware of. Before leaving, he had told them in Berlin that he was not to be approached: nor were such orders altogether unusual on the part of those in a position to give them. Autumn offered a faint respite.

Not that Elmo abstained from looking out over the lake from various upstairs windows. It seemed perfectly secure, provided that he took care to stand well back in the room; which was often, at that, an empty room as far as furniture or pictures or trophies were concerned. The panes in the windows were old and imperfect, not only defeating the intrusive stare from without, but also adding much to the fascination of the view across the water from within. Moreover, these upstairs windows were very imperfectly and infrequently cleaned. Sometimes Elmo would stand gazing and lost for hours at a time, oblivious at least; but in the end cramp and weariness would suddenly overcome him, in that it was, of course, impermissible to lean against the window frames themselves, as do most who look forth on life outside their abode.

"Jurgen!" Elmo went to the door of the big, empty room and shouted. He had expropriated all calendars, but supposed it to be now the end of September or the beginning of October: a phase of the twelvemonth when cold became noticeable. It was about eleven o'clock in the morning.

Jurgen, one of the resident peasants, came clambering up the several flights of imposing but uncarpeted stairs. Elmo had attached this man to his more personal needs, in the absence of the valet who had been his go-between or Mercury with Elvira, and who had therefore been left behind to rediscover himself in Berlin. The man was in late middle-age (or more), but had seemed sharper than his fellows.

"Jurgen. You see that boat?"

Jurgen looked through the discoloured window rather casually. "No, your Highness. I see no boat."

"Look again, man. Look harder. Look."

"Well, perhaps, your Highness."

"There's something I recognize about it. Something familiar."

Jurgen stared at his master, though only from the corner of his eye. He was not sure that he himself could see anything at all. However, his master's statement was all of a piece.

"Have you any ideas about it, Jurgen?"

"No, your Highness."

"I need to know. I should like the boat to be brought in, if necessary."

"That's not possible, your Highness."

"Why not? We've got Delphin and Haifisch, and men to row them. Or to sail them, if the wind's right."

"It's not that, your Highness."

"What is it, then?"

"If the boat your Highness speaks of out there is the boat I think I can see—though I'm not really sure about it, your Highness—she's not in territorial water."

"Not in *our* territorial water maybe, but I don't think we shall start a war."

Elmo, however, reflected for a moment. The Lake of Constance was adjoined by several different national territories, with varying statutes and rights. What did it really matter about the boat? What did it really matter about anything? What other thought mattered than that nothing mattered?

He was about to resign the pointless idea, as he had resigned other ideas, when Jurgen spoke again. "Your Highness, if the boat your Highness speaks of is where she seems to be, then, your Highness, she is on No Man's Water."

"What's that, Jurgen?"

"No Man's Water, your Highness," Jurgen said again.

"I don't know what you mean, Jurgen."

Jurgen looked as if taken aback; so much so that he seemed unable to speak.

"You've lived here all your life," said Elmo, "and your father before you, and so forth. I haven't. In any case, I never came here for history and geography lessons. Explain what you mean."

"Well, your Highness, everyone knows—I beg your Highness's pardon—that there's a part of the lake which belongs to no one, no king or emperor, and not to Switzerland either, and from what I can see of it, if I can see it at all, that boat out there is on that very piece of water."

"I don't believe there's any such spot, Jurgen. I'm sure you think it, but it's impossible."

"As your Highness says," replied Jurgen.

Elmo was again looking out. "Can't you see something familiar about that boat?" It was true that, like most members of his family, he had exceptionally long sight, but he was staring as if distracted. He had even drawn far too near to the glass, though fortunately there seemed none to see him, as he would have been visible only from the lake; and on the lake, that cold morning, there was only the single boat in question, very distant, if there at all. Often there were odd fishermen, and odd traders too, but at the moment none were in sight.

"What is familiar about it, if I may venture to ask your Highness?"

"I wish I knew," said Elmo slowly. "I simply don't know. And yet I know I do."

"Yes, your Highness," replied Jurgen.

His master's words were still all of a piece. Downstairs most had come to the view that their master was simply a little out of his mind, poor gentleman. It was common enough among the great families; and elsewhere for that matter. He was always identifying things and recollecting things and staring at things.

"How are you so sure where this piece of water is?" asked Elmo, not looking at Jurgen, but still staring. "How can you tell?"

"All of us know, your Highness. We know all our lives. Near enough leastways, your Highness. So that we don't find ourselves there by mistake like."

"Would it matter so much if you did?"

"Oh yes, your Highness. As I said to your Highness, it's a piece of water that belongs to no one. That's not natural, is it, your Highness?"

"If this had been a year ago," said Elmo, "I should first have had the whole story properly looked into, and then, if there had proved to be anything true about it, I should have sailed out there myself."

Jurgen was obviously about to demur, and there was a slight but detectable passage of time before he replied, "As your Highness says."

"But I don't believe a word of it," commented Elmo petulantly. It was difficult to decide to what extent he was still staring out at the lake and to what extent he was staring at the blackness inside him.

Jurgen bowed more formally and clattered downstairs again.

The survival of the lost beloved being so incomparably more afflicting than his or her death, the bereaved is the more likely to vary bitter grief with occasional episodes of hysterical elation, as the dying man, isolated amid the Polar or Himalayan snows, has quarter hours of almost peaceful confidence that of course he will emerge, even believing that he sees how.

So it was that afternoon with Elmo. He found himself growing more and more wildly excited by what Jurgen had asserted, nonsense though it was. The world seemed to be suddenly lighted up with liberation, as in that case of the Polar or Himalayan castaway. Inwardly he knew that any motion on his part, however minute or merely symbolic, would at once dim and then rapidly extinguish the light: he must simply hold on to the excitement as long as he could, for its own sake. Indeed, he had been through such interludes before during the past year, through two or three of them; and he knew how transitory they were. All the same, if the castle library had offered a modern reference book, he might have consulted it. As it was, it contained nothing of the kind later than works left behind (or "presented") by the French officers at the time of the Napoleonic occupation.

When one is dead as Elmo was dead, ideas cease to be big or small, true or false, weighty or trivial: the only distinction is between irritant and anodyne. Long after his false elation had worn off (such conditions seldom last as long as an hour), Jurgen's fantasy still lingered in Elmo's mind as anodyne.

Shortly after three o'clock that afternoon, he picked up the bell and shook it. The wiring of the castle bells had become so defective that Elmo found he did better with a handbell, but it had to be a big, heavy, and noisy one, a veritable crier's bell, or it would not have been heard through the thick walls, and down the corridors.

"Jurgen. I should like to see Herr Spalt. After dinner, of course."

"But, your Highness——" After all, Jurgen's master had not merely seen no one from the outside world for a twelvemonth, but had given particular directions, with serious penalties attached, that no one was even to be told he was in residence.

"After dinner, Jurgen, I should like to see Herr Spalt."

"I shall see what can be done, your Highness. I shall do my best."

"No man can do more," commented Elmo with a spectral smile.

Herr Spalt was the schoolmaster. In other days, Elmo had not infrequently asked him in, to share some evening concoction he, Elmo, had himself prepared according to regimental tradition. Indeed, Elmo considered that he had learned much from Spalt, whom he deemed to be palpably no ordinary village disciplinarian. He assumed that, at some point in his career or in his life, Spalt had been in trouble, so that he had sunk below his proper position in scholarship.

As has been said, the grief-stricken sometimes gorge and sometimes starve. That evening Elmo ate little. Some new impulse had entered his bloodstream, though he could not decide whether it helped or harmed, especially as there was so little difference between the two.

It was past eight o'clock when Spalt arrived. The walk from the village was not inconsiderable, notably in the dark. Spalt now was a corpulent man, grey-skinned and bald, and with an overall air of neglect. There was even a triangular tear in the left leg of his trousers. He was noticeably what is described as "a confirmed bachelor".

"Spalt, have some Schnapps." Elmo poured two large measures. "It's cold in the evenings. It's cold always."

Spalt made a fat little bow.

Elmo said: "I do not wish to go into things. There are reasons for all I do and all I do not."

Spalt bowed again, sucking at the Schnapps. "Your Highness's confidences are his own."

"Tell me how is Baron Viktor von Revenstein?"

"As before, your Highness. There is no change that we are aware of."

"What did *you* make of it, Spalt?"

"The baron endured a terrible experience, your Highness. Terrible." Spalt's expression had seldom been seen to change. Possibly this was a qualification for his profession. The young have to be strengthened, especially the young men and boys.

"If I remember rightly, you were among those who thought it was done by a shark?"

"Something like that, your Highness. What else could it have been?"

"A freshwater shark?"

Spalt said nothing.

"Are there such things? You are a well-informed man, Spalt. I have found that you know almost everything. Are there such things as freshwater sharks? Do they exist?"

"The ichthyologists do not know of them, your Highness. That is true. But there must have been something of the kind out there. If not exactly a shark, then something not dissimilar. What other explanation is possible?"

Elmo refilled the glasses, lavishly.

"Jurgen, my man here, rough, very rough, but not a conscious liar I should say, has been telling me a wild tale about there being a part of the lake which belongs to no one. To no state or ruler; to no one of any kind, as I gather. Have you ever heard of that?"

"Oh yes, your Highness," replied Spalt. "It is perfectly true."

"Really? You astonish me. How can it be possible?"

"There was not always an international law governing the ownership of open water between different states, and even now that law is very imperfect. It is distinctly controversial in various parts of the world. In our case, the international law has never been deemed to apply. The ownership of the lake's surface has been governed by treaty and even by convention. One consequence, doubtless unintended, is that part of the lake's surface belongs to no one. It is quite simple."

"What about beneath the water?"

"The same, your Highness, I imagine. Exactly the same."

"The lake is very deep, I have always understood?"

"In places, your Highness. Very deep indeed in places. There has never been a complete hydrographical survey."

"Indeed! Do you not think there should be?"

"It is hard to see what practical purpose could be served."

"The acquisition of new knowledge is surely a sufficient end in itself?"

"So it is said, your Highness."

"But you must agree? You are our local savant."

Instead of replying, Spalt said: "Your Highness was not then aware that the baron's terrible injury happened on that part of the lake?"

"Of course I was not. Though perhaps since this afternoon I may have suspected it. Perhaps that is why you are here now. But how do you know, in any case? You were not there."

"I was not there. And indeed I do not know in the ordinary sense. No one knows in that sense, except perhaps your Highness, who *was* there. None the less, I am sure of it."

"Why are you sure of it?"

"Because it is the part of the lake where all strange things happen."

"What else has happened there?"

"Fishermen have seen treasure ships there. Sailors in the service once fought a big battle there—suffered deaths and casualties too.

Men whose lives were due to end have crossed the lake on calm nights and perished there, or at least vanished there."

"Anything else, Spalt?"

"Yes, your Highness. A boy I was fond of, already a brilliant scholar, saw a phantom there, and is now screaming in the Margrave's madhouse."

"How often do you suggest that these things happen?"

"Rarely, your Highness. Or so I suppose. But when they do happen it is always in that region of the water. However infrequently it be. I have sometimes thought there have been unacknowledged reasons why that part of the lake has been left unpossessed."

"Yes," said Elmo. "I'm not sure I don't accept every word you say."

"There is believed to be a certain truth among us peasants," said Spalt quietly, and pulling heavily on the long glass of spirits, which, indeed, he emptied.

"I don't see you as a peasant, Spalt, splendid fellows though most of them are."

"None the less, I am a peasant, your Highness."

"Be that as it may," said Elmo, "you are a very deep man. I've always known that."

"There is hardly a man on the lakeside who cannot tell a story about No Man's Water, your Highness, often many stories."

"In that case, why have I never heard of this before?"

"It is *unheimlich*, your Highness. Men do not speak of it. It is like the secrets of the heart, the true secrets which one man only knows."

"An exalted comparison, Spalt."

"We are most of us two people, your Highness. There is something lacking in the man who is one man only, and so, as he believes, at peace with the world and with himself."

"Is there, Spalt?"

"And the two people within us seldom communicate. Even when both are present together in consciousness, there is little communication. Neither can confront the other without discomfort."

"One of the two sometimes dies before the other," observed Elmo.

"Life is primarily directed to seeing that that happens, your Highness. Life, as we know it, could hardly continue if men did not soon slay the dreamer inside them. There are the children to think of; the mothers who breed them and thus enable our race to endure; the economy; the ordered life of society. Of such factors as these your Highness will be always particularly aware, in view of your Highness's station and responsibilities."

"Yes," said Elmo. "As you say, it is my duty, which, naturally, we all perform as best we can." He came over with the bottle. "Fill up, Spalt. Let me rekindle the dying fire." But Elmo's hand was shaking as he poured, so that he splashed the drink on the table, already in need of a finer polish; and even on the schoolmaster's worn trousers, though Spalt remained motionless.

"Men's dreams, their inner truth, are *unheimlich* also, your Highness. If any man examines his inner truth with both eyes wide open, and his inner eye wide open also, he will be overcome with terror at what he finds. That, I have always supposed, is why we hear these stories about a region of our lake. Out there, on the water, in darkness, out of sight, men encounter the image within them. Or so they suppose. It is not to be expected that many will return unscathed."

"Thus with men, Spalt. What about women?"

"Women have no inner life that is so decisively apart. With women the inner life merges ever with the totality. That is why women seem to men either deceitful and elusive, or moralistic and uninteresting. Women have no problem comparable with the problem of merely being a man. They do not need our lake."

"Have you ever been married, Spalt? I imagine not at all."

"Certainly, I have been married, your Highness. As I reminded your Highness, I am but a peasant."

"And what happened?"

"She died in childbirth. Our first-born."

"I am sorry, Spalt."

"No doubt it also saved much sadness for both of us. There is always that to remember."

"Did the child die too?"

"No, your Highness. She did not. The father had no inclination to remarry; and a woman to look after the child—the little girl—would have led at once to malice when the father was a schoolmaster, and required to be an example. I was fortunate in being able to leave the child in a good home. As schoolmaster, I was of course informed about all the homes. She is now in your Highness's employ, but she has no idea that I am her father, and would suffer much if she knew, so that I request your Highness to be silent, if the occasion ever occurs."

"Of course, of course, Spalt. I grieve for you that things did not work out better."

"All things must go ill one day, your Highness, or what seems to be ill. That is the message of the *memento mori*. And usually it is one day soon." His long glass was empty again, and he was gazing with apparent absorption at the patches of discoloration on the backs of his hands.

The Bodensee is not precisely a mountain lake. Only at the eastern end, in the territory of the Austrian Empire, above and around Bregenz, are the mountains immediate. Elsewhere they are but background, sometimes distant; occasionally fanciful, as behind Bodman, where the primitives live; often invisible through the transforming atmosphere. None the less, around the wider perimeter the mountains wait and watch, as do the immense, unknowable entities that on and within them dwell. When the moon is clouded or withdrawn, there are those areas where the lake seems as large as the sea, as black, as treacherous, as omnipotent; and no one can tell how cold who has not been afloat there in a small boat alone.

So it was now with Elmo. There was no gleam or spark of light anywhere, but there was a faint swell on the surface of the water, and every now and then the clink of ice against the boat, though one might not have supposed the season for ice quite arrived. Never before in his life had he experienced such total darkness. Never in his childhood had he been locked in a dark cellar or cupboard, and never in manhood had he known serious action in the field. Somewhere between the rickety but, as he embarked, reasonably visible castle jetty, with its prohibitory notices, and the part of the lake where he now was, he had realized that the fabric of the boat had suffered from neglect; but he could not see the water that had seeped in, or for that matter yet hear it swill. It was merely that he could feel dampness, and a little more than dampness, when, having paused in his progress, he had placed his hand on the floor planks; which he had been led to do by the almost uncanny coldness of his ten toes.

Still it was no matter to go back for. Life's challenge (or menace) can, after all, never be evaded; and Elmo realized that, within his world of pain, he was fortunate that to him the contest presented itself in a shape so clear-cut, so four-square, defined with such comparative precision by a schoolmaster. Whatever else might happen (if anything did), the little boat would not sink yet awhile.

Indeed, it was perhaps not such a little boat at that: Elmo was finding it heavier and heavier to pull with every minute that passed, or was it with every hour? The darkness was so thick that it impeded his movements like frozen black treacle. The darkness also smelt. Whoever can tell what lies beneath deep waters after all the centuries and millennia; especially under such unmastered and comparatively remote waters as Elmo now traversed?

Soon it seemed as if not merely the darkness but the lake itself were holding him back. It was almost as if he were sweating to pull or push the vessel through frozen mud; through a waste such as only the earliest seekers for the North West Passage had had to include among their trials. For all his exertion, Elmo could feel the ice quickly forming not merely on his face, but all over his body. Soon he might be encased, and doubtless the ill-maintained boat also.

The boat was lower in the water. Elmo realized this as he tried to pull. And it was no matter of a possible leak in the hull. There was no more water in the bottom of the boat than formerly. It was still possible for Elmo to check that; which he did with his cold right hand. For the purpose he had to leave hold of the oar or scull; but the boat was so far down that somehow the oar left its rowlock, thereby left the boat also, and vanished into the darkness with an odd crash. Elmo in horror clutched at the other oar with both hands at once; but this action merely swung the boat's course many points to port, and the other oar vanished likewise as she twisted through the mysteriously resistant water. Elmo's hands were too frozen to hold on to the unwieldy object under such conditions.

Elmo realized that something had hold of the bottom of the boat. He could feel the straining of her timbers, robust enough looking on shore, but out here truly matchwood or less. Indeed, the drag and stress on the boat's planks was by now the only thing he could feel, and he felt it through all his muscles. Nor was there a thing to be seen; though the confused odours were being subtly alembicated into one single sweet perfume. The crackling of the ice against the boat seemed to Elmo to be rising to a roar, although, surely, it was yet but autumn.

It was not, he thought, the same lady that he had seen, however momentarily, however dreamily, above the lake in the *Tiergarten*. But she was visible all the same; and Elmo at once apprehended how and why. It must indeed be that many hours had passed, though previously he had not really thought so; because here, once more, was the first, faint, frightening light of dawn. This lady, too, had large eyes and a large mouth; but now the mouth was open, showing white and pointed teeth, as many teeth as a strange fish. Although her mouth was so very open, this lady smiled not.

And, of course, as in the earlier instance, she was gone almost as soon as come; but, also as in the earlier instance, she brought back to the eyes of the heart the vision of Elvira, dread and lethal and indestructible.

Elmo laid himself down in the boat. He was an ice-man. "Receive one who is dead already," he half whispered to the spirits of the lake and mountains.

The light was more yellow than grey; the surface ice by no means so dense, or even so serrated as Elmo supposed. It is to be repeated it was no later than autumn.

The few remains were far beyond identification. The body had been gnashed and gnawed and ripped, so that even the bones were mostly sliced away and splintered. And, of course, there was no proper head. All had in truth to be guesswork. "There's nothing *in* that coffin," men mouthed to each other when, in a few days' time, the hour came for the noble ceremony. Moreover, from first finding to last disposing, throughout it was freezing winter, authentically and accurately.

And what happened to Viktor, some have wondered? From the time of Elmo's presumed death, he seemed steadily to recapture his wits, until when the world war struck, a generation and a half later, he was deemed fit once more for service of a kind, and, though stationed far behind the lines, had the misfortune to be annihilated, with all who were with him, in consequence of a freakish hit by the British artillery; a lucky shot, the British might have called it. Thus Viktor's death too was not without distinction.

4

PAGES FROM A YOUNG GIRL'S
JOURNAL

---

3 OCTOBER. PADUA—FERRARA—RAVENNA. We've reached Ravenna only
four days after leaving that horrid Venice. And all in a hired carriage!
I feel sore and badly bitten too. It was the same yesterday, and the
day before, and the day before that. I wish I had someone to talk to.
This evening, Mamma did not appear for dinner at all. Papa just sat
there saying nothing and looking at least 200 years old instead of only
100, as he usually does. I wonder how old he *really* is? But it's no good
wondering. We shall never know, or at least I shan't. I often think
Mamma *does* know, or very nearly. I wish Mamma were someone I
could talk to, like Caroline's Mamma. I often used to think that Caroline and her Mamma were more like sisters together, though of course
I could never say such a thing. But then Caroline is pretty and gay,
whereas I am pale and quiet. When I came up here to my room after
dinner, I just sat in front of the long glass and stared and stared. I
must have done it for half an hour or perhaps an hour. I only rose to
my feet when it had become quite dark outside.

I don't like my room. It's much too big and there are only two
wooden chairs, painted in greeny-blue with gold lines, or once painted
like that. I hate having to lie on my bed when I should prefer to sit
and everyone knows how bad it is for the back. Besides, this bed,
though it's enormous, seems to be as hard as when the earth's dried up
in summer. Not that the earth's like that here. Far from it. The rain
has never stopped since we left Venice. Never once. Quite unlike what
Miss Gisborne said before we set out from my dear, dear Derbyshire.
This bed really is *huge*. It would take at least eight people my size. I
don't like to think about it. I've just remembered: it's the third of the

month so that we've been gone exactly half a year. What a lot of places I have been to in that time—or been through! Already I've quite forgotten some of them. I never properly saw them in any case. Papa has his own ideas and one thing I'm sure of is that they are quite unlike other people's ideas. To me the whole of Padua is just a man on a horse—stone or bronze, I suppose, but I don't even know which. The whole of Ferrara is a huge palace—castle—fortress that simply frightened me, so that I didn't *want* to look. It was as big as this bed—in its own way, of course. And those were two large, famous towns I have visited this very week. Let alone where I was perhaps two months ago! What a farce! as Caroline's Mamma always says. I wish she were here now and Caroline too. No one ever hugged and kissed me and made things happy as they do.

The contessa has at least provided me with no fewer than twelve candles. I found them in one of the drawers. I suppose there's nothing else to do but read—except perhaps to say one's prayers. Unfortunately, I finished all the books I brought with me long ago, and it's so difficult to buy any new ones, especially in English. However, I managed to purchase two very long ones by Mrs Radcliffe before we left Venice. Unfortunately, though there are twelve candles, there are only two candlesticks, both broken, like everything else. Two candles *should* be enough, but all they seem to do is make the room look even larger and darker. Perhaps they are not-very-good foreign candles. I noticed that they seemed very dirty and discoloured in the drawer. In fact, one of them looked quite black. That one must have lain in the drawer a very long time. By the way, there is a framework hanging from the ceiling in the middle of the room. I cannot truthfully describe it as a chandelier: perhaps as the ghost of a chandelier. In any case, it is a long way from even the foot of the bed. They do have the most *enormous* rooms in these foreign houses where we stay. Just as if it were very warm the whole time, which it certainly is not. What a farce!

As a matter of fact, I'm feeling quite cold at this moment, even though I'm wearing my dark-green woollen dress that in Derbyshire saw me through the whole of last winter. I wonder if I should be any warmer *in* bed? It is something I can never make up my mind about. Miss Gisborne always calls me "such a chilly mortal". I see I have used the present tense. I wonder if that is appropriate in the case of Miss Gisborne? Shall I ever see Miss Gisborne again? I mean in *this* life, of course.

Now that six days have passed since I have made an entry in this journal, I find that I am putting down *everything*, as I always do once I make a start. It is almost as if nothing horrid could happen to me as long as I keep on writing. That is simply silly, but I sometimes wonder whether the silliest things are not often the truest.

I write down words on the page, but what do I say? Before we started, everyone told me that, whatever else I did, I *must* keep a journal, a travel journal. I do not think this a travel journal at all. I find that when I am travelling with Papa and Mamma, I seem hardly to look at the outside world. Either we are lumbering along, with Papa and Mamma naturally in the places from which something can be seen, or at least from which things can be best seen; or I find that I am alone in some great vault of a bedroom for hours and hours and hours, usually quite unable to go to sleep, sometimes for the whole night. I should see so much more if I could sometimes walk about the different cities on my own—naturally, I do not mean at night. I wish that were possible. Sometimes I really hate being a girl. Even Papa cannot hate my being a girl more than I do sometimes.

And then when there *is* something to put down, it always seems to be the same thing! For example, here we are in still another of these households to which Papa always seems to have an entrée. Plainly it is very wicked of me, but I sometimes wonder *why* so many people should want to know Papa, who is usually so silent and disagreeable, and always so old! Perhaps the answer is simple enough: it is that they never meet him—or Mamma—or me. We drive up, Papa gives us all over to the major-domo or someone, and the family never sets eyes on us, because the family is never at home. These foreign families seem to have terribly many houses and always to be living in another of them. And when one of the family *does* appear, he or she usually seems to be almost as old as Papa and hardly able to speak a word of English. I think I have a pretty voice, though it's difficult to be quite sure, but I deeply wish I had worked harder at learning foreign languages. At least—the trouble is that Miss Gisborne is so bad at teaching them. I must say *that* in my own defence, but it doesn't help much now. I wonder how Miss Gisborne would be faring if she were in this room with me? Not much better than I am, if you ask me.

I have forgotten to say, though, that this is one of the times when we *are* supposed to be meeting the precious family; though, apparently, it consists only of two people, the contessa and her daughter. Sometimes I feel that I have already seen enough women without particularly wanting to meet any new ones, whatever their ages. There's something rather monotonous about women—unless, of course, they're like Caroline and her Mamma, which none of them are, or could be. So far the contessa and her daughter have not appeared. I don't know why not, though no doubt Papa knows. I am told that we are to meet them both tomorrow. I expect very little. I wonder if it will be warm enough for me to wear my green satin dress instead of my green woollen dress? Probably not.

And this is the town where the great, the immortal Lord Byron lives in sin and wildness! Even Mamma has spoken of it several times. Not that this melancholy house is actually *in* the town. It is a villa at some little distance away from it, though I do not know in which direction, and I am sure that Mamma neither knows nor cares. It seemed to me that after we passed through the town this afternoon, we travelled on for fifteen or twenty minutes. Still, to be even in the same *region* as Lord Byron must somewhat move even the hardest heart; and my heart, I am very sure, is not hard in the least.

I find that I have been scribbling away for nearly an hour. Miss Gisborne keeps on saying that I am too prone to the insertion of unnecessary hyphens, and that it is a weakness. If a weakness it is, I intend to cherish it.

I know that an hour has passed because there is a huge clock somewhere that sounds every quarter. It must be a *huge* clock because of the noise it makes, and because everything abroad *is* huge.

I am colder than ever and my arms are quite stiff. But I must drag off my clothes somehow, blow out the candles, and insinuate my tiny self into this enormous, frightening bed. I do hate the lumps you get all over your body when you travel abroad, and so much hope I don't get many more during the night. Also I hope I don't start feeling thirsty, as there's no water of any kind, let alone water safe to drink.

Ah, Lord Byron, living out there in riot and wickedness! It is impossible to forget him. I wonder what he would think of *me?* I do hope there are not too many biting things in this room.

4 October. What a surprise! The contessa has said it will be quite in order for me to go for short walks in the town, provided I have my maid with me; and when Mamma at once pointed out that I had no maid, offered the services of her own! To think of this happening the very day after I wrote down in this very journal that it could never happen! I am now quite certain that it would have been perfectly correct for me to walk about the other towns too. I daresay that Papa and Mamma suggested otherwise only because of the difficulty about the

maid. Of course I *should* have a maid, just as Mamma should have a maid too and Papa a man, and just as we should all have a proper carriage of our own, with our crest on the doors! If it was that we were too poor, it would be humiliating. As we are not too poor (I am sure we are not), it is farcical. In any case, Papa and Mamma went on making a fuss, but the contessa said we had now entered the States of the Church, and were, therefore, all living under the special beneficence of God. The contessa speaks English very well and even knows the English *idioms*, as Miss Gisborne calls them.

Papa screwed up his face when the contessa mentioned the States of the Church, as I knew he would. Papa remarked several times while we were on the way here that the Papal States, as he calls them, are the most misgoverned in Europe and that it was not only as a Protestant that he said so. I wonder. When Papa expresses opinions of that kind, they often seem to me to be just notions of his own, like his notions of the best way to travel. After the contessa had spoken as she did, I felt—very strongly—that it must be rather beautiful to be ruled directly by the Pope and his cardinals. Of course, the cardinals and even the Pope are subject to error, as are our own bishops and rectors, all being but men, as Mr Biggs-Hartley continually emphasizes at home; but, all the same, they simply *must* be nearer to God than the sort of people who rule us in England. I do not think Papa can be depended upon to judge such a question.

I am determined to act upon the contessa's kind offer. Miss Gisborne says that though I am a pale little thing, I have very much a will of my own. Here will be an opportunity to prove it. There may be certain difficulties because the contessa's maid can only speak Italian; but when the two of us shall be alone together, it is I who shall be mistress and she who will be maid, and nothing can change that. I have seen the girl. She is a pretty creature, apart from the size of her nose.

Today it has been wet, as usual. This afternoon we drove round Ravenna in the contessa's carriage: a proper carriage for once, with arms on the doors and a footman as well as the coachman. Papa has paid off our hired coach. I suppose it has lumbered away back to Fusina, opposite to Venice. I expect I can count upon our remaining in Ravenna for a week. That seems to be Papa's usual sojourn in one of our major stopping places. It is not very long, but often it is quite long enough, the way we live.

This afternoon we saw Dante's Tomb, which is simply by the side of the street, and went into a big church with the Throne of Neptune in it, and then into the Tomb of Galla Placidia, which is blue inside, and very beautiful. I was on the alert for any hint of where Lord Byron might reside, but it was quite unnecessary to speculate, because the contessa almost shouted it out as we rumbled along one of the streets: "The Palazzo Guiccioli. See the netting across the bottom of the door to prevent Lord Byron's animals from straying." "Indeed, indeed," said Papa, looking out more keenly than he had at Dante's Tomb. No more was said, because, though both Papa and Mamma had more than once alluded to Lord Byron's present way of life so that I should be able to understand things that might come up in conversation, yet neither the contessa nor Papa and Mamma knew how much I might really understand. Moreover, the little contessina was in the carriage, sitting upon a cushion on the floor at her Mamma's feet, making five of us in all, foreign carriages being as large as everything else foreign; and I daresay *she* knew nothing at all, sweet little innocent.

"Contessina" is only a kind of nickname or *sobriquet,* used by the family and the servants. The contessina is really a contessa: in foreign noble families, if one person is a duke, then all the other men seem to be dukes also, and all the women duchesses. It is very confusing and nothing like such a good arrangement as ours, where there is only one duke and one duchess to each family. I do not know the little contessina's age. Most foreign girls look far older than they really are, whereas most of our girls look younger. The contessa is *very* slender, a veritable sylph. She has an olive complexion, with no blemish of any kind. People often write about "olive complexions": the contessina really has one. She has absolutely enormous eyes, the shape of broad beans, and not far off that in colour; but she never uses them to look at anyone. She speaks so little and often has such an empty, lost expression that one might think her more than slightly simple; but I do not think she is. Foreign girls are raised quite differently from the way our girls are raised. Mamma frequently refers to this, pursing her lips. I must admit that I cannot see myself finding in the contessina a friend, pretty though she is in her own way, with feet about half the size of mine or Caroline's.

When foreign girls grow up to become women, they usually continue, poor things, to look older than they are. I am sure this applies to the contessa. The contessa has been very kind to me—in the few hours that I have so far known her—and even seems to be a little sorry for me—as, indeed, I am for her. But I do not understand the contessa. Where was she last night? Is the little contessina her only child? What

has become of her husband? Is it because he is dead that she seems—
and looks—so sad? Why does she want to live in such a big house—it is
called a villa, but one might think it a palazzo—when it is all falling to
bits, and much of it barely even furnished? I should like to ask
Mamma these questions, but I doubt whether she would have the
right answers, or perhaps any answers.

The contessa did appear for dinner this evening, and even the little
contessina. Mamma was there too: in that frock I dislike. It really is
the wrong kind of red—especially for Italy, where *dark* colours seem
to be so much worn. The evening was better than last evening; but
then it could hardly have been worse. (Mr Biggs-Hartley says we
should never say that: things can *always* be worse.) It was not a *good*
evening. The contessa was trying to be quite gay, despite her own obvious trouble, whatever that is; but neither Papa nor Mamma know
how to respond and I know all too well that I myself am better at
thinking about things than at casting a spell in company. What I like
most is just a few friends I know really well and whom I can truly
trust and love. Alas, it is long since I have had even one such to clasp
by the hand. Even letters seem mostly to lose themselves en route, and
I can hardly wonder; supposing people are still bothering to write
them in the first place, needless to say, which it is difficult to see why
they should be after all this time. When dinner was over, Papa and
Mamma and the contessa played an Italian game with both playing
cards and dice. The servants had lighted a fire in the salone and the
contessina sat by it doing nothing and saying nothing. If given a
chance, Mamma would have remarked that "the child should have
been in bed long ago", and I am sure she should. The contessa wanted
to teach me the game, but Papa said at once that I was too young,
which is absolutely farcical. Later in the evening, the contessa, after
playing a quite long time with Papa and Mamma, said that tomorrow
she would put her foot down (the contessa knows so many such ex-
pressions that one would swear she must have *lived* in England) and
would *insist* on my learning. Papa screwed his face up and Mamma
pursed her lips in the usual way. I had been doing needlework, which
I shall never like nor see any point in when servants can always do it
for us; and I found that I was thinking many deep thoughts. And then
I noticed that a small tear was slowly falling down the contessa's face.
Without thinking, I sprang up; but then the contessa smiled, and I sat
down. One of my deep thoughts was that it is not so much particular
disasters that make people cry, but something always there in life it-

self, something that a light falls on when we are trying to enjoy ourselves in the company of others.

I must admit that the horrid lumps are going down. I certainly do not seem to have acquired any more, which is an advantage when compared with what happened every night in Dijon, that smelly place. But I wish I had a more cheerful room, with better furniture, though tonight I have succeeded in bringing to bed one of our bottles of mineral water and even a glass from which to drink it. It is only the Italian mineral water, of course, which Mamma says may be very little safer than the ordinary water; but as all the ordinary water seems to come from the dirty wells one sees down the side streets, I think that Mamma exaggerates. I admit, however, that it is not like the bottled water one buys in France. How farcical to have to buy water in a bottle, anyway! All the same, there are some things that I have grown to *like* about foreign countries; perhaps even to prefer. It would never do to let Papa and Mamma hear me talk in such a way. I often wish I were not so sensitive, so that the rooms I am given and things of that kind did not matter so much. And yet Mamma is more sensitive about the water than I am! I am sure it is not so *important*. It can't be. To me it is *obvious* that Mamma is *less* sensitive than I am, where *important* things are concerned. My entire life is based on that obvious fact; my real life, that is.

I rather wish the contessina would invite me to share *her* room, because I think she is sensitive in the same way that I am. But perhaps the little girl sleeps in the contessa's room. I should not really mind that. I do not *hate* or even dislike the little contessina. I expect she already has troubles herself. But Papa and Mamma would never agree to it anyway, and now I have written all there is to write about this perfectly ordinary, but somehow rather odd, day. In this big cold room, I can hardly move with chilliness.

5 October. When I went in to greet Mamma this morning, Mamma had the most singular news. She told me to sit down (Mamma and Papa have more chairs in their rooms than I have, and more of other things too), and then said that there was to be a party! Mamma spoke as though it would be a dreadful ordeal, which it was impossible for us to avoid; and she seemed to take it for granted that I should receive the announcement in the same way. I do not know what I really thought about it. It is true that I have never enjoyed a party yet (not that I have been present at many of them); but all day I have been

aware of feeling different inside myself, lighter and swifter in some way, and by this evening I cannot but think it is owing to the knowledge that a party lies before me. After all, foreign parties may be different from parties at home, and probably are. I keep pointing that out to myself. This particular party will be given by the contessa, who, I feel sure, knows more about it than does Mamma. If she does, it will not be the only thing that the contessa knows more about than Mamma.

The party is to be the day after tomorrow. While we were drinking our coffee and eating our panini (always very flaky and powdery in Italy), Mamma asked the contessa whether she was sure there would be time enough for the preparations. But the contessa only smiled—in a very polite way, of course. It is probably easier to do things quickly in Italy (when one really wants to, that is), because everyone has so many servants. It is hard to believe that the contessa has much money, but she seems to keep more servants than we do, and, what is more, they behave more like slaves than like servants, quite unlike our Derbyshire keel-the-pots. Perhaps it is simply that everyone is so fond of the contessa. That I should entirely understand. Anyway, preparations for the party have been at a high pitch all day, with people hanging up banners, and funny smells from the kitchen quarters. Even the Bath House at the far end of the formal garden (it is said to have been built by the Byzantines) has had the spiders swept out and been populated with cooks, perpetrating I know not what. The transformation is quite bewildering. I wonder when Mamma first knew of what lay ahead? Surely it must at least have been before we went to bed last night?

I feel I should be vexed that a new dress is so impracticable. A train of seamstresses would have to work day and night for 48 hours, as in the fairy tales. I should like that (who would not?), but I am not at all sure that *I* should be provided with a new dress even if whole weeks were available in which to make it. Papa and Mamma would probably still agree that I had quite enough dresses already even if it were the Pope and his cardinals who were going to entertain me. All the same, I am not really vexed. I sometimes think that I am deficient in a proper interest in clothes, as Caroline's Mamma calls it. Anyway, I have learned from experience that new dresses are more often than not thoroughly disappointing. I keep reminding myself of that.

The other important thing today is that I have been out for my first walk in the town with the contessa's maid, Emilia. I just swept through what Papa had to say on the subject, as I had promised myself. Mamma was lying down at the time, and the contessa simply smiled her sweet smile and sent for Emilia to accompany me.

I must admit that the walk was not a *complete* success. I took with me our copy of Mr Grubb's *Handbook to Ravenna and Its Antiquities* (Papa could hardly say No, lest I do something far worse), and began looking places up on the map with a view to visiting them. I felt that this was the best way to start, and that, once started, I could wait to see what life would lay before me. I am often quite resolute when there is some specific situation to be confronted. The first difficulty was the quite long walk into Ravenna itself. Though it was nothing at all to me, and though it was not raining, Emilia soon made it clear that she was unaccustomed to walking a step. This could only have been an affectation, or rather pretension, because everyone knows that girls of that kind come from peasant families, where I am quite sure they have to walk about all day, and much more than merely walk about. Therefore, I took no notice at all, which was made easier by my hardly understanding a word that Emilia actually said. I simply pushed and dragged her forward. Sure enough, she soon gave up all her pretences, and made the best of the situation. There were some rough carters on the road and large numbers of horrid children, but for the most part they stopped annoying us as soon as they saw who we were, and in any case it was as nothing to the roads into Derby, where they have lately taken to throwing stones at the passing carriages.

The next trouble was that Emilia was not in the least accustomed to what I had in mind when we reached Ravenna. Of course people do not go again and again to look at their own local antiquities, however old they may be; and least of all, I suspect, Italian people. When she was not accompanying her mistress, Emilia was used to going to town only for some precise purpose: to buy something, to sell something, or to deliver a letter. There was that in her attitude which made me think of the saucy girls in the old comedies: whose only work is to fetch and carry billets-doux, and sometimes to take the places of their mistresses, with their mistresses' knowledge or otherwise. I did succeed in visiting another of these Bath Houses, this one a public spectacle and called the Baptistry of the Orthodox, because it fell into Christian hands after the last days of the Romans, who built it. It was, of course, far larger than the Bath House in the contessa's garden, but in the interior rather dark and with a floor so uneven that it was difficult not to fall. There was also a horrible dead animal inside. Emilia began laughing, and it was quite plain what she was laughing at. She was striding about as if she were back on her mountains and the kind of thing she seemed to be suggesting was that if I proposed to walk all the way to the very heel or toe of Italy she was quite prepared to walk with me, and perhaps to walk ahead of me. As an English girl, I did not care for this, nor for the complete reversal of Emilia's original attitude, almost suggesting that she has a deliberate and impertinent policy of keeping the situation between us under her own control. So, as I have said, the walk was not a complete success. All the same, I have made a start. It is obvious that the world has more to offer than would be likely to come my way if I were to spend my whole life creeping about with Papa at one side of me and Mamma at the other. I shall think about how best to deal with Emilia now that I better understand her ways. I was not in the least tired when we had walked back to the villa. I despise girls who get tired, quite as much as Caroline despises them.

Believe it or not, Mamma was still lying down. When I went in, she said that she was resting in preparation for the party. But the party is not until the day after tomorrow. Poor dear Mamma might have done better not to have left England in the first place! I must take great care that I am not like that when I reach the same time of life and am married, as I suppose I shall be. Looking at Mamma in repose, it struck me that she would still be quite pretty if she did not always look so tired and worried. Of course she was once far prettier than I am now. I know that well. I, alas, am not really pretty at all. I have to cultivate other graces, as Miss Gisborne puts it.

I saw something unexpected when I was going upstairs to bed. The little contessina had left the salone before the rest of us and, as usual, without a word. Possibly it was only I who saw her slip out, she went so quietly. I noticed that she did not return and supposed that, at her age, she was quite worn out. Assuredly, Mamma would have said so. But then when I myself was going upstairs, holding my candle, I saw for myself what had really happened. At the landing, as we in England should call it, there is in one of the corners an odd little closet or cabinet, from which two doors lead off, both locked, as I know because I have cautiously turned the handles for myself. In this corner, by the light of my candle, I saw the contessina, and she was being hugged by a man. I think it could only have been one of the servants, though I was not really able to tell. Perhaps I am wrong about that, but I am not wrong about it being the contessina. They had been there in complete darkness, and, what is more, they never moved a muscle as I came up the stairs and walked calmly along the passage in

the opposite direction. I suppose they hoped I should fail to see them
in the dimness. They must have supposed that no one would be coming to bed just yet. Or perhaps they were lost to all sense of time, as
Mrs Radcliffe expresses it. I have very little notion of the contessina's
age, but she often looks about twelve or even less. Of course I shall
say nothing to anybody.

6 October. I have been thinking on and off all day about the
differences between the ways we are supposed to behave and the
ways we actually do behave. And both are different from the ways in
which God calls upon us to behave, and which we can never achieve
whatever we do and however hard we apply ourselves, as Mr Biggs-
Hartley always emphasizes. We seem, every one of us, to be at least
three different people. And that's just to start with.

I am disappointed by the results of my little excursion yesterday
with Emilia. I had thought that there was so much of which I was
deprived by being a girl and so being unable to go about on my own,
but now I am not sure that I have been missing anything. It is almost
as if the nearer one approaches to a thing, the less it proves to be
there, to exist at all. Apart, of course, from the bad smells and bad
words and horrid rough creatures from which and from whom we
women are supposed to be "shielded". But I am waxing metaphysical;
against which Mr Biggs-Hartley regularly cautions us. I wish Caroline
were with us. I believe I might feel quite differently about things if
she were here to go about with me, just the two of us. Though, needless to say, it would make no difference to what the things truly were—
or were not. It is curious that things should seem not to exist when
visited with one person, and then to exist after all if visited with another person. Of course it is all just fancy, but what (I think at moments like this) is not?

I am so friendless and alone in this alien land. It occurs to me that I
must have great inner strength to bear up as I do and to fulfil my
duties with so little complaint. The contessa has very kindly given me
a book of Dante's verses, with the Italian on one side and an English
translation on the page opposite. She remarked that it would aid me
to learn more of her language. I am not sure that it will. I have du-
tifully read through several pages of the book, and there is nothing in
this world that I like more than reading, but Dante's ideas are so
gloomy and complicated that I suspect he is no writer for a woman,
certainly not for an English woman. Also his face frightens me, so crit-

ical and severe. After looking at his portrait, beautifully engraved at the beginning of the book, I begin to fear that I shall see that face looking over my shoulder as I sit gazing into the looking glass. No wonder Beatrice would have nothing to do with him. I feel that he was quite deficient in the graces that appeal to our sex. Of course one must not even hint such a thing to an Italian, such as the contessa, for to all Italians Dante is as sacred as Shakespeare or Dr Johnson is to us.

For once I am writing this during the afternoon. I suspect that I am suffering from ennui and, as that is a sin (even though only a minor one), I am occupying myself in order to drive it off. I know by now that I am much more prone to such lesser shortcomings as ennui and indolence than to such vulgarities as letting myself be embraced and kissed by a servant. And yet it is not that I feel myself wanting in either energy or passion. It is merely that I lack for anything or anyone worthy of such feelings, and refuse to spend them upon what is unworthy. But what a "merely" is that! How well I understand the universal ennui that possesses our neighbour, Lord Byron! I, a tiny slip of a girl, feel, at least in this particular, at one with the great poet! There might be consolation in the thought, were I capable of consolation. In any case, I am sure that there will be nothing more that is worth record before my eyes close tonight in slumber.

Later. I was wrong! After dinner tonight, it struck me simply to ask the contessa whether she had ever *met* Lord Byron. I suppose it might not be a thing she would proclaim unsolicited, either when Papa and Mamma were present, or, for reasons of delicacy, on one of the two rare occasions when she and I were alone; but I thought that I might now be sufficiently simpatica to venture a discreet enquiry.

I fear that I managed it very crudely. When Papa and Mamma had become involved in one of their arguments together, I walked across the room and sat down at the end of the sofa on which the contessa was reclining; and when she smiled at me and said something agreeable, I simply blurted out my question, quite directly. "Yes, *mia cara,*" she replied, "I have met him, but we cannot invite him to our party because he is too political, and many people do not agree with his politics. Indeed, they have already led to several deaths; which some are reluctant to accept at the hands of a straniero, however eminent." And of course it *was* the wonderful possibility of Lord Byron attending the contessa's party that *had been* at the back of my thoughts. Not for the first time, the contessa showed her fascinating insight into the minds of others—or assuredly into my mind.

7 October. The day of the party! It is quite early in the morning and the sun is shining as I have not seen it shine for some time. Perhaps it regularly shines at this time of the day, when I am still asleep? "What you girls miss by not getting up!" as Caroline's Mamma always exclaims, though she is the most indulgent of parents. The trouble is that one *always* awakens early just when it is most desirable that one should slumber longest; as today, with the party before us. I am writing this now because I am *quite certain* that I shall be nothing but a tangle of nerves all day and, after everything is over, utterly spent and exhausted. So, for me, it always is with parties! I am glad that the day after tomorrow will be Sunday.

8 October. I met a man at the party who, I must confess, interested me very much; and, beside that, what matters, as Mrs Fremlinson enquires in *The Hopeful and the Despairing Heart, almost* my favourite of all books, as I truly declare?

Who could believe it? Just now, while I was still asleep, there was a knocking at my door, just loud enough to awaken me, but otherwise so soft and discreet, and there was the contessa *herself*, in the most beautiful negligée, half-rose-coloured and half-mauve, with a tray on which were things to eat and drink, a complete foreign breakfast, in fact! I must acknowledge that at that moment I could well have devoured a complete English breakfast, but what could have been kinder or more thoughtful on the part of the charming contessa? Her dark hair (but not so dark as with the majority of the Italians) had not yet been dressed, and hung about her beautiful, though sad, face, but I noticed that all her rings were on her fingers, flashing and sparkling in the sunshine. "Alas, *mia cara*," she said, looking round the room, with its many deficiencies; "the times that were and the times that are." Then she actually bent over my face, rested her hand lightly on the top of my night-gown, and kissed me. "But how pale you look!" she continued. "You are white as a lily on the altar." I smiled. "I am English," I said, "and I lack strong colouring." But the contessa went on staring at me. Then she said: "The party has quite fatigued you?" She seemed to express it as a question, so I replied, with vigour: "Not in the least, I assure you, Contessa. It was the most beautiful evening of my life" (which was unquestionably the truth and no more than the truth). I sat up in the big bed and, so doing, saw myself in the glass. It was true that I *did* look pale, unusually pale. I was about to remark upon the earliness of the hour, when the contessa suddenly seemed to draw herself together with a gasp and turn remarkably pale herself, considering the native hue of her skin. She stretched out her hand and pointed. She seemed to be pointing at the pillow behind me. I looked round, disconcerted by her demeanour; and I saw an irregular red mark upon the pillow, not a very large mark, but undoubtedly a mark of blood. I raised my hands to my throat. *"Dio Illustrissimo!"* cried out the contessa. *"Ell' e stregata!"* I know enough Italian, from Dante and from elsewhere, to be informed of what that means: "She is bewitched." I leapt out of bed and threw my arms round the contessa before she could flee, as she seemed disposed to do. I besought her to say more, but I was all the time fairly sure that she would not. Italians, even educated ones, still take the idea of "witchcraft" with a seriousness that to us seems unbelievable; and regularly fear even to speak of it. Here I knew by instinct that Emilia and her mistress would be at one. Indeed, the contessa seemed most uneasy at my mere embrace, but she soon calmed herself, and left the room saying, quite pleasantly, that she must have a word with my parents about me. She even managed to wish me *"Buon appetito"* of my little breakfast.

I examined my face and throat in the looking-glass and there, sure enough, was a small scar on my neck which explained everything—except, indeed, how I had come by such a mark, but for that the novelties, the rigours, and the excitements of last night's party would *entirely* suffice. One cannot expect to enter the tournament of love and emerge unscratched: and it is into the tournament that, as I thrill to think, I verily have made my way. I fear it is perfectly typical of the Italian manner of seeing things that a perfectly natural, and very tiny, mishap should have such a disproportionate effect upon the contessa. For myself, an English girl, the mark upon my pillow does not even disturb me. We must hope that it does not cast into screaming hysterics the girl whose duty it will be to change the linen.

If I look especially pale, it is partly because the very bright sunlight makes a contrast. I returned at once to bed and rapidly consumed every scrap and drop that the contessa had brought to me. I seemed quite weak from lack of sustenance, and indeed I have but the slenderest recollection of last night's fare, except that, naturally, I drank far more than on most previous days of my short life, probably more than on *any*.

And now I lie here in my pretty night-gown and nothing else, with my pen in my hand and the sun on my face, and think about *him!* I did not believe such people existed in the real world. I thought that such writers as Mrs Fremlinson and Mrs Radcliffe *improved* men̄, in order to reconcile their female readers to their lot, and to put their less numerous male readers in a good conceit of themselves. Caroline's Mamma and Miss Gisborne, in their quite different ways, have both indicated as much most clearly; and my own observation hitherto of the opposite sex has confirmed the opinion. But now I have actually met a man at whom even Mrs Fremlinson's finest creation does but hint! He is an Adonis! an Apollo! assuredly a god! Where he treads, sprouts asphodel!

The first romantic thing was that he was not properly presented to me—indeed, he was not presented at all. I know this was very incorrect, but it cannot be denied that it was very exciting. Most of the guests were dancing an old-fashioned *minuetto,* but as I did not know the steps, I was sitting at the end of the room with Mamma, when Mamma was suddenly overcome in some way and had to leave. She emphasized that she would be back in only a minute or two, but almost as soon as she had gone, *he* was standing there, quite as if he had emerged from between the faded tapestries that covered the wall or even from the tapestries themselves, except that he looked very far from faded, though later, when more candles were brought in for supper, I saw that he was older than I had at first supposed, with such a wise and experienced look as I have never seen on any other face.

Of course he had not only to speak to me at once, or I should have risen and moved away, but to *compel* me, with his eyes and words, to remain. He said something pleasant about my being the only rosebud in a garden otherwise autumnal, but I am not such a goose as never to have heard speeches like that before, and it was what he said next that made me fatally hesitate. He said (and never, *never* shall I forget his words): "As we are both visitants from a world that is not this one, we should know one another". It was so exactly what I always feel about myself, as this journal (I fancy) makes clear, that I could not but yield a trifle to his apperceptiveness in finding words for my deepest conviction, extremely irregular and dangerous though I well knew my position to be. *And* he spoke in beautiful English; his accent (not, I think, an Italian one) only making his words the more choice-sounding and delightful!

I should remark here that it was not true that *all* the contessa's guests were "autumnal", even though most of them certainly were. Sweet creature that she is, she had invited several *cavalieri* from the local nobility *expressly* for my sake, and several of them had duly been presented to me, but with small conversation resulting, partly because there was so little available of a common tongue, but more because each single *cavaliero* seemed to me very much what in Derbyshire we call a peg-Jack. It was typical of the contessa's sympathetic nature that she perceived the unsuccess of these *rencontres,* and made no attempt to fan flames that were never so much as faint sparks. How unlike the matrons of Derbyshire, who, when they have set their minds to the task, will work the bellows in such cases not merely for a whole single evening, but for weeks, months, or, on occasion, years! But then it would be unthinkable to apply the word "matron" to the lovely contessa! As it was, the four *cavalieri* were left to make what they could of the young contessina and such other *bambine* as were on parade.

I pause for a moment seeking words in which to describe him. He is above the average tall, and, while slender and elegant, conveys a wondrous impression of force and strength. His skin is somewhat pallid, his nose aquiline and commanding (though with quivering, sensitive nostrils), his mouth scarlet and (I must apply the word) passionate. Just to look at his mouth made me think of great poetry and wide seas. His fingers are very long and fine, but powerful in their grip: as I learned for myself before the end of the evening. His hair I at first thought quite black, but I saw later that it was delicately laced with grey, perhaps even white. His brow is high, broad, and noble. Am I describing a god or a man? I find it hard to be sure.

As for his conversation I can only say that, indeed, it was not of this world. He proffered none of the empty chatter expected at social gatherings; which, in so far as it has any meaning at all, has a meaning quite different from that which the words of themselves convey—a meaning often odious to me. Everything he said (at least after that first conventional compliment) spoke to something deep within me, and everything I said in reply was what I really wanted to say. I have been able to talk in that way before with no man of any kind, from Papa downwards; and with very few women. And yet I find it difficult to recall what subjects we discussed. I think that may be a *consequence* of the feeling with which we spoke. The feeling I not merely recollect but feel still—all over and through me—deep and warm—transfiguring. The subjects, no. They were life, and beauty, and art, and nature, and myself: in fact, *everything.* Everything, that is, except the very different and very silly things that almost everyone else talks about all the time, chatter and chump without stopping this side of the churchyard. He did once observe that "Words are what prevail with women", and I could only smile, it was so true.

Fortunately, Mamma *never* re-appeared. As for the rest of them, I daresay they were more relieved than otherwise to find the gauche little English girl off their hands, so to speak, and apparently provided for. With Mamma indisposed, the obligation to watch over me would descend upon the contessa, but her I saw only in the distance. Perhaps she was resolved not to intrude where *I* should not wish it. If so, it would be what I should expect of her. I do not know.

Then came supper. Much to my surprise (and chagrin), my friend, if so I may call him, excused himself from participating. His explanation, lack of appetite, could hardly be accepted as sufficient or courteous, but the words he employed, succeeded (as always, I feel, with him) in purging the offence. He affirmed most earnestly that I must sustain myself even though he were unable to escort me, and that he would await my return. As he spoke, he gazed at me so movingly that I could but accept the situation, though I daresay I had as little appetite (for the coarse foods of this world) as he. I perceive that I have so far omitted to refer to the beauty and power of his eyes; which are so dark as to be almost black—at least by the light of candles. Glancing back at him, perhaps a little keenly, it occurred to me that he might be bashful about showing himself in his full years by the bright lights of the supper tables. It is a vanity *by no means* confined to my own sex. Indeed he seemed almost to be shrinking away from the augmented brightness even at this far end of the room. And this for all the impression of strength which was the most marked thing about him. Tactfully I made to move off. "You will return?" he asked, so anxiously and compellingly. I remained calm. I merely smiled.

And then Papa caught hold of me. He said that Mamma, having gone upstairs, had succumbed totally, as I might have known in advance she would do, and in fact *did* know; and that, when I had supped, I had "better come upstairs also". At that Papa elbowed me through to the tables and started trying to stuff me like a turkey, but, as I have said, I had little gusto for it, so little that I cannot now name a single thing that I ate, or that Papa ate either. Whatever it was, I "washed it down" (as we say in Derbyshire) with an unusual quantity (for me) of the local wine, which people, including Papa, always say is so "light", but which always seems to me no "lighter" than any other, but noticeably "heavier" than some I could name. What is more, I had already consumed a certain amount of it earlier in the evening when I was supposed to be flirting with the local peg-Jacks. One curious thing is that Papa, who never fails to demur at my doing almost anything else, seems to have no objection to my drinking wine quite heavily. I do not think I have ever known him even try to impose a limit. That is material, of course, only in the rare absence of Mamma, to whom this observation does not apply. But Mamma herself is frequently unwell after only two or three glasses. At supper last night, I was in a state of "trance": eating food was well-nigh impossible, but drinking wine almost fatally facile. Then Papa started trying to push me off to bed again—or perhaps to hold Mamma's head. After all that wine, and with my new friend patiently waiting for me, it was farcical. But I had to dispose of Papa somehow, so I promised him faithfully, and forgot my promise (whatever it was) immediately. Mercifully, I have not so far set eyes upon Papa since that moment.

Or, in reality, upon *anyone* until the contessa waked me this morning: on anyone but *one*.

There he was quietly awaiting me among the shadows cast by the slightly swaying tapestries and by the flapping bannerets ranged round the walls above us. This time he actually clutched my hand in his eagerness. It was only for a moment, of course, but I felt the firmness of his grip. He said he hoped he was not keeping me from the dance floor, but I replied No, oh No. In truth, I was barely even capable of dancing at that moment; and I fancy that the measures trod by the musty relics around us were, at the best of times, not for me. Then he said, with a slight smile, that once he had been a great dancer. Oh, I said idly and under the power of the wine; where was that? At Versailles, he replied; and in Petersburg. I must say that, wine or no wine, this surprised me; because surely, as everyone knows, Versailles was burned down by the incendiaries in 1789, a good thirty years ago? I must have glanced at him significantly, because he then said, smiling once more, though faintly: "Yes, I am very, *very* old." He said it with such curious emphasis that he did not seem to demand some kind of denial, as such words normally do. In fact, I could find nothing immediate to say at all. And yet it was nonsense, and denial would have been sincere. I do not know his age, and find even an approximation difficult, but "very, very old" he most certainly is not, but in all important ways one of the truly youngest people that can be imagined, and one of the most truly ardent. He was wearing the most beautiful black clothes, with a tiny Order of some kind, I am sure *most* distinguished, because so unobtrusive. Papa has often remarked that the flashy display of Honours is no longer correct.

In some ways the most romantic thing of all is that I do not even know his name. As people were beginning to leave the party, not so very late, I suppose, as most of the people were, after all, quite old, he took my hand and this time held it, nor did I even affect to resist. "We shall meet again," he said, "many times;" looking so deeply and steadily into my eyes that I felt he had penetrated my inmost heart and soul. Indeed, there was something so powerful and mysterious about my own feelings at that moment that I could only murmur "Yes," in a voice so weak that he could hardly have heard me, and then cover my eyes with my hands, those eyes into which he had been gazing so piercingly. For a moment (it cannot have been longer, or my discomposure would have been observed by others), I sank down into a chair with all about me black and swimming, and when I had recovered myself, he was no longer there, and there was nothing to do but be kissed by the contessa, who said "You're looking tired, child," and be hastened to my big bed, immediately.

And though new emotions are said to deprive us of rest (as I have myself been able to confirm on one or two occasions), I seem to have *slept* immediately too, and very deeply, and for a very long time. I know, too, that I dreamed remarkably, but I cannot at all recollect of what. Perhaps I do not need the aid of memory, for surely I can surmise?

On the first occasion since I have been in Italy, the sun is truly very hot. I do not think I shall write any more today. I have already covered pages in my small, clear handwriting, which owes so much to Miss Gisborne's patience and severity, and to her high standards in all matters touching young girlhood. I am rather surprised that I have been left alone for so long. Though Papa and Mamma do not seem to me to accomplish very much in proportion to the effort they expend, yet they are very inimical to "lying about and doing nothing", especially in my case, but in their own cases also, as I must acknowledge. I wonder how Mamma is faring after the excitement of last night? I am sure I should arise, dress, and ascertain; but instead I whisper to myself that once more I feel powerfully drawn towards the embrace of Morpheus.

9 October. Yesterday morning I decided that I had already recorded enough for one single day (though for what wonderful events I had to try, however vainly, to find words!), but there are few private occupations in this world about which I care more than inscribing the thoughts and impressions of my heart in this small, secret journal, which no one else shall ever in this world see (I shall take good care of that), so that I am sure I should again have taken up my pen in the

evening, had there been any occurrence sufficiently definite to write about. *That,* I fear, is what Miss Gisborne would call one of my overloaded sentences, but overloaded sentences can be the reflection, I am sure, of overloaded spirits, and even be their only relief and outlet! How well at this moment do I recall Miss Gisborne's moving counsel: Only find the right words for your troubles, and your troubles become half-joys. Alas, for me at this hour there can be no right words: in some strange way that I can by no means grasp hold of, I find myself fire and ice in equal parts. I have never before felt so greatly alive and yet I catch in myself an eerie conviction that my days are now closely numbered. It does not frighten me, as one would expect it to do. Indeed, it is very nearly a relief. I have never moved at my ease in this world, despite all the care that has been lavished on me; and if I had never known Caroline, I can only speculate what would have become of me. And now! What is Caroline, hitherto my dearest friend (and sometimes her Mamma too), by comparison with . . . Oh, there *are* no words. Also I have not completely recovered from the demands which last night made upon me. This is something I am rather ashamed of and shall admit to no one. But it is true. As well as being torn by emotion, I am worn to a silken thread.

The contessa, having appeared in my room yesterday morning, then disappeared and was not seen again all day, as on the day we arrived. All the same she seemed to have spoken to Mamma about me, as she had said she would be doing. This soon became clear.

It was already afternoon before I finally rose from my bed and ventured from my sunny room. I was feeling very hungry once more, and I felt that I really must find out whether Mamma was fully recovered. So I went first and knocked at the door of Mamma and Papa's rooms. As there was no answer, I went downstairs, and, though there was no one else around (when it is at all sunny, most Italians simply lie down in the shade), there was Mamma, in full and blooming health, on the terrace overlooking the garden. She had her workbox with her and was sitting in the full sun trying to do two jobs at once, perhaps three, in her usual manner. When Mamma is feeling quite well, she always fidgets terribly. I fear that she lacks what the gentleman we met in Lausanne called "the gift of repose". (I have never forgotten that expression.)

Mamma set about me at once. "Why didn't you dance with even one of those nice young men whom the contessa had gone to the trouble of inviting simply for your sake? The contessa is very upset about it. Besides, what have you been doing all the morning? This lovely,

sunny day? And what is all this other rubbish the contessa has been
trying to tell me about you? I cannot understand a word of it. Perhaps
you can enlighten me? I suppose it is something I ought to know
about. No doubt it is a consequence of your father and mother agreeing to your going into the town on your own?"

Needless to say, I know by this time how to reply to Mamma when
she rants on in terms such as these.

"The contessa is very upset about it all," Mamma exclaimed again
after I had spoken; as if a band of knaves had stolen all the spoons,
and I had been privy to the crime. "She is plainly hinting at something
which courtesy prevents her putting into words, and it is something to
do with you. I should be obliged if you would tell me what it is. Tell
me at once," Mamma commanded very fiercely.

Of course I was aware that something had taken place between the
contessa and me that morning, and by now I knew very well what lay
behind it: in one way or another the contessa had divined my *ren-
contre* of the evening before and had realized something (though how
far from the whole!) of the effect it had made upon me. Even to me
she had expressed herself in what English people would regard as an
overwrought, Italianate way. It was clear that she had said something
to Mamma on the subject, but of a veiled character, as she did not
wish actually to betray me. She had, indeed, informed me that she
was going to do this, and I now wished that I had attempted to dis-
suade her. The fact is that I had been so somnolent as to be half without my wits.

"Mamma," I said, with the dignity I have learned to display at
these times, "if the contessa has anything to complain of in my conduct, I am sure she will complain only when I am present." And, indeed, I *was* sure of that; though doubtful whether the contessa would
ever consider complaining about me at all. Her addressing herself to
Mamma in the present matter was, I could be certain, an attempt to
aid me in some way, even though possibly misdirected, as was almost
inevitable with someone who did not know Mamma very well.

"You are defying me, child," Mamma almost screamed. "You are
defying your own mother." She had so worked herself up (surely
about nothing? Even less than usual?) that she managed to prick herself. Mamma is constantly pricking herself when she attempts needlework, mainly, I always think, because she *will* not concentrate upon
any one particular task; and she keeps a wad of lint in her box against
the next time it occurs. This time, however, the lint seemed to be missing, and she appeared to have inflicted quite a gash. Poor Mamma

flapped about like a bird beneath a net, while the blood was beginning to flow quite freely. I bent forward and sucked it away with my tongue. It was really strange to have Mamma's blood in my mouth. The strangest part was that it tasted delightful; almost like an exceptionally delicious sweetmeat! I feel my own blood mantling to my cheek as I write the words now.

Mamma then managed to staunch the miniature wound with her pocket handkerchief: one of the pretty ones she had purchased in Besançon. She was looking at me in her usual critical way, but all she said was: "It is perhaps fortunate that we are leaving here on Monday."

Though it was our usual routine, nothing had been said on the present occasion, and I was aghast. (Here, I suppose, *was* something definite to record yesterday evening!)

"What!" I cried. "Leave the sweet contessa so soon! Leave, within only a week, the town where Dante walked and wrote!" I smile a little as I perceive how, without thinking, I am beginning to follow the flamboyant, Italian way of putting things. I am not really sure that Dante did *write* anything much in Ravenna, but to Italians such objections have little influence upon the choice of words. I realize that it is a habit I must guard against taking to an extreme.

"Where Dante walked may be not at all a suitable place for you to walk," rejoined Mamma, uncharitably, but with more sharpness of phrase and thought than is customary with her. She was fondling her injured thumb the while, and had nothing to mollify her acerbity towards me. The blood was beginning to redden the impromptu bandage, and I turned away with what writers call "very mixed feelings".

All the same, I did manage to see some more of the wide world before we left Ravenna; and on the very next day, this day, Sunday, and even though it is a Sunday. Apparently, there is no English church in Ravenna, so that all we could compass was for Papa to read a few prayers this morning and go through the Litany, with Mamma and me making the responses. The major-domo showed the three of us to a special room for the purpose. It had nothing in it but an old table with shaky legs and a line of wooden chairs: all dustier and more decrepit even than other things I have seen in the villa. Of course all this has happened in previous places when it was a Sunday, but never before under such dispiriting conditions—even, as I felt, *unhealthy* conditions. I was *most* disagreeably affected by the entire experience and *entirely* unable to imbibe the Word of God, as I should have done. I have never felt like that before even at the least uplifting of Family

Prayers. Positively *irreverent* thoughts raced uncontrolledly through my little head: for example, I found myself wondering how efficacious God's Word could be for Salvation when droned and stumbled over by a mere uncanonized layman such as Papa—no, I mean, of course, *unordained*, but I have let the first word stand because it is so comic when applied to Papa, who is always denouncing "the Roman Saints" and all they represent, such as frequent days of public devotion in their honour. English people speak so unkindly of the Roman Catholic priests, but at least they have all, including the most unworthy of them, been touched by hands that go back and back and back to Saint Peter and so to the Spurting Fountain of Grace itself. You can hardly say the same for Papa, and I believe that even Mr Biggs-Hartley's consecrationary position is a matter of dispute. I feel very strongly that the Blood of the Lamb cannot be mediated unless by the Elect or washed in by hands that are not strong and white.

Oh, how can he fulfil his promise that "We shall meet again", if Papa and Mamma drag me, protesting, from the place where we met first? Let alone meet "Many times"? These thoughts distract me, as I need not say; and yet I am quite sure that they distract me less than one might expect. For that the reason is simple enough: deep within me I *know* that some wondrous thing, some special election, has passed between him and me, and that meet again we shall in consequence, and no doubt "Many times". Distracted about it all though I am, I am simultaneously so sure as to be almost at peace: fire and ice, as I have said. I find I can still sometimes think about other things, which was by no means the case when I fancied, long, long ago, that I was "in love" (perish the thought!) with Mr Franklin Stobart. Yes, yes, my wondrous friend has brought to my wild soul a measure of peace at last! I only wish I did not feel so tired. Doubtless it will pass when the events of the night before last are more distant (what sadness, though, when they are! What sadness, happen what may!), and, I suppose, this afternoon's tiring walk also. No, *not* "tiring". I refuse to admit the word, and that malapert Emilia returned home "fresh as a daisy", to use the expression her kind of person uses where I come from.

But what a walk it proved to be, none the less! We wandered through the *Pineta di Classe:* a perfectly enormous forest between Ravenna and the sea, with pine trees like very thick, dark, bushy umbrellas, and, so they say, either a brigand or a bear hiding behind each one of them! I have never seen such pine trees before; not in France or Switzerland or the Low Countries, let alone in England. They are more like trees in the *Thousand Nights and a Night* (not that I have read that work), dense enough at the top and stout-trunked enough for rocks to nest in! And such countless numbers of them, all so old! Left without a guide, I should easily have found myself lost within only a few minutes, so many and so vague are the different tracks among the huge conifers but I have to admit that Emilia, quite shed now of her *bien élevée* finicking, strode out almost like a boy, and showed a knowledge of the best routes that I could only wonder at and take advantage of. There is now almost an understanding between me and Emilia, and it is mainly from her that I am learning an amount of Italian that is beginning quite to surprise me. All the time I recall, however, that it is a very simple language: the great poet of *Paradise Lost* (not that I have read that work either) remarked that it was unnecessary to set aside special periods for instruction in Italian, because one could simply pick it up as one went along. So it is proving between me and Emilia.

The forest routes are truly best suited to gentlemen on horseback, and at one place two such emerged from one of the many tracks going off to our left. "*Guardi!*" cried out Emilia and clutched my arm as if she were my intimate. "Milord Byron and Signor Shelley!" (I do not attempt to indicate Emilia's funny approximation to the English names.) What a moment in my life—or in anyone's life! To see at the same time two persons both so great and famous and both so irrevocably doomed! There was not, of course, time enough for any degree of close observation, though Mr Shelley seemed slightly to acknowledge with his crop our standing back a little to allow him and his friend free passage, but I fear that my main impression was of both *giaours* looking considerably older than I had expected and Lord Byron considerably more corpulent (as well as being quite grey-headed, though I believe only at the start of his life's fourth decade). Mr Shelley was remarkably untidy in his dress and Lord Byron most comical: in that respect at least, the reality was in accord with the report. Both were without hats or caps. They cantered away down the track up which we had walked. They were talking in loud voices (Mr Shelley's noticeably high in pitch), both together, above the thudding of their horses' hoofs. Neither of them really stopped talking even when slowing in order to wheel, so to speak, round the spot where we stood.

And so I have at length set eyes upon the fabled Lord Byron! A wondrous moment indeed; but how much more wondrous for me if it had occurred before that recent most wondrous of all possible moments! But it would be very wrong of me to complain because the red

and risen moon has quite dimmed my universal nightlight! Lord
Byron, that child of destiny, is for the whole world and, no doubt, for
all time, or at least for a great deal of it! My fate is a different one and
I draw it to my breast with a young girl's eager arms!

"Come gentili!" exclaimed Emilia, gazing after our two horsemen.
It was not perhaps the most appropriate comment upon Lord Byron,
or even upon Mr Shelley, but there was nothing for me to reply (even
if I could have found the Italian words), so on went our walk, with
Emilia now venturing so far as to sing, in a quite pretty voice, and me
lacking heart to chide her, until in the end the pine-trees parted and I
got my first glimpse of the Adriatic Sea, and, within a few more paces,
a whole wide prospect of it. (The Venetian Lagoon I refuse to take
seriously.) The Adriatic Sea is linked with the Mediterranean Sea, indeed quite properly a part or portion of it, so that I can now say to
myself that I have "seen the Mediterranean"; which good old Doctor
Johnson defined as the true object of all travel. It was almost as if at
long last my own eyes had seen the Holy Grail, with the Redemptive
Blood streaming forth in golden splendour; and I stood for whole moments quite lost in my own deep thoughts. The world falls from me
once more in a moment as I muse upon that luminous, rapturous
flood.

But I can write no more. So unwontedly weary do I feel that the
vividness of my vision notwithstanding is something to be marvelled
at. It is as if my hand were guided as was Isabella's by the distant
Traffio in Mrs Fremlinson's wonderful book; so that Isabella was enabled to leave a record of the strange events that preceded her death—
without which record, as it now occurs to me, the book, fiction though
it be, could hardly with sense have been written at all. The old moon
is drenching my sheets and my night-gown in brightest crimson. In
Italy, the moon is always full and always so red.

Oh, when next shall I see my friend, my paragon, my genius!

10 October. I have experienced so sweet and great a dream that I
must write down the fact before it is forgotten, and even though I find
that already there is almost nothing left that *can* be written. I have
dreamed that he was with me; that he indued my neck and breast
with kisses that were at once the softest and the sharpest in the world;
that he filled my ears with thoughts so strange that they could have
come only from a world afar.

And now the Italian dawn is breaking: all the sky is red and purple.

The rains have gone, as if for ever. The crimson sun calls to me to take flight before it is once more autumn and then winter. Take flight! Today we are leaving for Rimini! Yes, it is but to Rimini that I am to repair. It is farcical.

And in my dawn-red room there is once again blood upon my person. But this time I know. It is at his embrace that my being springs forth, in joy and welcome; his embrace that is at once the softest and the sharpest in the world. How strange that I could ever have failed to recall such bliss!

I rose from my bed to look for water, there being, once more, none in my room. I found that I was so weak with happiness that I all but fainted. But after sinking for a moment upon my bed, I somewhat recovered myself and succeeded in gently opening the door. And what should I find there? Or, rather, whom? In the faintly lighted corridor, at some distance, stood silently none other than the little contessina, whom I cannot recollect having previously beheld since her Mamma's *soirée à danse*. She was dressed in some kind of loose dark wrapper, and I may only leave between her and her conscience what she can have been doing. No doubt for some good reason allied therewith, she seemed turned to stone by the sight of *me*. Of course I was in *déshabillé* even more complete than her own. I had omitted even to cover my night-gown. And upon that there was blood—as if I had suffered an injury. When I walked towards her reassuringly (after all, we are but two young girls and I am not her judge—nor anyone's), she gave a low croaking scream and fled from me as if I had been the Erl Queen herself, but still almost silently, no doubt for her same good reasons. It was foolish of the little contessina, because all I had in mind to do was to take her in my arms, and then to kiss her in token of our common humanity and the strangeness of our encounter at such an hour.

I was disconcerted by the contessina's childishness (these Italians manage to be shrinking *bambine* and hardened women of the world at one and the same time), and, again feeling faint, leaned against the passage wall. When I stood full on my feet once more, I saw by the crimson light coming through one of the dusty windows that I had reached out to stop myself falling and left a scarlet impression of my hand on the painted plaster. It is difficult to excuse and impossible to remove. How I weary of these *règles* and conventionalities by which I have hitherto been bound! How I long for the measureless liberty that has been promised me and of which I feel so complete a future assurance!

But I managed to find some water (the contessa's villa is no longer of the kind that has servitors alert—or supposedly alert—all night in the larger halls), and with this water I did what I could, at least in my own room. Unfortunately I had neither enough water nor enough strength to do all. Besides, I begin to grow reckless.

11 October. No dear dream last night!

Considerable crafty unpleasantness, however, attended our departure yesterday from Ravenna. Mamma disclosed that the contessa was actually lending us her own carriage. "It's because she wants to see the last of us," said Mamma to me, looking at the cornice. "How can that be, Mamma?" I asked. "Surely, she's hardly seen us at all? She was invisible when we arrived, and now she's been almost invisible again for days." "There's no connection between those two things," Mamma replied. "At the time we arrived, the contessa was feeling unwell, as we mothers often do, you'll learn that for yourself soon. But for the last few days, she's been very upset by your behaviour, and now she wants us to go." As Mamma was still looking at the wall instead of at me, I put out the tip of my tongue, only the merest scrap of it, but *that* Mamma did manage to see, and had lifted her hand several inches before she recollected that I was now as good as an adult and so not to be corrected by a simple cuff.

And then when we were all about to enter the draggled old carriage, lo and behold the contessa did manage to haul herself into the light, and I caught her actually crossing herself behind my back, or what she no doubt thought was behind my back. I had to clench my hands to stop myself spitting at her. I have since begun to speculate whether she did not really *intend* me to see what she did. I was once so fond of the contessa, so drawn to her—I can still *remember* that quite well—but *all* is now changed. A week, I find, can sometimes surpass a lifetime; and so, for that matter, can one single indelible night. The contessa took great care to prevent her eyes once meeting mine, though, as soon as I perceived this, I never for a moment ceased glaring at her like a little basilisk. She apologised to Papa and Mamma for the absence of the contessina whom she described as being in bed with screaming megrims or the black cramp or some other malady (I truly cared not what! nor care now!) no doubt incident to girlish immaturity in Italy! And Papa and Mamma made response as if they really minded about the silly little child! Another way of expressing their disapproval of *me*, needless to observe. My considered opinion is that the contessina and her Mamma are simply two of a kind, but that the contessa has had time to become more skilled in concealment and duplicity. I am sure that all Italian females are alike, when one really knows them. The contessa had made me dig my finger-nails so far into my palms that my hands hurt all the rest of the day and still look as if I had caught a dagger in each of them, as in Sir Walter Scott's tale.

We had a coachman and a footman on the box, neither of them at all young, but more like two old wiseacres; and, when we reached Classe, we stopped in order that Papa, Mamma, and I could go inside the church, which is famous for its mosaics, going back, as usual to the Byzantines. The big doors at the western end were open in the quite hot sunshine and indeed the scene inside did look very pretty, all pale azure, the colour of Heaven, and shining gold; but I saw no more of it than that, because as I was about to cross the threshold, I was again overcome by my faintness, and sitting down on a bench, bade Papa and Mamma go in without me, which they immediately did, in the sensible English way, instead of trying to make an ado over me, in the silly Italian way. The bench was of marble, with arms in the shape of lions, and though the marble was worn, and cut, and pock-marked, it was a splendid, heavy object, carved, if I mistake not, by the Romans themselves. Seated on it, I soon felt better once more, but then I noticed the two fat old men on the coach doing something or other to the doors and windows. I supposed they were greasing them, which I am sure would have been very much in order, as would have been a considerable application of paint to the entire vehicle. But when Papa and Mamma at last came out of the church, and we all resumed our places, Mamma soon began to complain of a smell, which she said was, or at least resembled, that of the herb, garlic. Of course when one is abroad, the smell of garlic is *everywhere*, so that I quite understood when Papa merely told Mamma not to be fanciful; but then I found that I myself was more and more affected, so that we completed the journey in almost total silence, none of us, except Papa, having much appetite for the very crude meal set before us en route at Cesenatico. "You're looking white," said Papa to me, as we stepped from the coach. Then he added to Mamma, but hardly attempting to prevent my hearing, "I can see why the contessa spoke to you as she did". Mamma merely shrugged her shoulders: something she would never have thought of doing before we came abroad, but which now she does frequently. I nearly said something spiteful. At the end, the contessa, when she condescended to appear at all, was constantly disparaging my appearance, and indeed I am pale, paler than I once was, though always I have been pale enough, pale as a little phantom; but only I know the reason for the change in me, and no one else shall know it ever, because no one else ever can. It is not so much a "secret". Rather is it a revelation.

In Rimini we are but stopping at the inn; and we are almost the only persons to be doing so. I cannot wonder at this: the inn is a gaunt, forbidding place; the *padrona* has what in Derbyshire we call a "hare-lip"; and the attendance is of the worst. Indeed, no one has so far ventured to come near me. All the rooms, including mine, are very large; and all lead into one another, in the style of 200 years ago. The building resembles a palazzo that has fallen upon hard times, and perhaps that is what it is. At first I feared that my dear Papa and Mamma were to be ensconced in the apartment adjoining my own, which would have suited me not at all, but, for some reason, it has not happened, so that between my room and the staircase are two dark and empty chambers, which would once have caused me alarm, but which now I welcome. Everything is poor and dusty. Shall I ever repose abroad in such ease and *bien-être* as one takes for granted in Derbyshire? Why No, I shall not: and a chill runs down my back as I inscribe the words; but a chill more of excitement than of fear. Very soon now shall I be entirely elsewhere and entirely above such trivia.

I have opened a pair of the big windows, a grimy and, I fear, a noisy task. I flitted out in the moonlight on to the stone balcony, and gazed down into the *piazza*. Rimini seems now to be a very poor town, and there is nothing of the nocturnal uproar and riot which are such usual features of Italian existence. At this hour, all is completely silent—even strangely so. It is still very warm, but there is a mist between the earth and the moon.

I have crept into another of these enormous Italian beds. He is winging towards me. There is no further need for words. I have but to slumber, and that will be simple, so exhausted I am.

12 13 14 October. Nothing to relate but him, and of him nothing that can be related.

I am very tired, but it is tiredness that follows exaltation, not the vulgar tiredness of common life. I noticed today that I no longer have either shadow or reflection. Fortunately Mamma was quite destroyed (as the Irish simpletons express it) by the journey from Ravenna, and has not been seen since. How many, many hours one's elders pass in retirement! How glad I am never to have to experience such bondage! How I rejoice when I think about the new life which spreads before me into infinity, the new ocean which already laps at my feet, the new vessel with the purple sail and the red oars upon which I shall at any moment embark! When one is confronting so tremendous a transformation, how foolish seem words, but the habit of them lingers even when I have hardly strength to hold the pen! Soon, soon, new force will be mine, fire that is inconceivable; and the power to assume any night-shape that I may wish, or to fly through the darkness with none. What love is his! How chosen among all women am I; and I am just a little English girl! It is a miracle, and I shall enter the halls of Those Other Women with pride.

Papa is so beset by Mamma that he has failed to notice that I am eating nothing and drinking only water; that at our horrid, odious meals I am but feigning.

Believe it or not, yesterday we visited, Papa and I, the Tempio Malatestiano. Papa went as an English Visitor: I (at least by comparison with Papa) as a Pythoness. It is a beautiful edifice, among the most beautiful in the world, they say. But for me a special splendour lay in the noble and amorous dead it houses, and in the control over them which I feel increase within me. I was so rent and torn with new power that Papa had to help me back to the inn. Poor Papa, burdened, as he supposes, by *two* weak invalid women! I could almost pity him.

I wish I had reached the pretty little contessina and kissed her throat.

15 October. Last night I opened my pair of windows (the other pair resists me, weak—in terms of this world—as I am), and, without quite venturing forth, stood there in nakedness and raised both my arms. Soon a soft wind began to rustle, where all had previously been still as death. The rustling steadily rose to roaring, and the faint chill of the night turned to heat as when an oven door is opened. A great crying out and weeping, a buzzing and screaming and scratching, swept in turmoil past the open window, as if invisible (or almost invisible) bodies were turning around and around in the air outside, always lamenting and accusing. My head was split apart by the sad sounds and my body as moist as if I were an Ottoman. Then, on an instant, all had passed by. *He* stood there before me in the dim embrasure of the window. "That," he said, "is Love as the elect of this world know it."

"The *elect?*" I besought him, in a voice so low that it was hardly a voice at all (but what matter?). "Why yes," he seemed to reaffirm. "Of this world, the elect."

16 October. The weather in Italy changes constantly. Today once more it is cold and wet.

They have begun to suppose me ill. Mamma, back on her legs for a spell, is fussing like a blowfly round a dying lamb. They even called in a *medico*, after discussing at length in my presence whether an Italian physician could be regarded as of any utility. With what voice I have left, I joined in vigorously that he could not. All the same, a creature made his appearance: wearing fusty black, and, believe it or not, a grey *wig*—in all, a veritable Pantalone. What a farce! With my ever sharper fangs, I had him soon despatched, and yelling like the Old Comedy he belonged to. Then I spat forth his enfeebled, senile lymph, cleaning my lips of his skin and smell, and returned, hugging myself, to my couch.

Janua mortis vita, as Mr Biggs-Hartley says in his funny dog latin. And to think that today is Sunday! I wonder why no one has troubled to pray over me?

17 October. I have been left alone all day. Not that it matters.

Last night came the strangest and most beautiful event of my life, a seal laid upon my future.

I was lying here with my double window open, when I noticed that mist was coming in. I opened my arms to it, but my blood began to trickle down my bosom from the wound in my neck, which of course no longer heals—though I seem to have no particular trouble in concealing the mark from the entire human race, not forgetting learned men with certificates from the University of Sciozza.

Outside in the *piazza* was a sound of shuffling and nuzzling, as of sheep being folded on one of the farms at home. I climbed out of bed, walked across, and stepped on to the balcony.

The mist was filtering the moonlight into a silver-grey that I have never seen elsewhere.

The entire *piazza*, a very big one, was filled with huge, grizzled wolves, all perfectly silent, except for the small sounds I have mentioned, all with their tongues flopping and lolling, black in the silvery light, and all gazing up at my window.

Rimini is near to the Apennine Mountains, where wolves notoriously abound, and commonly devour babies and small children. I suppose that the coming cold is drawing them into the towns.

I smiled at the wolves. Then I crossed my hands on my little bosom and curtsied. They will be prominent among my new people. My blood will be theirs, and theirs mine.

I forgot to say that I have contrived to lock my door. Now, I am assisted in such affairs.

Somehow I have found my way back to bed. It has become exceedingly cold, almost icy. For some reason I think of all the empty rooms in this battered old palazzo (as I am sure it once was), so fallen from their former stateliness. I doubt if I shall write any more. I do not think I shall have any more to say.

5

THE HOSPICE

IT WAS SOMEWHERE at the back of beyond. Maybury would have found it difficult to be more precise.

He was one who, when motoring outside his own territory, preferred to follow a route "given" by one of the automobile organizations, and, on this very occasion, as on other previous ones, he had found reasons to deplore all deviation. This time it had been the works manager's fault. The man had not only poured ridicule on the official route, but had stood at the yard gate in order to make quite certain that Maybury set off by the short cut which, according to him, all the fellows in the firm used, and which departed in the exactly opposite direction.

The most that could be said was that Maybury was presumably at the outer edge of the immense West Midlands conurbation. The outer edge it by now surely must be, as he seemed to have been driving for hours since he left the works, going round and round in large or small circles, asking the way and being unable to understand the answers (when answers were vouchsafed), all the time seemingly more off-course than ever.

Maybury looked at his watch. He *had* been driving for hours. By rights he should have been more than halfway home—considerably more. Even the dashboard light seemed feebler than usual; but by it Maybury saw that soon he would be out of petrol. His mind had not been on that particular matter of petrol.

Dark though it was, Maybury was aware of many trees, mountainous and opaque. It was not, however, that there were no houses. Houses there must be, because on both sides of the road, there were gates; broad single gates, commonly painted white: and, even where there were no gates, there were dim entrances. Presumably it was a costly nineteenth-century housing estate. Almost identical roads seemed to curve away in all directions. The straightforward had been genteelly avoided. As often in such places, the racer-through, the taker of a short cut, was quite systematically penalized. Probably this attitude accounted also for the failure to bring the street lighting fully up-to-date.

Maybury came to a specific bifurcation. It was impossible to make any reasoned choice, and he doubted whether it mattered much in any case.

Maybury stopped the car by the side of the road, then stopped the engine in order to save the waning petrol while he thought. In the end, he opened the door and stepped out into the road. He looked upwards. The moon and stars were almost hidden by the thick trees. It was quiet. The houses were set too far back from the road for the noise of the television sets to be heard, or the blue glare thereof seen. Pedestrians are nowadays rare in such a district at any hour, but now there was no traffic either, nor sound of traffic more remote. Maybury was disturbed by the silence.

He advanced a short distance on foot, as one does at such times. In any case, he had no map, but only a route, from which he had departed quite hopelessly. None the less, even that second and locally preferred route, the one used by all the fellows, had seemed perfectly clear at the time, and as the manager had described it. He supposed that otherwise he might not have been persuaded to embark upon it; not even overpersuaded. As things were, his wonted expedient of merely driving straight ahead until one found some definite sign or other indication, would be dubious, because the petrol might run out first.

Parallel with each side of each road was a narrow made-up footway, with a central gravelly strip. Beyond the strip to Maybury's left was a wilderness of vegetation, traversed by a ditch, beyond which was the hedge-line of the different properties. By the light of the occasional street-lamp, Maybury could see that sometimes there was an owner who had his hedge trimmed, and sometimes an owner who did not. It would be futile to walk any further along the road, though the air was pleasantly warm and aromatic. There were Angela and their son, Tony, awaiting him; and he must resume the fight to rejoin them.

Something shot out at him from the boskage on his left.

He had disturbed a cat, returned to its feral habitude. The first he knew of it was its claws, or conceivably its teeth, sunk into his left leg.

There had been no question of ingratiation or cuddling up. Maybury kicked out furiously. The strange sequel was total silence. He must have kicked the cat a long way, because on the instant there was no hint of it. Nor had he seen the colour of the cat, though there was a pool of light at that point on the footway. He fancied he had seen two flaming eyes, but he was not sure even of that. There had been no mew, no scream.

Maybury faltered. His leg really hurt. It hurt so much that he could not bring himself to touch the limb, even to look at it in the lamplight.

He faltered back to the car, and, though his leg made difficulties even in starting it, set off indecisively down the road along which he had just walked. It might well have become a case of its being wise for him to seek a hospital. The deep scratch or bite of a cat might well hold venom, and it was not pleasant to think where the particular cat had been treading, or what it might have been devouring. Maybury again looked at his watch. It was fourteen minutes past eight. Only nine minutes had passed since he had looked at it last.

The road was beginning to straighten out, and the number of entrances to diminish, though the trees remained dense. Possibly, as so often happens, the money had run out before the full development had reached this region of the property. There were still occasional houses, with entries at long and irregular intervals. Lamp posts were becoming fewer also, but Maybury saw that one of them bore a hanging sign of some kind. It was most unlikely to indicate a destination, let alone a destination of use to Maybury, but he eased and stopped none the less, so urgently did he need a clue of some kind. The sign was shaped like a club in a pack of cards, and read:

THE HOSPICE

S   N

O   GOOD FARE   O

M   I

E ACCOMMODA T

The modest words relating to accommodation were curved round the downward pointing extremity of the club.

Maybury decided almost instantly. He was hungry. He was injured. He was lost. He was almost without petrol.

He would enquire for dinner and, if he could telephone home, might even stay the night, though he had neither pyjamas nor electric razor. The gate, made of iron, and more suited, Maybury would have

thought, to a farmyard bullpen, was, none the less, wide open. Maybury drove through.

The drive had likewise been surfaced with rather unattractive concrete, and it appeared to have been done some time ago, since there
were now many potholes, as if heavy vehicles passed frequently. Maybury's headlights bounced and lurched disconcertingly as he proceeded, but suddenly the drive, which had run quite straight, again as
on a modern farm, swerved, and there, on Maybury's left, was The
Hospice. He realized that the drive he had come down, if indeed it
had been a drive, was not the original main entrance. There was an
older, more traditional drive, winding away between rhododendron
bushes. All this was visible in bright light from a fixture high above
the cornice of the building: almost a floodlight, Maybury thought. He
supposed that a new entry had been made for the vehicles of the various suppliers when the place had became—whatever exactly it had become, a private hotel? a guest house? a club? No doubt the manage-
ment aspired to cater for the occupants of the big houses, now that
there were no longer servants in the world.

Maybury locked the car and pushed at the door of the house. It was
a solid Victorian door, and it did not respond to Maybury's pressure.
Maybury was discouraged by the need to ring, but he rang. He noticed that there was a second bell, lower down, marked NIGHT. Surely
it could not yet be Night? The great thing was to get in, to feed (the
works had offered only packeted sandwiches and flavourless coffee by
way of luncheon), to ingratiate himself: before raising questions of
petrol, whereabouts, possible accommodation for the night, a telephone call to Angela, disinfectant for his leg. He did not much care for
standing alone in a strange place under the bright floodlight, uncertain what was going to happen.

But quite soon the door was opened by a lad with curly fair hair
and an untroubled face. He looked like a young athlete, as Maybury
at once thought. He was wearing a white jacket and smiling helpfully.

"Dinner? Yes, certainly, sir. I fear we've just started, but I'm sure
we can fit you in."

To Maybury, the words brought back the seaside boarding houses
where he had been taken for holidays when a boy. Punctuality in
those days had been almost as important as sobriety.

"If you can give me just a couple of minutes to wash . . ."

"Certainly, sir. This way, please."

Inside, it was not at all like those boarding houses of Maybury's
youth. Maybury happened to know exactly what it *was* like. The

effect was that produced by the efforts of an expensive and, therefore, rather old-fashioned, furniture emporium if one placed one's whole abode and most of one's cheque-book in its hands. There were hangings on all the walls, and every chair and sofa was upholstered. Colours and fabrics were harmonious but rich. The several standard lamps had immense shades. The polished tables derived from Italian originals. One could perhaps feel that a few upholstered occupants should have been designed and purveyed to harmonize also. As it was, the room was empty, except for the two of them.

The lad held open the door marked "Gentlemen" in script, but then followed Maybury in, which Maybury had not particularly expected. But the lad did not proceed to fuss tiresomely, with soap and towel, as happens sometimes in very expensive hotels, and happened formerly in clubs. All he did was stand about. Maybury reflected that doubtless he was concerned to prevent all possible delay, dinner having started.

The dining-room struck Maybury, immediately he entered, as rather too hot. The central heating must be working with full efficiency. The room was lined with hangings similar to those Maybury had seen in the hall, but apparently even heavier. Possibly noise reduction was among the objects. The ceiling of the room had been brought down in the modern manner, as if to serve the stunted; and any window or windows had disappeared behind swathes.

It is true that knives and forks make a clatter, but there appeared to be no other immediate necessity for costly noise abatement, as the diners were all extremely quiet; which at first seemed the more unexpected in that most of them were seated, fairly closely packed, at a single long table running down the central axis of the room. Maybury soon reflected, however, that if he had been wedged together with a party of total strangers, he might have found little to say to them either.

This was not put to the test. On each side of the room were four smaller tables, set endways against the walls, every table set for a single person, even though big enough to accommodate four, two on either side; and at one of these, Maybury was settled by the handsome lad in the white jacket.

Immediately, soup arrived.

The instantaneity of the service (apart from the fact that Maybury was late) could be accounted for by the large number of the staff. There were quite certainly four men, all, like the lad, in white jackets; and two women, both in dark blue dresses. The six of them were noticeably deft and well set-up, though all were past their first youth.

Maybury could not see more because he had been placed with his back to the end wall which contained the service door (as well as, on the other side, the door by which the guests entered from the lounge). At every table, the single place had been positioned in that way, so that the occupant saw neither the service door opening and shutting, nor, in front of him, the face of another diner.

As a matter of fact, Maybury was the only single diner on that side of the room (he had been given the second table down, but did not think that anyone had entered to sit behind him at the first table); and, on the other side of the room, there was only a single diner also, he thought, a lady, seated at the second table likewise, and thus precisely parallel with him.

There was an enormous quantity of soup, in what Maybury realized was an unusually deep and wide plate. The amplitude of the plate had at first been masked by the circumstance that round much of its wide rim was inscribed, in large black letters, THE HOSPICE; rather in the style of a baby's plate, Maybury thought, if both lettering and plate had not been so immense. The soup itself was unusually weighty too: it undoubtedly contained eggs as well as pulses, and steps have been taken to add "thickening" also.

Maybury was hungry, as has been said, but he was faintly disconcerted to realize that one of the middle-aged women was standing quietly behind him as he consumed the not inconsiderable number of final spoonfuls. The spoons seemed very large also, at least for modern usages. The woman removed his empty plate with a reassuring smile.

The second course was there. As she set it before him, the woman spoke confidentially in his ear of the third course: "It's turkey tonight." Her tone was exactly that in which promise is conveyed to a little boy of his favourite dish. It was as if she were Maybury's nanny; even though Maybury had never had a nanny, not exactly. Meanwhile, the second course was a proliferating elaboration of pasta; plainly home-made pasta, probably fabricated that morning. Cheese, in fairly large granules, was strewn across the heap from a large porcelain bowl without Maybury being noticeably consulted.

"Can I have something to drink? A lager will do."

"We have nothing like that, sir." It was as if Maybury knew this perfectly well, but she was prepared to play with him. There might, he thought, have been some warning that the place was unlicensed.

"A pity," said Maybury.

The woman's inflections were beginning to bore him; and he was wondering how much the rich food, all palpably fresh, and home-grown, and of almost unattainable quality, was about to cost him. He doubted very much whether it would be sensible to think of staying the night at The Hospice.

"When you have finished your second course, you may have the opportunity of a word with Mr Falkner." Maybury recollected that, after all, he had started behind all the others. He must doubtless expect to be a little hustled while he caught up with them. In any case, he was not sure whether or not the implication was that Mr Falkner might, under certain circumstances, unlock a private liquor store.

Obviously it would help the catching-up process if Maybury ate no more than two-thirds of the pasta fantasy. But the woman in the dark blue dress did not seem to see it like that.

"Can't you eat any more?" she enquired baldly, and no longer addressing Maybury as sir.

"Not if I'm to attempt another course," replied Maybury, quite equably.

"It's turkey tonight," said the woman. "You know how turkey just slips down you?" She still had not removed his plate.

"It's very good," said Maybury firmly. "But I've had enough."

It was as if the woman were not used to such conduct, but, as this was no longer a nursery, she took the plate away.

There was even a slight pause, during which Maybury tried to look round the room without giving an appearance of doing so. The main point seemed to be that everyone was dressed rather formally: all the men in "dark suits", all the women in "long dresses". There was a wide variety of age, but, curiously again, there were more men than women. Conversation still seemed far from general. Maybury could not help wondering whether the solidity of the diet did not contribute here. Then it occurred to him that it was as if most of these people had been with one another for a long time, during which things to talk about might have run out, and possibly with little opportunity for renewal through fresh experience. He had met that in hotels. Naturally, Maybury could not, without seeming rude, examine the one-third of the assembly which was seated behind him.

His slab of turkey appeared. He had caught up, even though by cheating. It was an enormous pile, steaming slightly, and also seeping slightly with a colourless, oily fluid. With it appeared five separate varieties of vegetable in separate dishes, brought on a tray; and a sauceboat, apparently for him alone, of specially compounded fluid, dark red and turgid. A sizeable mound of stuffing completed the repast. The middle-aged woman set it all before him swiftly but, this time, silently, with unmistakable reserve.

The truth was that Maybury had little appetite left. He gazed around, less furtively, to see how the rest were managing. He had to admit that, as far as he could see, they were one and all eating as if their lives depended on it: old as well as young, female as well as male; it was as if all had spent a long, unfed day in the hunting field. "Eating as if their lives depended on it," he said again to himself; then, struck by the absurdity of the phrase when applied to eating, he picked up his knife and fork with resolution.

"Is everything to your liking, Mr Maybury?"

Again he had been gently taken by surprise. Mr Falkner was at his shoulder: a sleek man in the most beautiful dinner jacket, an instantly ameliorative mâitre d'hôtel.

"Perfect, thank you," said Maybury. "But how did you know my name?"

"We like to remember the names of all our guests," said Falkner, smiling.

"Yes, but how did you find out *my* name in the first place?"

"We like to think we are proficient at that too, Mr Maybury."

"I am much impressed," said Maybury. Really he felt irritated (irritated, at least), but his firm had trained him never to display irritation outside the family circle.

"Not at all," said Falkner genially. "Whatever our vocation in life, we may as well do what we can to excel." He settled the matter by dropping the subject. "Is there anything I can get for you? Anything you would like?"

"No, thank you very much. I have plenty."

"Thank *you*, Mr Maybury. If you wish to speak to me at any time, I am normally available in my office. Now I will leave you to the enjoyment of your meal. I may tell you, in confidence, that there is steamed fruit pudding to follow."

He went quietly forward on his round of the room, speaking to perhaps one person in three at the long, central table; mainly, it seemed, to the older people, as was no doubt to be expected. Falkner wore very elegant black suède shoes, which reminded Maybury of the injury to his own leg, about which he had done nothing, though it might well be septic, even endangering the limb itself, perhaps the whole system.

He was considerably enraged by Falkner's performance about his name, especially as he could find no answer to the puzzle. He felt that

he had been placed, almost deliberately, at an undignified disadvantage. Falkner's patronizing conduct in this trifling matter was of a
piece with the nannying attitude of the waitress. Moreover, was the
unexplained discovery of his name such a trifle, after all? Maybury felt
that it had made him vulnerable in other matters also, however
undefined. It was the last straw in the matter of his eating any more
turkey. He no longer had any appetite whatever.

He began to pass everything systematically through his mind, as he
had been trained to do; and almost immediately surmised the answer.
In his car was a blue-bound file which on its front bore his name: "Mr
Lucas Maybury"; and this file he supposed that he must have left,
name-upwards, on the driving seat, as he commonly did. All the same,
the name was merely typed on a sticky label, and would not have
been easy to make out through the car window. But he then remembered the floodlight. Even so, quite an effort had been necessary on
someone's part, and he wondered who had made that effort. Again he
guessed the answer: it was Falkner himself who had been snooping.
What would Falkner have done if Maybury had parked the car outside the floodlighted area, as would have been perfectly possible?
Used a torch? Perhaps even skeleton keys?

That was absurd.

And how much did the whole thing matter? People in business
often had these little vanities, and often had he encountered them.
People would do almost anything to feed them. Probably he had one
or two himself. The great thing when meeting any situation was to extract the essentials and to concentrate upon them.

To some of the people Falkner was speaking for quite a period of
time, while, as Maybury noticed, those seated next to them, previously
saying little in most cases, now said nothing at all, but confined themselves entirely to eating. Some of the people at the long table were not
merely elderly, he had observed, but positively senile: drooling, wa-
tery-eyed, and almost hairless; but even they seemed to be eating
away with the best. Maybury had the horrid idea about them that eating was all they did do. "They lived for eating": another nursery expression, Maybury reflected; and at last he had come upon those of
whom it might be true. Some of these people might well relate to rich
foods as alcoholics relate to excisable spirits. He found it more nau-
seating than any sottishness; of which he had seen a certain amount.

Falkner was proceeding so slowly, showing so much professional
consideration, that he had not yet reached the lady who sat by herself parallel with Maybury, on the other side of the room. At her

Maybury now stared more frankly. Black hair reached her shoulders, and she wore what appeared to be a silk evening dress, a real "model", Maybury thought (though he did not really know), in many colours; but her expression was of such sadness, suffering, and exhaustion that Maybury was sincerely shocked, especially as once she must, he was sure, have been beautiful, indeed, in a way, still was. Surely so unhappy, even tragic, a figure as that could not be ploughing through a big slab of turkey with five vegetables? Without caution or courtesy, Maybury half rose to his feet in order to look.

"Eat up, sir. Why you've hardly started!" His tormentor had quietly returned to him. What was more, the tragic lady *did* appear to be eating.

"I've had enough. I'm sorry, it's very good, but I've had enough."

"You said that before, sir, and, look, here you are, still eating away." He knew that he had, indeed, used those exact words. Crises are met by clichés.

"I've eaten quite enough."

"That's not necessarily for each of us to say, is it?"

"I want no more to eat of any kind. Please take all this away and just bring me a black coffee. When the time comes, if you like. I don't mind waiting." Though Maybury did mind waiting, it was necessary to remain in control.

The woman did the last thing Maybury could have expected her to do. She picked up his laden plate (he had at least helped himself to everything) and, with force, dashed it on the floor. Even then the plate itself did not break, but gravy and five vegetables and rich stuffing spread across the thick, patterned, wall-to-wall carpet. Complete, in place of comparative, silence followed in the whole room; though there was still, as Maybury even then observed, the muted clashing of cutlery. Indeed, his own knife and fork were still in his hands.

Falkner returned round the bottom end of the long table.

"Mulligan," he asked, "how many more times?" His tone was as quiet as ever. Maybury had not realized that the alarming woman was Irish.

"Mr Maybury," Falkner continued. "I entirely understand your difficulty. There is naturally no obligation to partake of anything you do not wish. I am only sorry for what has happened. It must seem very poor service on our part. Perhaps you would prefer to go into our lounge? Would you care simply for some coffee?"

"Yes," said Maybury, concentrating upon the essential. "I should, please. Indeed, I had already ordered a black coffee. Could I possibly have a pot of it?"

He had to step with care over the mess on the floor, looking downwards. As he did so, he saw something most curious. A central rail ran the length of the long table a few inches above the floor. To this rail, one of the male guests was attached by a fetter round his left ankle.

Maybury, now considerably shaken, had rather expected to be alone in the lounge until the coffee arrived. But he had no sooner dropped down upon one of the massive sofas (it could easily have seated five in a row, at least two of them stout), than the handsome boy appeared from somewhere and proceeded merely to stand about, as at an earlier phase of the evening. There were no illustrated papers to be seen, nor even brochures about Beautiful Britain, and Maybury found the lad's presence irksome. All the same, he did not quite dare to say, "There's nothing I want." He could think of nothing to say or to do; nor did the boy speak, or seem to have anything particular to do either. It was obvious that his presence could hardly be required there when everyone was in the dining room. Presumably they would soon be passing on to fruit pudding. Maybury was aware that he had yet to pay his bill. There was a baffled but considerable pause.

Much to his surprise, it was Mulligan who in the end brought him the coffee. It was a single cup, not a pot; and even the cup was of such a size that Maybury, for once that evening, could have done with a bigger. At once he divined that coffee was outside the régime of the place, and that he was being specially compensated, though he might well have to pay extra for it. He had vaguely supposed that Mulligan would have been helping to mop up in the dining-room. Mulligan, in fact, seemed quite undisturbed.

"Sugar, sir?" she said.

"One lump, please," said Maybury, eyeing the size of the cup.

He did not fail to notice that, before going, she exchanged a glance with the handsome lad. He was young enough to be her son, and the glance might mean anything or nothing.

While Maybury was trying to make the most of his meagre coffee and to ignore the presence of the lad, who must surely be bored, the door from the dining-room opened, and the tragic lady from the other side of the room appeared.

"Close the door, will you?" she said to the boy. The boy closed the door, and then stood about again, watching them.

"Do you mind if I join you?" the lady asked Maybury.

"I should be delighted."

She was really rather lovely in her melancholy way, her dress was
as splendid as Maybury had supposed, and there was in her demeanour an element that could only be called stately. Maybury was unaccustomed to that.

She sat, not at the other end of the sofa, but at the centre of it. It
struck Maybury that the rich way she was dressed might almost have
been devised to harmonize with the rich way the room was decorated.
She wore complicated, oriental-looking earrings, with pink translucent
stones, like rosé diamonds (perhaps they *were* diamonds); and silver
shoes. Her perfume was heavy and distinctive.

"My name is Cécile Céliména," she said. "How do you do? I am
supposed to be related to the composer, Chaminade."

"How do you do?" said Maybury. "My name is Lucas Maybury,
and my only important relation is Solway Short. In fact, he's my
cousin."

They shook hands. Her hand was very soft and white, and she wore
a number of rings, which Maybury thought looked real and valuable
(though he could not really tell). In order to shake hands with him,
she turned the whole upper part of her body towards him.

"Who is that gentleman you mention?" she asked.

"Solway Short? The racing motorist. You must have seen him on the
television."

"I do not watch the television."

"Quite right. It's almost entirely a waste of time."

"If you do not wish to waste time, why are you at The Hospice?"

The lad, still observing them, shifted, noticeably, from one leg to
the other.

"I am here for dinner. I am just passing through."

"Oh! You are going then?"

Maybury hesitated. She was attractive and, for the moment, he did
not wish to go. "I suppose so. When I've paid my bill and found out
where I can get some petrol. My tank's almost empty. As a matter of
fact, I'm lost. I've lost my way."

"Most of us here are lost."

"Why here? What makes you come here?"

"We come for the food and the peace and the warmth and the rest."

"A tremendous *amount* of food, I thought."

"That's necessary. It's the restorative, you might say."

"I'm not sure that I quite fit in," said Maybury. And then he added:
"I shouldn't have thought that you did either."

"Oh, but I do! Whatever makes you think not?" She seemed quite anxious about it, so that Maybury supposed he had taken the wrong line.

He made the best of it. "It's just that you seem a little different from what I have seen of the others."

"In what way, different?" she asked, really anxious, and looking at him with concentration.

"To start with, more beautiful. You are very beautiful," he said, even though the lad was there, certainly taking in every word.

"That is kind of you to say." Unexpectedly she stretched across the short distance between them and took his hand. "What did you say your name was?"

"Lucas Maybury."

"Do people call you Luke?"

"No, I dislike it. I'm not a Luke sort of person."

"But your wife can't call you Lucas?"

"I'm afraid she does." It was a fishing question he could have done without.

"Lucas? Oh no, it's such a cold name." She was still holding his hand.

"I'm very sorry about it. Would you like me to order you some coffee?"

"No, no. Coffee is not right; it is stimulating, wakeful, overexciting, unquiet." She was gazing at him again with sad eyes.

"This is a curious place," said Maybury, giving her hand a squeeze. It was surely becoming remarkable that none of the other guests had yet appeared.

"I could not live without The Hospice," she replied.

"Do you come here often?" It was a ludicrously conventional form of words.

"Of course. Life would be impossible otherwise. All those people in the world without enough food, living without love, without even proper clothes to keep the cold out."

During dinner it had become as hot in the lounge, Maybury thought, as it had been in the dining-room.

Her tragic face sought his understanding. None the less, the line she had taken up was not a favourite of his. He preferred problems to which solutions were at least possible. He had been warned against the other kind.

"Yes," he said. "I know what you mean, of course."

"There are millions and millions of people all over the world with no clothes at all," she cried, withdrawing her hand.

"Not quite," Maybury said, smiling. "Not quite that. Or not yet."

He knew the risks perfectly well, and thought as little about them as possible. One had to survive, and also to look after one's dependents.

"In any case," he continued, trying to lighten the tone, "that hardly applies to you. I have seldom seen a more gorgeous dress."

"Yes," she replied with simple gravity. "It comes from Rome. Would you like to touch it?"

Naturally, Maybury would have liked, but, equally naturally, was held back by the presence of the watchful lad.

"Touch it," she commanded in a low voice. "God, what are you waiting for? Touch it." She seized his left hand again and forced it against her warm, silky breast. The lad seemed to take no more and no less notice than of anything else.

"Forget. Let go. What is life for, for God's sake?" There was a passionate earnestness about her which might rob any such man as Maybury of all assessment, but he was still essentially outside the situation. As a matter of fact, he had never in his life lost *all* control, and he was pretty sure by now that, for better or for worse, he was incapable of it.

She twisted round until her legs were extended the length of the sofa, and her head was on his lap, or more precisely on his thighs. She had moved so deftly as not even to have disordered her skirt. Her perfume wafted upwards.

"Stop glancing at Vincent," she gurgled up at him. "I'll tell you something about Vincent. Though you may think he looks like a Greek God, the simple fact is that he hasn't got what it takes, he's impotent."

Maybury was embarrassed, of course. All the same, what he reflected was that often there were horses for courses, and often no more to be said about a certain kind of situation than that one thing.

It did not matter much what he reflected, because when she had spoken, Vincent had brusquely left the room through what Maybury supposed to be the service door.

"Thank the Lord," he could not help remarking naïvely.

"He's gone for reinforcements," she said. "We'll soon see."

Where were the other guests? Where, by now, could they be? All the same, Maybury's spirits were authentically rising, and he began caressing her more intimately.

Then, suddenly, it seemed that everyone was in the room at once, and this time all talking and fussing.

She sat herself up, none too precipitately, and with her lips close to his ear, said, "Come to me later. Number 23."

It was quite impossible for Maybury to point out that he was not staying the night in The Hospice.

Falkner had appeared.

"To bed, all," he cried genially, subduing the crepitation on the instant.

Maybury, unentangled once more, looked at his watch. It seemed to be precisely ten o'clock. That, no doubt, was the point. Still it seemed very close upon a heavy meal.

No one moved much, but no one spoke either.

"To bed, all of you," said Falkner again, this time in a tone which might almost be described as roguish. Maybury's lady rose to her feet.

All of them filtered away, Maybury's lady among them. She had spoken no further word, made no further gesture.

Maybury was alone with Falkner.

"Let me remove your cup," said Falkner courteously.

"Before I ask for my bill," said Maybury, "I wonder if you could tell me where I might possibly find some petrol at this hour?"

"Are you out of petrol?" enquired Falkner.

"Almost."

"There's nothing open at night within twenty miles. Not nowadays. Something to do with our new friends, the Arabs, I believe. All I can suggest is that I syphon some petrol from the tank of our own vehicle. It is a quite large vehicle and it has a large tank."

"I couldn't possibly put you to that trouble." In any case, he, Maybury, did not know exactly how to do it. He had heard of it, but it had never arisen before in his own life.

The lad, Vincent, reappeared, still looking pink, Maybury thought, though it was difficult to be sure with such a glowing skin. Vincent began to lock up; a quite serious process, it seemed, rather as in great-grandparental days, when prowling desperadoes were to be feared.

"No trouble at all, Mr Maybury," said Falkner. "Vincent here can do it easily, or another member of my staff."

"Well," said Maybury, "if it would be all right . . ."

"Vincent," directed Falkner, "don't bolt and padlock the front door yet. Mr Maybury intends to leave us."

"Very good," said Vincent, gruffly.

"Now if we could go to your car, Mr Maybury, you could then drive it round to the back. I will show you the way. I must apologise for putting you to this extra trouble, but the other vehicle takes some time to start, especially at night."

Vincent had opened the front door for them.

"After you, Mr Maybury," said Falkner.

Where it had been excessively hot within, it duly proved to be excessively cold without. The floodlight had been turned off. The moon had "gone in", as Maybury believed the saying was; and all the stars had apparently gone in with it.

Still, the distance to the car was not great. Maybury soon found it in the thick darkness, with Falkner coming quietly step by step behind him.

"Perhaps I had better go back and get a torch?" remarked Falkner.

So there duly was a torch. It brought to Maybury's mind the matter of the office file with his name on it, and, as he unlocked the car door, there the file was, exactly as he had supposed, and, assuredly, name uppermost. Maybury threw it across to the back seat.

Falkner's electric torch was a heavy service object which drenched a wide area in cold, white light.

"May I sit beside you, Mr Maybury?" He closed the offside door behind him.

Maybury had already turned on the headlights, torch or no torch, and was pushing at the starter, which seemed obdurate.

It was not, he thought, that there was anything wrong with it, but rather that there was something wrong with him. The sensation was exactly like a nightmare. He had of course done it hundreds of times, probably thousands of times; but now, when after all it really mattered, he simply could not manage it, had, quite incredibly, somehow lost the simple knack of it. He often endured bad dreams of just this kind. He found time with part of his mind to wonder whether this was not a bad dream. But it was to be presumed not, since now he did not wake, as we soon do when once we realize that we are dreaming.

"I wish I could be of some help," remarked Falkner, who had shut off his torch, "but I am not accustomed to the make of car. I might easily do more harm than good." He spoke with his usual bland geniality.

Maybury was irritated again. The make of car was one of the commonest there is: trust the firm for that. All the same, he knew it was entirely his own fault that he could not make the car start, and not in the least Falkner's. He felt as if he were going mad. "I don't quite know what to suggest," he said; and added: "If, as you say, there's no garage."

"Perhaps Cromie could be of assistance," said Falkner. "Cromie has been with us quite a long time and is a wizard with any mechanical problem."

No one could say that Falkner was pressing Maybury to stay the night, or even hinting towards it, as one might expect. Maybury wondered whether the funny place was not, in fact, full up. It seemed the most likely answer. Not that Maybury wished to stay the night: far from it.

"I'm not sure," he said, "that I have the right to disturb anyone else."

"Cromie is on night duty," replied Falkner. "He is always on night duty. That is what we employ him for. I will fetch him."

He turned on the torch once more, stepped out of the car, and disappeared into the house, shutting the front door behind him, lest the cold air enter.

In the end, the front door reopened, and Falkner re-emerged. He still wore no coat over his dinner suit, and seemed to ignore the cold. Falkner was followed by a burly but shapeless and shambling figure, whom Maybury first saw indistinctly standing behind Falkner in the light from inside the house.

"Cromie will soon put things to rights," said Falkner, opening the door of the car. "Won't you, Cromie?" It was much as one speaks to a friendly retriever.

But there was little, Maybury felt, that was friendly about Cromie. Maybury had to admit to himself that on the instant he found Cromie alarming, even though, what with one thing and another, there was little to be seen of him.

"Now what exactly seems wrong, Mr Maybury?" asked Falkner. "Just tell Cromie what it is."

Falkner himself had not attempted to re-enter the car, but Cromie forced himself in and was sprawling in the front seat, next to Maybury, where Angela normally sat. He really did seem a very big, bulging person, but Maybury decisively preferred not to look at him, though the glow cast backwards from the headlights provided a certain illumination.

Maybury could not acknowledge that for some degrading reason he was unable to operate the starter, and so had to claim there was something wrong with it. He was unable not to see Cromie's huge, badly misshapen, yellow hands, both of them, as he tugged with both of them at the knob, forcing it in and out with such violence that Maybury cried out: "Less force. You'll wreck it."

"Careful, Cromie," said Falkner from outside the car. "Most of Cromie's work is on a big scale," he explained to Maybury.

But violence proved effective, as so often. Within seconds, the car engine was humming away.

"Thank you very much," said Maybury.

Cromie made no detectable response, nor did he move.

"Come on out, Cromie," said Falkner. "Come on out of it."

Cromie duly extricated himself and shambled off into the darkness.

"Now," said Maybury, brisking up as the engine purred. "Where do we go for the petrol?"

There was the slightest of pauses. Then Falkner spoke from the dimness outside. "Mr Maybury, I have remembered something. It is not petrol that we have in our tank. It is, of course, diesel oil. I must apologise for such a stupid mistake."

Maybury was not merely irritated, not merely scared: he was infuriated. With rage and confusion he found it impossible to speak at all. No one in the modern world could confuse diesel oil and petrol in that way. But what could he possibly do?

Falkner, standing outside the open door of the car, spoke again. "I am extremely sorry, Mr Maybury. Would you permit me to make some amends by inviting you to spend the night with us free of charge, except perhaps for the dinner?"

Within the last few minutes Maybury had suspected that this moment was bound to come in one form or another.

"Thank you," he said less than graciously. "I suppose I had better accept."

"We shall try to make you comfortable," said Falkner.

Maybury turned off the headlights, climbed out of the car once more, shut and, for what it was worth, locked the door, and followed Falkner back into the house. This time Falkner completed the locking and bolting of the front door that he had instructed Vincent to omit.

"I have no luggage of any kind," remarked Maybury, still very much on the defensive.

"That may solve itself," said Falkner, straightening up from the bottom bolt and smoothing his dinner jacket. "There's something I ought to explain. But will you first excuse me a moment?" He went out through the door at the back of the lounge.

Hotels really have become far too hot, thought Maybury. It positively addled the brain.

Falkner returned. "There is something I ought to explain," he said again. "We have no single rooms, partly because many of our visitors prefer not to be alone at night. The best we can do for you in your emergency, Mr Maybury, is to offer you the share of a room with another guest. It is a large room and there are two beds. It is a sheer stroke of good luck that at present there is only one guest in the room, Mr Bannard. Mr Bannard will be glad of your company, I am certain, and you will be quite safe with him. He is a very pleasant person, I can assure you. I have just sent a message up asking him if he can possibly come down, so that I can introduce you. He is always very helpful, and I think he will be here in a moment. Mr Bannard has been with us for some time, so that I am sure he will be able to fit you up with pyjamas and so forth."

It was just about the last thing that Maybury wanted from any point of view, but he had learned that it was of a kind that is peculiarly difficult to protest against, without somehow putting oneself in the wrong with other people. Besides he supposed that he was now committed to a night in the place, and therefore to all the implications, whatever they might be, or very nearly so.

"I should like to telephone my wife, if I may," Maybury said. Angela had been steadily on his mind for some time.

"I fear that's impossible, Mr Maybury," replied Falkner. "I'm so sorry."

"How can it be impossible?"

"In order to reduce tension and sustain the atmosphere that our guests prefer, we have no external telephone. Only an internal link between my quarters and the proprietors."

"But how can you run an hotel in the modern world without a telephone?"

"Most of our guests are regulars. Many of them come again and again, and the last thing they come for is to hear a telephone ringing the whole time with all the strain it involves."

"They must be half round the bend," snapped Maybury, before he could stop himself.

"Mr Maybury," replied Falkner, "I have to remind you of two things. The first is that I have invited you to be our guest in the fuller sense of the word. The second is that, although you attach so much importance to efficiency, you none the less appear to have set out on a long journey at night with very little petrol in your tank. Possibly you should think yourself fortunate that you are not spending the night stranded on some motorway."

"I'm sorry," said Maybury, "but I simply must telephone my wife. Soon she'll be out of her mind with worry."

"I shouldn't think so, Mr Maybury," said Falkner smiling. "Concerned, we must hope; but not quite out of her mind."

Maybury could have hit him, but at that moment a stranger entered.

"Ah, Mr Bannard," said Falkner, and introduced them. They actually shook hands. "You won't mind, Mr Bannard, if Mr Maybury shares your room?"

Bannard was a slender, bony little man, of about Maybury's age. He was bald, with a rim of curly red hair. He had slightly glaucous grey-green eyes of the kind that often go with red hair. In the present environment, he was quite perky, but Maybury wondered how he would make out in the world beyond. Perhaps, however, this was because Bannard was too shrimp-like to look his best in pyjamas.

"I should be delighted to share my room with anyone," replied Bannard. "I'm lonely by myself."

"Splendid," said Falkner coolly. "Perhaps you'd lead Mr Maybury upstairs and lend him some pyjamas? You must remember that he is a stranger to us and doesn't yet know all our ways."

"Delighted, delighted," exclaimed Bannard.

"Well, then," said Falkner. "Is there anything you would like, Mr Maybury, before you go upstairs?"

"Only a telephone," rejoined Maybury, still recalcitrant. He simply did not believe Falkner. No one in the modern world could live without a telephone, let alone run a business without one. He had begun uneasily to wonder if Falkner had spoken the whole truth about the petrol and the diesel fuel either.

"Anything you would like that we are in a position to provide, Mr Maybury?" persisted Falkner, with offensive specificity.

"There's no telephone *here*," put in Bannard, whose voice was noticeably high, even squeaky.

"In that case, nothing," said Maybury. "But I don't know what my wife will do with herself."

"None of us knows that," said Bannard superfluously, and cackled for a second.

"Good-night, Mr Maybury. Thank you, Mr Bannard."

Maybury was almost surprised to discover, as he followed Bannard upstairs, that it seemed a perfectly normal hotel, though overheated and decorated over-heavily. On the first landing was a full-size reproduction of a chieftain in scarlet tartan by Raeburn. Maybury knew the picture, because it had been chosen for the firm's calendar one year, though ever since they had used girls. Bannard lived on the second

floor, where the picture on the landing was smaller, and depicted ladies and gentlemen in riding dress taking refreshments together.

"Not too much noise," said Bannard. "We have some very light
sleepers amongst us."

The corridors were down to half-illumination for the night watches,
and distinctly sinister. Maybury crept foolishly along and almost stole
into Bannard's room.

"No," said Bannard in a giggling whisper. "Not Number 13, not yet
Number 12 A."

As a matter of fact Maybury had not noticed the number on the
door that Bannard was now cautiously closing, and he did not feel
called upon to rejoin.

"Do be quiet taking your things off, old man," said Bannard softly.
"When once you've woken people who've been properly asleep, you
can never quite tell. It's a bad thing to do."

It was a large square room, and the two beds were in exactly opposite corners, somewhat to Maybury's relief. The light had been on
when they entered. Maybury surmised that even the unnecessary
clicking of switches was to be eschewed.

"That's your bed," whispered Bannard, pointing jocularly.

So far Maybury had removed only his shoes. He could have done
without Bannard staring at him and without Bannard's affable grin.

"Or perhaps you'd rather we did something before settling down?"
whispered Bannard.

"No, thank you," replied Maybury. "It's been a long day." He was
trying to keep his voice reasonably low, but he absolutely refused to
whisper.

"To be sure it has," said Bannard, rising to much the volume that
Maybury had employed. "Night-night then. The best thing is to get to
sleep quickly." His tone was similar to that which seemed habitual
with Falkner.

Bannard climbed agilely into his own bed, and lay on his back peering at Maybury over the sheets.

"Hang your suit in the cupboard," said Bannard, who had already
done likewise. "There's room."

"Thank you," said Maybury. "Where do I find the pyjamas?"

"Top drawer," said Bannard. "Help yourself. They're all alike."

And, indeed, the drawer proved to be virtually filled with apparently identical suits of pyjamas.

"It's between seasons," said Bannard. "Neither proper summer, nor
proper winter."

"Many thanks for the loan," said Maybury, though the pyjamas were considerably too small for him.

"The bathroom's in there," said Bannard.

When Maybury returned, he opened the door of the cupboard. It was a big cupboard and it was almost filled by a long line of (presumably) Bannard's suits.

"There's room," said Bannard once more. "Find yourself an empty hanger. Make yourself at home."

While balancing his trousers on the hanger and suspending it from the rail, Maybury again became aware of the injury to his leg. He had hustled so rapidly into Bannard's pyjamas that, for better or for worse, he had not even looked at the scar.

"What's the matter?" asked Bannard on the instant. "Hurt yourself, have you?"

"It was a damned cat scratched me," replied Maybury, without thinking very much.

But this time he decided to look. With some difficulty and some pain, he rolled up the tight pyjama leg. It was a quite nasty gash and there was much dried blood. He realized that he had not even thought about washing the wound. In so far as he had been worrying about anything habitual, he had been worrying about Angela.

"Don't show it to me," squeaked out Bannard, forgetting not to make a noise. All the same, he was sitting up in bed and staring as if his eyes would pop. "It's bad for me to see things like that. I'm upset by them."

"Don't worry," said Maybury. "I'm sure it's not as serious as it looks." In fact, he was far from sure; and he was aware also that it had not been quite what Bannard was concerned about.

"I don't want to know anything about it," said Bannard.

Maybury made no reply but simply rolled down the pyjama leg. About his injury too there was plainly nothing to be done. Even a request for Vaseline might lead to hysterics. Maybury tried to concentrate upon the reflection that if nothing worse had followed from the gash by now, then nothing worse might ever follow.

Bannard, however, was still sitting up in bed. He was looking pale. "I come here to forget things like that," he said. "We all do." His voice was shaking.

"Shall I turn the light out?" enquired Maybury. "As I'm the one who's still up?"

"I don't usually do that," said Bannard, reclining once more, none the less. "It can make things unnecessarily difficult. But there's you to be considered too."

"It's your room," said Maybury, hesitating.

"All right," said Bannard. "If you wish. Turn it out. Tonight anyway." Maybury did his injured leg no good when stumbling back to his bed. All the same, he managed to arrive there.

"I'm only here for one night," he said more to the darkness than to Bannard. "You'll be on your own again tomorrow."

Bannard made no reply, and, indeed, it seemed to Maybury as if he were no longer there, that Bannard was not an organism that could function in the dark. Maybury refrained from raising any question of drawing back a curtain (the curtains were as long and heavy as elsewhere), or of letting in a little night air. Things, he felt, were better left more or less as they were.

It was completely dark. It was completely silent. It was far too hot.

Maybury wondered what the time was. He had lost all touch. Unfortunately, his watch lacked a luminous dial.

He doubted whether he would ever sleep, but the night had to be endured somehow. For Angela it must be even harder—far harder. At the best, he had never seen himself as a first-class husband, able to provide a superfluity, eager to be protective. Things would become quite impossible, if he were to lose a leg. But, with modern medicine, that might be avoidable, even at the worst: he should be able to continue struggling on for some time yet.

As stealthily as possible he insinuated himself from between the burning blankets and sheets on to the surface of the bed. He lay there like a dying fish, trying not to make another movement of any kind.

He became almost cataleptic with inner exertion. It was not a promising recipe for slumber. In the end, he thought he could detect Bannard's breathing, far, far away. So Bannard was still there. Fantasy and reality are different things. No one could tell whether Bannard slept or waked, but it had in any case become a quite important aim not to resume general conversation with Bannard. Half a lifetime passed.

There could be no doubt, now, that Bannard was both still in the room and also awake. Perceptibly, he was on the move. Maybury's body contracted with speculation as to whether Bannard in the total blackness was making towards his corner. Maybury felt that he was only half his normal size.

Bannard edged and groped interminably. Of course Maybury had been unfair to him in extinguishing the light, and the present anxiety was doubtless no more than the price to be paid.

Bannard himself seemed certainly to be entering into the spirit of the situation: possibly he had not turned the light on because he could not reach the switch; but there seemed more to it than that. Bannard could be thought of as committed to a positive effort in the direction of silence, in order that Maybury, the guest for a night, should not be disturbed. Maybury could hardly hear him moving at all, though perhaps it was a gamble whether this was consideration or menace. Maybury would hardly have been surprised if the next event had been hands on his throat.

But, in fact, the next event was Bannard reaching the door and opening it, with vast delicacy and slowness. It was a considerable anti-climax, and not palpably outside the order of nature, but Maybury did not feel fully reassured as he rigidly watched the column of dim light from the passage slowly widen and then slowly narrow until it vanished with the faint click of the handle. Plainly there was little to worry about, after all, but Maybury had probably reached that level of anxiety where almost any new event merely causes new stress. Soon, moreover, there would be the stress of Bannard's return. Maybury half realized that he was in a grotesque condition to be so upset, when Bannard was, in fact, showing him all possible consideration. Once more he reflected that poor Angela's plight was far worse.

Thinking about Angela's plight, and how sweet, at the bottom of everything, she really was, Maybury felt more wakeful than ever, as he awaited Bannard's return, surely imminent, surely. Sleep was impossible until Bannard had returned.

But still Bannard did not return. Maybury began to wonder whether something had gone wrong with his own time faculty, such as it was; something, that is, of medical significance. That whole evening and night, from soon after his commitment to the recommended route, he had been in doubt about his place in the universe, about what people called the state of his nerves. Here was evidence that he had good reason for anxiety.

Then, from somewhere within the house, came a shattering, ear-piercing scream, and then another, and another. It was impossible to tell whether the din came from near or far; still less whether it was female or male. Maybury had not known that the human organism could make so loud a noise, even in the bitterest distress. It was shattering to listen to; especially in the enclosed, hot, total darkness. And this was nothing momentary: the screaming went on and on, a paroxysm, until Maybury had to clutch at himself not to scream in response.

He fell off the bed and floundered about for the heavy curtains. Some light on the scene there must be; if possible, some new air in the room. He found the curtains within a moment, and dragged back first one, and then the other.

There was no more light than before.

Shutters, perhaps? Maybury's arm stretched out gingerly. He could feel neither wood nor metal.

The light switch. It must be found.

While Maybury fell about in the darkness, the screaming stopped on a ghoulish gurgle: perhaps as if the sufferer had vomited immensely and then passed out; or perhaps as if the sufferer had in mercy passed away altogether. Maybury continued to search.

It was harder than ever to say how long it took, but in the end he found the switch, and the immediate mystery was explained. Behind the drawn-back curtains was, as the children say, just wall. The room apparently had no window. The curtains were mere decoration.

All was silent once more: once more extremely silent. Bannard's bed was turned back as neatly as if in the full light of day.

Maybury cast off Bannard's pyjamas and, as quickly as his state permitted, resumed his own clothes. Not that he had any very definite course of action. Simply it seemed better to be fully dressed. He looked vaguely inside his pocket-book to confirm that his money was still there.

He went to the door and made cautiously to open it and seek some hint into the best thing for him to do, the best way to make off.

The door was unopenable. There was no movement in it at all. It had been locked at the least; perhaps more. If Bannard had done it, he had been astonishingly quiet about it: conceivably experienced.

Maybury tried to apply himself to thinking calmly.

The upshot was that once more, and even more hurriedly, he removed his clothes, disposed of them suitably, and resumed Bannard's pyjamas.

It would be sensible once more to turn out the light; to withdraw to bed, between the sheets, if possible; to stand by, as before. But Maybury found that turning out the light, the resultant total blackness, were more than he could face, however expedient.

Ineptly, he sat on the side of his bed, still trying to think things out, to plan sensibly. Would Bannard, after all this time, ever, in fact, return? At least during the course of that night?

He became aware that the electric light bulb had begun to crackle and fizzle. Then, with no further sound, it simply failed. It was not, Maybury thought, some final authoritative lights-out all over the house. It was merely that the single bulb had given out, however unfortunately from his own point of view: an isolated industrial incident.

He lay there, half in and half out, for a long time. He concentrated on the thought that nothing had actually happened that was dangerous. Ever since his schooldays (and, indeed, during them) he had become increasingly aware that there were many things strange to him, most of which had proved in the end to be apparently quite harmless.

Then Bannard was creeping back into the dark room. Maybury's ears had picked up no faint sound of a step in the passage, and, more remarkable, there had been no noise, either, of a turned key, let alone, perhaps, of a drawn bolt. Maybury's view of the bulb failure was confirmed by a repetition of the widening and narrowing column of light, dim, but probably no dimmer than before. Up to a point, lights were still on elsewhere. Bannard, considerate as before, did not try to turn on the light in the room. He shut the door with extraordinary skill, and Maybury could just, though only just, hear him slithering into his bed.

Still, there was one unmistakable development: at Bannard's return, the dark room had filled with perfume; the perfume favoured, long ago, as it seemed, by the lady who had been so charming to Maybury in the lounge. Smell is, in any case, notoriously the most recollective of the senses.

Almost at once, this time, Bannard not merely fell obtrusively asleep, but was soon snoring quite loudly.

Maybury had every reason to be at least irritated by everything that was happening, but instead he soon fell asleep himself. So long as Bannard was asleep, he was at least in abeyance as an active factor in the situation; and many perfumes have their own drowsiness, as Iago remarked. Angela passed temporarily from the forefront of Maybury's mind.

Then he was awake again. The light was on once more, and Maybury supposed that he had been awakened deliberately, because Bannard was standing there by his bed. Where and how had he found a new light bulb? Perhaps he kept a supply in a drawer. This seemed so likely that Maybury thought no more of the matter.

It was very odd, however, in another way also.

When Maybury had been at school, he had sometimes found difficulty in distinguishing certain boys from certain other boys. It had been a very large school, and boys do often look alike. None the less, it was a situation that Maybury thought best to keep to himself, at the time and since. He had occasionally made responses or approaches based upon misidentifications: but had been fortunate in never being made to suffer for it bodily, even though he had suffered much in his self-regard.

And now it was the same. Was the man standing there really Bannard? One obvious thing was that Bannard had an aureole or fringe of red hair, whereas this man's fringe was quite grey. There was also a different expression and general look, but Maybury was more likely to have been mistaken about that. The pyjamas seemed to be the same, but that meant little.

"I was just wondering if you'd care to talk for a bit," said Bannard. One had to assume that Bannard it was; at least to start off with. "I didn't mean to wake you up. I was just making sure."

"That's all right, I suppose," said Maybury.

"I'm over my first beauty sleep," said Bannard. "It can be lonely during the night." Under all the circumstances it was a distinctly absurd remark, but undoubtedly it was in Bannard's idiom.

"What was all that screaming?" enquired Maybury.

"I didn't hear anything," said Bannard. "I suppose I slept through it. But I can imagine. We soon learn to take no notice. There are sleepwalkers for that matter, from time to time."

"I suppose that's why the bedroom doors are so hard to open?"

"Not a bit," said Bannard, but he then added, "Well, partly, perhaps. Yes, partly. I think so. But it's just a knack really. We're not actually locked in, you know." He giggled. "But what makes you ask? You don't need to leave the room in order to go to the loo. I showed you, old man."

So it really must be Bannard, even though his eyes seemed to be a different shape, and even a different colour, as the hard light caught them when he laughed.

"I expect I was sleepwalking myself," said Maybury warily.

"There's no need to get the wind up," said Bannard, "like a kid at a new school. All that goes on here is based on the simplest of natural principles: eating good food regularly, sleeping long hours, not taxing the overworked brain. The food is particularly important. You just wait for breakfast, old man, and see what you get. The most tremendous spread, I promise you."

"How do you manage to eat it all?" asked Maybury. "Dinner alone was too much for me."

"We simply let Nature have its way. Or rather, perhaps, *her* way. We give Nature her head."

"But it's not *natural* to eat so much."

"That's all you know," said Bannard. "What you are old man, is effete." He giggled as Bannard had giggled, but he looked somehow unlike Maybury's recollection of Bannard. Maybury was almost certain there was some decisive difference.

The room still smelt of the woman's perfume; or perhaps it was largely Bannard who smelt of it, Bannard who now stood so close to Maybury. It was embarrassing that Bannard, if he really had to rise from his bed and wake Maybury up, did not sit down; though preferably not on Maybury's blanket.

"I'm not saying there's no suffering here," continued Bannard. "But where in the world are you exempt from suffering? At least no one rots away in some attic—or wretched bed-sitter, more likely. Here there are no single rooms. We all help one another. What can you and I do for one another, old man?"

He took a step nearer and bent slightly over Maybury's face. His pyjamas really reeked of perfume.

It was essential to be rid of him; but essential to do it uncontentiously. The prospect should accept the representative's point of view as far as possible unawares.

"Perhaps we could talk for just five or ten minutes more," said Maybury, "and then I should like to go to sleep again, if you will excuse me. I ought to explain that I slept very little last night owing to my wife's illness."

"Is your wife pretty?" asked Bannard. "Really pretty? With this and that?" He made a couple of gestures, quite conventional though not aforetime seen in drawing rooms.

"Of course she is," said Maybury. "What do you think?"

"Does she really turn you on? Make you lose control of yourself?"

"Naturally," said Maybury. He tried to smile, to show he had a sense of humour which could help him to cope with tasteless questions.

Bannard now not merely sat on Maybury's bed, but pushed his frame against Maybury's legs, which there was not much room to withdraw, owing to the tightness of the blanket, as Bannard sat on it.

"Tell us about it," said Bannard. "Tell us exactly what it's like to be a married man. Has it changed your whole life? Transformed everything?"

"Not exactly. In any case, I married years ago."

"So now there is someone else. *I* understand."

"No, actually there is not."

"Love's old sweet song still sings to you?"

"If you like to put it like that, yes. I love my wife. Besides she's ill. And we have a son. There's him to consider too."

"How old is your son?"

"Nearly sixteen."

"What colour are his hair and eyes?"

"Really, I'm not sure. No particular colour. He's not a baby, you know."

"Are his hands still soft?"

"I shouldn't think so."

"Do you love your son, then?"

"In his own way, yes, of course."

"I should love him, were he mine, and my wife too." It seemed to Maybury that Bannard said it with real sentiment. What was more, he looked at least twice as sad as when Maybury had first seen him: twice as old, and twice as sad. It was all ludicrous, and Maybury at last felt really tired, despite the lump of Bannard looming over him, and looking different.

"Time's up for me," said Maybury. "I'm sorry. Do you mind if we go to sleep again?"

Bannard rose at once to his feet, turned his back on Maybury's corner, and went to his bed without a word, thus causing further embarrassment.

It was again left to Maybury to turn out the light, and to shove his way back to bed through the blackness.

Bannard had left more than a waft of the perfume behind him; which perhaps helped Maybury to sleep once more almost immediately, despite all things.

Could the absurd conversation with Bannard have been a dream? Certainly what happened next was a dream: for there was Angela in her nightdress with her hands on her poor head, crying out "Wake up! Wake up! Wake up!" Maybury could not but comply, and in Angela's place, there was the boy, Vincent, with early morning tea for him. Perforce the light was on once more: but that was not a matter to be gone into.

"Good morning, Mr Maybury."

"Good morning, Vincent."

Bannard already had his tea.

Each of them had a pot, a cup, jugs of milk and hot water, and a plate of bread and butter, all set on a tray. There were eight large triangular slices each.

"No sugar," cried out Bannard genially. "Sugar kills appetite."

Perfect rubbish, Maybury reflected; and squinted across at Bannard, recollecting his last rubbishy conversation. By the light of morning, even if it were but the same electric light, Bannard looked much more himself, fluffy red aureole and all. He looked quite rested. He munched away at his bread and butter. Maybury thought it best to go through the motions of following suit. From over there Bannard could hardly see the details.

"Race you to the bathroom, old man," Bannard cried out.

"Please go first," responded Maybury soberly. As he had no means of conveying the bread and butter off the premises, he hoped, with the aid of the towel, to conceal it in his skimpy pyjamas jacket, and push it down the water closet. Even Bannard would probably not attempt to throw his arms round him and so uncover the offence.

Down in the lounge, there they all were, with Falkner presiding indefinably but genially. Wan though authentic sunlight trickled in from the outer world, but Maybury observed that the front door was still bolted and chained. It was the first thing he looked for. Universal expectation was detectable: of breakfast, Maybury assumed. Bannard, at all times shrimpish, was simply lost in the throng. Cécile he could not see, but he made a point of not looking very hard. In any case, several of the people looked new, or at least different. Possibly it was a further example of the phenomenon Maybury had encountered with Bannard.

Falkner crossed to him at once: the recalcitrant but still privileged outsider. "I can promise you a good breakfast, Mr Maybury," he said confidentially. "Lentils. Fresh fish. Rump steak. Apple pie made by ourselves, with lots and lots of cream."

"I mustn't stay for it," said Maybury. "I simply mustn't. I have my living to earn. I must go at once."

He was quite prepared to walk a couple of miles; indeed, all set for it. The automobile organisation, which had given him the route from which he should never have diverged, could recover his car. They had done it for him before, several times.

A faint shadow passed over Falkner's face, but he merely said in a low voice, "If you really insist, Mr Maybury——."

"I'm afraid I have to," said Maybury.

"Then I'll have a word with you in a moment."

None of the others seemed to concern themselves. Soon they all filed off, talking quietly among themselves, or, in many cases, saying nothing.

"Mr Maybury," said Falkner, "you can respect a confidence?"

"Yes," said Maybury steadily.

"There was an incident here last night. A death. We do not talk about such things. Our guests do not expect it."

"I am sorry," said Maybury.

"Such things still upset me," said Falkner. "None the less I must not think about that. My immediate task is to dispose of the body. While the guests are preoccupied. To spare them all knowledge, all pain."

"How is that to be done?" enquired Maybury.

"In the usual manner, Mr Maybury. The hearse is drawing up outside the door even as we speak. Where you are concerned, the point is this. If you wish for what in other circumstances I could call a lift, I could arrange for you to join the vehicle. It is travelling quite a distance. We find that best." Falkner was progressively unfastening the front door. "It seems the best solution, don't you think, Mr Maybury? At least it is the best I can offer. Though you will not be able to thank Mr Bannard, of course."

A coffin was already coming down the stairs, borne on the shoulders of four men in black, with Vincent, in his white jacket, coming first, in order to leave no doubt of the way and to prevent any loss of time.

"I agree," said Maybury. "I accept. Perhaps you would let me know my bill for dinner?"

"I shall waive that too, Mr Maybury," replied Falkner, "in the present circumstances. We have a duty to hasten. We have others to think of. I shall simply say how glad we have all been to have you with us." He held out his hand. "Good-bye, Mr Maybury."

Maybury was compelled to travel with the coffin itself, because there simply was not room for him on the front seat, where a director of the firm, a corpulent man, had to be accommodated with the driver. The nearness of death compelled a respectful silence among the company in the rear compartment, especially when a living stranger was in the midst; and Maybury alighted unobtrusively when a bus stop was reached. One of the undertaker's men said that he should not have to wait long.

6

THE SAME DOG

THOUGH THERE WERE three boys, there were also twelve long years between Hilary Brigstock and his immediately elder brother, Gilbert. On the other hand, there was only one year and one month between Gilbert and the future head of the family, Roger.

Hilary could not remember when first the suggestion entered his ears that his existence was the consequence of a "mistake". Possibly he had in any case hit upon the idea already, within his own head. Nor did his Christian name help very much: people always supposed it to be the name of a girl, even though his father asserted loudly on all possible occasions that the idea was a complete mistake, a product of etymological and historical ignorance, and of typical modern sloppiness.

And his mother was dead. He was quite unable to remember her, however hard he tried; as he from time to time did. Because his father never remarried, having as clear and definite views about women as he had about many other things, Hilary grew up against an almost entirely male background. In practice, this background seemed to consist fundamentally of Roger and Gilbert forever slugging and bashing at one another, with an occasional sideswipe at their kid brother. So Hilary, though no milksop, tended to keep his own counsel and his own secrets. In particular, there are few questions asked by a young boy when there is no woman to reply to them; or, at least, few questions about anything that matters.

The family lived in the remoter part of Surrey. There was a very respectable, rather expensive, semi-infant school, Briarside, to which most of the young children were directed from the earliest age practicable. Hilary was duly sent there, as had been his brothers ahead of

him, in order to learn some simple reading and figuring, and how to
catch a ball, before being passed on to the fashionable preparatory
school, Gorselands, on his way to Cheltenham or Wellington. Some of
the family went to the one place, some to the other. It was an unusual
arrangement, and outsiders could never see the sense in it.

Almost unavoidably, Briarside was a mixed establishment (though
it would have been absurd to describe it as co-educational), and there
Hilary formed a close and remarkable friendship with a girl, two years
older than himself, named Mary Rossiter. The little girls at the school
were almost the first Hilary had ever met. Even his young cousins
were all boys, as happens in some families.

Mary had dark, frizzy hair, which stuck out round her head; and a
rather flat face, with, however, an already fine pair of large, dark eyes,
which not only sparkled, but seemed to move from side to side in surprising jerks as she spoke, which, if permitted, she did almost continuously. Generally she wore a shirt or sweater and shorts, as little
girls were beginning to do at that time, and emanated extroversion;
but occasionally, when there was a school celebration, more perhaps
for the parents than for the tots, she would appear in a really beautiful silk dress, eclipsing everyone, and all the more in that the dress
seemed not precisely right for her, but more like a stage costume.
Mary Rossiter showed promise of natural leadership (some of the
mums already called her "bossy"), but her fine eyes were for Hilary
alone; and not only her eyes, but hands and lips and tender words as
well.

From within the first few days of his arrival, Hilary was sitting next
to Mary at the classes (if such they could be called) and partnering
her inseparably in the playrooms and the garden. The establishment
liked the boys to play with the boys, the girls with the girls, and normally no admonition whatever was needed in those directions; but
when it came to Hilary and Mary, the truth was that already Mary
was difficult to resist when she was set upon a thing. She charmed, she
smiled, and she persisted. Moreover, her father was very rich; and it
was obvious from everything about her that her parents doted on her.

There were large regions of the week which the school did not
claim to fill. Most of the parents awaited the release of their boys and
girls and bore them home in small motor cars of the wifely kind. But
Mary was left, perhaps dangerously, with her freedom; simply because she wanted it to be like that. At least, she wanted it to be like
that after she had met Hilary. It is less certain where she had stood
previously. As for Hilary, no one greatly cared—within a wide span of

hours—whether he was home or not. There was a woman named Mrs Parker who came in each day and did all that needed to be done and did it as well as could be expected (Hilary's father would not even have considered such a person "living in"); but she had no authority to exercise discipline over Hilary, and, being thoroughly modern in her ideas, no temperamental inclination either. If Hilary turned up for his tea, it would be provided. If he did not, trouble was saved.

Hilary and Mary went for long, long walks; for much of the distance, hand in hand. In the midst of the rather droopy and distorted southern-Surrey countryside (or one-time countryside), they would find small, worked-out sandpits, or, in case of rain, disused, collapsing huts, and there they would sit close together, or one at the other's feet, talking without end, and gently embracing. He would force his small fingers through her wiry mop and make jokes about electricity coming out at the ends. She would touch the back of his neck, inside his faded red shirt, with her lips, and nuzzle into the soft, fair thicket on top of his head. They learned the southern-Surrey byways and bridlepaths remarkably thoroughly, for six or eight miles to the south-east, and six or eight miles to the south-west; and, in fact, collaborated in drawing a secret map of them. That was one of the happiest things they ever did. They were always at work revising the secret map, by the use of erasers, and adding to it, and colouring it with crayons borrowed from Briarside. They never tired of walking, because no one had ever said they should.

One day they were badly frightened.

They were walking down a sandy track, which they did not exactly know, when they came upon a large property with a wall round it. The wall was high and apparently thick. It had been covered throughout its length with plaster, but much of the plaster had either flaked, or fallen completely away, revealing the yellow bricks within, themselves tending to crumble. The wall was surmounted by a hipped roofing, which projected, in order to throw clear as much as possible of any rain that might descend; and this roofing also was much battered and gapped. One might have thought the wall to be in a late stage of disease. It was blotched and mottled in every direction. None the less, it continued to be very far from surmountable, even by a fully grown person.

Hilary took a run at it, clutching at a plant which protruded from a gap in the exposed pointing, and simultaneously setting his foot upon the plaster at the bottom of a large space where the rest of the plaster had fallen away. The consequence was instant disaster. The plant leapt from its rooting, and at the same time the plaster on which Hilary's small weight rested fell off the wall in an entire large slab, and shattered into smaller pieces among the rank grass and weeds below, where Hilary lay also.

"Hilary!" It was an authentic scream, and of authentic agony.

"It's all right, Mary." Hilary resolutely raised himself, resolutely refused to weep. "I'm all right. Really I am."

She had run to him and was holding him tightly.

"Mary, please. I'll choke."

Her arms fell away from him, but uncertainly.

"We'd better go home," she said.

"No, of course not. I'm perfectly all right, I tell you. It was nothing." But this last he did not really believe.

"It was *terrible*," said Mary, with solemnity. She was wearing a skirt that day, a small-scale imitation of an adult woman's tweed skirt, and he could see her knees actually knocking together.

He put his arm round her shoulder, but, as he did so, became aware that he was shaking himself. "Silly," he said affectionately. "It wasn't anything much. Let's go on."

But she merely stood there, quivering beneath his extended arm.

There was a perceptible pause. Then she said: "I don't like this place."

It was most unlike her to say such a thing. He had never before known her to do so.

But always he took her seriously. "What's the matter?" he asked. "I *am* all right, you know. I truly am. You can feel me if you like."

And then the dog started barking—if, indeed, one could call it a bark. It was more like a steady growling roar, with a clatter mixed up in it, almost certainly of gnashing teeth: altogether something more than barking, but unmistakably canine, all the same—horribly so. Detectably it came from within the domain behind the high wall.

"Hilary," said Mary, "let's run."

But her unusual attitude had put Hilary on his mettle.

"I don't know," he said. "Not yet."

"What d'you mean?" she asked.

"I see it like this," said Hilary, rubbing a place on his knee. "Either the dog is chained up, or shut in behind that wall, and we're all right. Or else he isn't, and it's no good our running."

It was somewhat the way that Mary's own influence had taught him to think, and she responded to it.

"Perhaps we should look for some big stones," she suggested.

"Yes," he said. "Though I shouldn't think it'll be necessary. I think he must be safely shut up in some way. He'd have been out by now otherwise."

"*I'm* going to look," said Mary.

There are plenty of stones in the worn earth of southern Surrey, and many old bricks and other constructional detritus also. Within two or three minutes, Mary had assembled a pile of such things.

In the meantime, Hilary had gone on a little along the track. He stood there, listening to the clamorous dog almost calmly.

Mary joined him, holding up the front part of her skirt, which contained four of the largest stones, more than she could carry in her hands.

"We won't need them," said Hilary, with confidence. "And if we do, they're everywhere."

Mary leaned forward and let the stones fall to the ground, taking care that they missed her toes. Possibly the quite loud thuds made the dog bark more furiously than ever.

"Perhaps he's standing guard over buried treasure?" suggested Mary.

"Or over some fairy kingdom that mortals may not enter," said Hilary.

They talked about such things for much of the time when they were together. Once they had worked together upon an actual map of Fairyland, and with Giantland adjoining.

"He might have lots of heads," said Mary.

"Come on, let's look," said Hilary.

"Quietly," said Mary, making no other demur.

He took her hand.

"There *must* be a gate," she remarked, after they had gone a little further, with the roaring, growling bark as obstreperous as ever.

"Let's hope it's locked then," he replied. At once he added: "Of course it's locked. He'd have been out by now otherwise."

"You said that before," said Mary. "But perhaps the answer is that there is no gate. There can't always be a gate, you know."

But there was a gate; a pair of gates, high, wrought iron, scrolled, rusted, and heavily padlocked. Through them, Hilary and Mary could see a large, palpably empty house, with many of the windows glassless, and the paint on the outside walls surviving only in streaks and smears, pink, green, and blue, as the always vaguely polluted atmosphere added its corruption to that inflicted by the weather. The house was copiously mock-battlemented and abundantly ogeed: a structure, without doubt, in the Gothic Revival taste, though of a period uncertain over at least a hundred years. Some of the heavy chimney-stacks had broken off and fallen. The front door, straight before them, was a recessed shadow. It was difficult to see whether it was open or shut. The paving stones leading to it were lost in mossy dampness.

"Haunted house," said Mary.

"What's that?" enquired Hilary.

"Don't exactly know," said Mary. "But Daddy says they're *everywhere*, though people don't realize it."

"But how can you tell?" asked Hilary, looking at her seriously and a little anxiously.

"Just by the look," replied Mary with authority. "You can tell at once when you know. It's a mistake to look for too long, though."

"Ought we to put it on the map?"

"I suppose so. I'm not sure."

"Is that dog going to bark all day, d'you think?"

"He'll stop when we go away. Let's go, Hilary."

"Look!" cried Hilary, clutching at her. "Here he is. He must have managed to break away. We must show no sign of fear. That's the important thing."

Curiously enough, Mary seemed in no need of this vital guidance. She was already standing rigidly, with her big eyes apparently fixed on the animal, almost as if hypnotized.

Of course, the tall, padlocked bars stood between them and the dog; and another curious thing was that the dog seemed to realize the fact, and to make allowance for it, in a most undoglike manner. Instead of leaping up at the bars in an endeavour to reach the two of them, and so to caress or bite them, it stood well back and simply stared at them, as if calculating hard. It barked no longer, but instead emitted an almost continuous sound halfway between a growl and a whine, and quite low.

It was a big, shapeless, yellow animal, with long, untidy legs, which shimmered oddly, perhaps as it sought a firm grip on the buried and slippery stones. The dog's yellow skin seemed almost hairless. Blotchy and draggled, it resembled the wall outside. Even the dog's eyes were a flat, dull yellow. Hilary felt strange and uneasy when he observed them; and next he felt upset as he realized that Mary and the dog were gazing at one another as if under a spell.

"Mary!" he cried out. "Mary, don't look like that. Please don't look like that."

He no longer dared to touch her, so alien had she become.

"Mary, let's go. You said we were to go." Now he had begun to cry, while all the time the dog kept up its muffled internal commotion, almost like soft singing.

In the end, but not before Hilary had become very wrought up, the tension fell away from Mary, and she was speaking normally.

"Silly," she said, caressing Hilary. "It's quite safe. You said so yourself."

He had no answer to that. The careful calculations by which earlier he had driven off the thought of danger had now proved terrifyingly irrelevant. All he could do was subside to the ground and lose himself in tears, his head between his knees.

Mary knelt beside him. "What are you crying about, Hilary? There's no danger. He's a friendly dog, really."

"He's not, he's not."

She tried to draw his hands away from his face. "Why are you crying, Hilary?" One might have felt that she quite urgently needed to know.

"I'm frightened."

"What are you frightened of? It can't be the dog. He's gone."

At that, Hilary slowly uncurled, and forgetting, on the instant, to continue weeping, directed his gaze at the rusty iron gates. There was no dog visible.

"Where's he gone, Mary? Did you see him go?"

"No, I didn't actually *see* him," she replied. "But he's gone. And that's what you care about, isn't it?"

"But *why* did he go? We're still here."

"I expect he had business elsewhere." He knew that she had acquired that explanation too from her father, because she had once told him so.

"Has he found a way out?"

"Of course he hasn't."

"How can you tell?"

"He's simply realized that we don't mean any harm."

"I don't believe you. You're just saying that. Why are you saying that, Mary? You were more scared than I was when we came here. What's happened to you, Mary?"

"What's happened to me is that I've got back a little sense." From whom, he wondered, had she learned to say *that*? It was so obviously insincere, that it first hurt, and then once more frightened him.

"I want to go home," he said.

She nodded, and they set off, but not hand in hand.

There was one more incident before they had left the area behind them.

As they returned up the gently sloping, sandy track, Hilary kept his eyes on the ground, carefully not looking at the yellow wall on his left, or looking at it as little as possible, and certainly not looking backwards over his shoulder. At the place where the wall bore away leftwards at a right angle, the track began to ascend rather more steeply for perhaps a hundred yards, to a scrubby tableland above. They were walking in silence, and Hilary's ears, always sharper than the average, were continuously strained for any unusual sound, probably from behind the wall, but possibly, and even more alarmingly, not. When some way up the steeper slope, he seemed to hear something, and could not stop himself from looking back.

There was indeed something to see, though Hilary saw it for only an instant.

At the corner of the wall, there was no special feature, as one might have half-expected, such as a turret or an obelisk. There was merely the turn in the hipped roofing. But now Hilary saw, at least for half a second, that a man was looking over, installed at the very extremity of the internal angle. There was about half of him visible, and he seemed tall and slender and bald. Hilary failed to notice how he was dressed: if, indeed, he was dressed at all.

Hilary jerked back his head. He did not feel able to mention what he had seen to Mary, least of all now.

He did not feel able, in fact, to mention the sight to anyone. Twenty years later, he was once about to mention it, but even then decided against doing so. In the meantime, and for years after these events, the thought and memory of them lay at the back of his mind; partly because of what had already happened, partly because of what happened soon afterwards.

The outing must have upset Hilary more than he knew, because the same evening he felt ill, and was found by Mrs Parker to have a temperature. That was the beginning of it, and the end of it was not for a period of weeks; during which there had been two doctors, and, on some of the days and nights, an impersonal nurse, or perhaps two of them also. There had also been much bluff jollying along from Hilary's father; Hilary's brothers being both at Wellington. Even Mrs Parker had to be reinforced by a blowsy teenager named Eileen.

In the end, and quite suddenly, Hilary felt as good as new: either owing to the miracles of modern medicine, or, more probably, owing to the customary course of nature.

"You may feel right, old son," said Doctor Morgan-Vaughan; "but you're *not* right, not yet."

"When can I go back to school?"

"Do you want to go back, son?"

"Yes," said Hilary.

"Well, well," said Doctor Morgan-Vaughan. "Small boys felt differently in my day."

"When can I?" asked Hilary.

"One fine day," said Doctor Morgan-Vaughan. "There's no hurry about it. You've been ill, son, really ill, and you don't want to do things in a rush."

So a matter of two months had passed before Hilary had any inkling of the fact that something had happened to Mary also. He would have liked to see her, but had not cared, rather than dared, to suggest it. At no time had he even mentioned her at home. There was no possibility of his hearing anything about her until his belated return to school.

Even then, the blowsy teenager was sent with him on the first day, lest, presumably, he faint at the roadside or vanish upwards to Heaven. His heart was heavy and confused, as he walked; and Eileen found difficulty in conversing with a kid of his kind anyway. He was slightly relieved by the fact that when they arrived at the school, she had no other idea than to hasten off with alacrity.

The headmistress (if so one might term her), who was also part-proprietor of the establishment, a neat lady of 36, was waiting specially for Hilary's arrival after his illness; and greeted him with kindness and a certain understanding. The children also felt a new interest in him, though with most of them it was only faint. But there was a little girl with two tight plaits and a gingham dress patterned with asters and sunflowers, who seemed more sincerely concerned about what had been happening to him. Her name was Valerie Watkinson.

"Where's Mary?" asked Hilary.

"Mary's dead," said Valerie Watkinson solemnly.

Hilary's first response was merely hostile. "I don't believe you," he said.

Valerie Watkinson nodded three or four times, even more solemnly.

Hilary clutched hold of both her arms above the elbows. "I don't believe you," he said again.

Valerie Watkinson began to cry. "You're hurting me."

Hilary took away his hands. Valerie did not move or make any further complaint. They stood facing one another in silence for a perceptible pause, with Valerie quietly weeping.

"Is it true?" said Hilary in the end.

Valerie nodded again behind her tiny handkerchief with a pinky-blue Swiss milkmaid on one corner. "You're very pale," she gasped out, her mouth muffled.

She stretched out a small damp hand. "Poor Hilary. Mary was your friend. I'm sorry for you, Hilary."

"Did she go to bed with a temperature?" asked Hilary. He was less unaccustomed than most children to the idea of death because he was perfectly well aware that of late he himself was said to have escaped death but narrowly.

This time Valerie shook her head, though with equal solemnity. "No," she said. "At least, I don't think so. It's all a mystery. We haven't been *told* she's dead. We thought she was ill, like you. Then Sandy saw something in the paper." Sandy Stainer was a podgy sprawling boy with, as one might suppose, vaguely reddish hair.

"What did he see?"

"Something nasty," said Valerie with confidence. "I don't know what it was. We're not supposed to know."

"Sandy knows."

"Yes," said Valerie.

"Hasn't he told?"

"He's been told not to. Miss Milland had him in her room."

"But don't you want to know yourself?"

"No, I don't," said Valerie, with extreme firmness. "My mummy says it's enough for us to know that poor Mary's dead. She says that's what really matters."

It was certainly what really mattered to Hilary. He passed his first day back at school looking very pallid and speaking no further word except when directly addressed by Miss Milland or Mrs Everson; both of whom agreed, after school hours, that Hilary Brigstock had been sent back before he should have been. It was something to which they were entirely accustomed: the children often seemed to divide into those perpetually truant and those perpetually in seeming need of more care and attention than they were receiving at home. That it should be so was odd in such a professional and directorial area; though Mrs Cartier, who looked in every now and then to teach elementary French, and was a Maoist, said it was just what one always found.

Hilary had never spoken to Sandy Stainer, nor ever wanted to. The present matter was not one which he would care to enquire about in such a quarter. Moreover, he knew perfectly well that he would be told nothing, but merely tormented. Sandy Stainer's lips had somehow been sealed in some remarkably effective way; and he would be likely to find, in such a situation, clear conscience and positive social sanction for quiet arm-twisting and general vexing of enquirers, especially of enquirers known to be as vulnerable as Hilary. And Mary had been so much to Hilary that he had no other close friend in the school —probably no other friend there at all. Perhaps Hilary was one of those men who are designed for one woman only.

Certainly he had no little friends outside the school; nor had ever been offered any. Nor, as usual, was the death of Mary a matter that could be laid before his father. In any case, what could his father permit himself to tell him; when all was so obscure, and so properly so?

Within a day or two, Hilary was back in bed once more, and again missing from school.

Doctor Morgan-Vaughan could not but suspect this time that the trouble contained a marked element of "the psychological"; but it was an aspect of medicine that had always struck him as almost entirely unreal, and certainly as a therapeutic dead end, except for those resolved to mine it financially. He preferred to treat visibly physiological disturbances with acceptably physiological nostra. In the present case, he seriously thought of again calling in Doctor Oughtred, who had undoubtedly made a very real contribution in the earlier manifestation of the child's illness.

"Do you read the local paper, Mrs Parker?" asked Hilary, whiter than the sheets between which he lay.

"I don't get round to it," replied Mrs Parker, in her carefully uncommitted way. "We take it in. Mr Parker feels we should."

"Why does he feel that?"

"Well, you want to know what's going on around you, don't you?"

"Yes," said Hilary.

"Not that Mr Parker reads anything very much. Why should he, when he's got the wireless? The *Advertiser* just piles up in heaps till the waste people come for it from the hospital."

"What do they do with it at the hospital?"

"Pulp it, I believe. You've got to do what you can for charity, haven't you?"

"Bring me all the local papers in the heap, Mrs Parker. I'm ill too. It's just like the hospital."

"You couldn't read them," said Mrs Parker, as before; carefully not conceding.

"I *could*," said Hilary.

"How's that? You can't read."

"I can," said Hilary. "I can read anything. Well, almost anything. Bring me the papers, Mrs Parker."

She expressed no surprise that he should want to read something so boring even to her; nor did it seem to strike her that there might be anything significant in his demand. In fact, she could think of nothing to say; and as, in any case, she was always wary about what she let fall in the ambience of her employment, she left Hilary's room without one word more.

But, as much as three days later, Eileen had something to say when she brought him his midday meal (not a very imaginative one) and an assembly of pills.

"You *are* old-fashioned," remarked Eileen. "At least that's what Mrs Parker thinks."

"What d'you mean?" asked Hilary in a sulky tone, because he disliked Eileen.

"Asking for the *Advertiser*, when you can't even read it."

"I *can* read it," said Hilary.

"I know more than Mrs Parker knows," said Eileen. "It's that little girl, isn't it? Mary Rossiter, your little sweetheart."

Hilary said nothing.

"I've seen you together. I know. Not that I've told Mrs Parker."

"You *haven't*?"

"Not likely. Why should I tell *her*?"

Hilary considered that.

"She's a silly cow," said Eileen casually.

Hilary was clutching with both hands at the sheet. "Do you know what happened to Mary?" he asked, looking as far away from Eileen as he could look.

"Not exactly. She was interfered with, and mauled about. Bitten all over, they say, poor little thing. But it's been hushed up proper, and you'd better hurry and forget all about her. That's all you *can* do, isn't it?"

In the end, having passed at Briarside and at Gorselands through the more difficult years of the Second World War, Hilary went to Wellington also. His father thought it a tidier arrangement: better adapted to more restricted times. By then, of course, Hilary's brothers, Roger and Gilbert, had left the school, though in neither case for the university. There seemed no point, they both decided; and their father had had no difficulty in agreeing. He had been to a university himself, and it had seemed to him more of a joke than anything else, and a not particularly useful one.

Despite the intermittent connection with Wellington, theirs had not been a particularly army family, and it was with surprise that Mr Brigstock learned of his youngest son's decision to make the army his career, especially as the war was not so long concluded. Hilary, as we have said, was no milksop, and no doubt the Wellington ethos had its influence; but, in any case, it is a mistake to think that an officers' mess is manned solely by good-class rowdies. There are as many (and, naturally, as few) sensitive people in the army as in most other places; and some of them find their way there precisely because they are so.

A further complexity is that the sensitive are sometimes most at their ease with the less sensitive. Among Hilary's friends at the depot, was a youth named Callcutt, undisguisedly extrovert, very dependable. On one occasion, Hilary Brigstock took Callcutt home for a few days of their common leave.

It was not a thing he did often, even now. The atmosphere of his home still brought out many reserves in him. It would hardly be too much to say that he himself went there as little as possible. But by now both Roger and Gilbert were married, and had homes of their own, as they frequently mentioned; so that Hilary was beginning to expect qualms within him on the subject of his father's isolation, and, surely, loneliness. Late middle-aged people living by themselves were always nowadays said to be lonely. Unlike most sons, Hilary at times positively wished that his father would marry again, as people in his situation were expected to do; that his father's views on the subject of women had somehow become less definite.

And really the place was dull. Stranded there with Callcutt, Hilary perceived luminously, as in a minutely detailed picture, how entirely dull, in every single aspect, his home was.

More secrets are improperly disclosed from boredom than from any other motive; and more intimacies imparted, with relief resulting, or otherwise.

"I love it here," said Callcutt, one day after lunch, when Mr Brigstock had gone upstairs for the afternoon, as he normally did.

"That's fine," replied Hilary. "What do you love in particular about
it?"

"The quiet," said Callcutt immediately. "I think one's home should
be a place where one can go for some quiet. You're a lucky chap."

"Yes," agreed Hilary. "Quiet it certainly is. Nowadays, at least.
When my two elder brothers were here, it wasn't quiet at all."

"Remind me where they are now?"

"Married. Both of them. With homes of their own."

"Nice girls?"

"So-so."

"Kids?"

"Two each."

"Boys?"

"All boys. We only breed boys."

"*Only?*"

"There hasn't been a girl in the Brigstock family within living memory."

"Saves a lot of trouble," said Callcutt.

"Loses a lot of fun," said Hilary.

"Not at that age."

"*Particularly*, perhaps, at that age."

"How's that? You're not one of these Lolita types, like old what-
not?"

"When I was a child I knew a girl who meant more to me than any
girl has meant to me since. More, indeed, than anyone at all. Remember that I never knew my mother."

"Lucky chap again," said Callcutt. "Well, in some ways. No, I
shouldn't have said that. I apologize. Forget it."

"That's all right."

"Tell me about your girl friend. I'm quite serious. As a matter of
fact, I know perfectly well what you meant about her."

Hilary hesitated. Almost certainly, if it had not been for the absence
of other topics, other possible activities, other interests, he would
never have mentioned Mary Rossiter at all. He had never spoken of
her to a soul for the twenty years since she had vanished, and for at
least half that time he had thought of her but infrequently.

"Well, if you like, I *will* tell you. For what it's worth, which isn't
much, especially to a third party. But we've nothing else to do."

"Thank the Lord!" commented Callcutt.

"I feel the Brigstocks should do more to provide entertainment."

"Good God!" rejoined Callcutt.

So, for the first time, Hilary imparted much of the story to another. He told how sweet Mary Rossiter had been, how they used to go for surprisingly long walks together, how they found the crumbling wall, and heard, and later saw, the shapeless, slithery dog, which seemed the colour of the wall, and saw also the collapsing mansion or near-mansion, which Mary, just like a kid, had immediately said must be a haunted house. Hilary even told Callcutt about the maps that the two children had drawn together, and that they had been maps not only of Surrey, but of Fairyland, and Giantland, and the Land of Shades also.

"Good preparation for the army," observed Callcutt.

But Hilary did not tell Callcutt about the lean, possibly naked, man he had so positively seen at the extremest angle of the wall. He had been about to tell him, simply without thinking, at the point where the incident came in the narrative; but he passed over the matter.

"Bloody savage dogs!" said Callcutt. "I'm against them. Especially in towns. Straining at the leash, and defecating all over the pavements. Something wrong with the owner's virility, I always think."

"This was the worst dog you ever saw," Hilary responded. "I'm quite confident of that."

"I hate them all," said Callcutt sweepingly. "They carry disease."

"That was the least in the case of the dog I was talking about," observed Hilary. And he told Callcutt of what had happened next—as far as he could tell it.

"Oh, God!" exclaimed Callcutt.

"I suppose it was what people used to call a mad dog."

"But that was well before your time, even if you *were* a kid. There aren't so many mad dogs these days. Anyway, what happened to the dog? Shot, I take it?"

"I have no idea."

"But surely it must have been shot? Things couldn't just have been left at that."

"Well, probably it was shot. I just don't know. I wasn't supposed to know anything at all about what had happened."

"Good God, it *should* have been shot. After doing a thing like that."

"I daresay it *was*."

There was a pause while Callcutt wrestled with his thoughts and

Hilary with his memories; memories of which he had remembered little for some longish time past.

"It was the most frightful thing," Callcutt summed up at last. "I say: could we pay a visit to the scene of the crime? Or would that be too much?"

"Not too much if I can find the place." This was indeed how one thing led to another. "I haven't been there since."

"I suppose not," said Callcutt, who hadn't thought of that. Then had added: "What, never?"

"Never," said Hilary. "After all, I'm not here very often."

"Whose car shall we take?"

"As far as I can recall the lie of the land, we had better walk. I daresay it's all caravans and bungalows by now."

And so, substantially, it proved. It would no doubt be wrong to suggest that the municipal authority or statutory body or honorary trustees responsible for the conservation of an open space had in any major degree permitted the public heritage to diminish in area or beauty, but whereas formerly the conserved terrain had merged off into pastures and semi-wild woodland, now it seemed to be encircled almost up to the last inch with houses. They were big, expensive houses, but they had converted the wilderness of Hilary's childhood into something more like a public park, very beaten down, and with the usual close network of amateur footpaths, going nowhere in particular, because serving no function. Round the edge of this slightly sad area Hilary and Callcutt prowled and prospected.

"It was somewhere about here," said Hilary. "Certainly on this side."

"I should have said it had all changed so much that we were unlikely to get far without comparative maps. None of these houses can be more than ten or twelve years old."

They varied greatly in style: from Cotswold to Moroccan, from Ernest George to Frank Lloyd Wright. Some seemed still to value seclusion, but more went in for neighbourliness and open plan. Despite all the desperation of discrepancy, there was a uniformity of tone which was even more depressing.

"I agree that my place has disappeared," said Hilary. "Been built over. Of course it was pretty far gone even then."

The houses were served by a rough road, almost certainly "unadopted". It assured them a precarious degree of freedom from casual motor traffic.

One of the biggest houses was in the Hollywood style: a garish structure with brightly coloured faience roof, much Spanish ironwork, mass-produced but costly, and a flight of outside steps in bright red tiles. The property was surrounded by a scumbled white wall. Hilary and Callcutt stared in through the elaborate, garden-of-remembrance gates.

"It's like a caricature of the old place," said Hilary. "Much smaller, and much louder—but still . . ."

The windows were all shut and there was no one in sight. Even the other houses seemed all to lie silent, and on the rough road nothing and no one passed. The two men continued to peer through the bars of the gate, ornate but trivial.

From round the back of the house to their left emerged, in like silence, a large, moulting, yellow dog. They could hardly even hear the patter of its large feet on the composition flagstones.

Hilary said nothing until the dog, which originally they saw head on, had turned and, with apparent indifference to them, displayed the full length of its right flank. Then he spoke: "Bogey," he said, "that's the same dog." Callcutt was known to his intimates as Bogey, following some early incident in his military life.

Callcutt thought before speaking. Then he said: "Rubbish, Hilary. Dogs don't live twenty years." But he wasn't quite sure of that.

"That one has."

But now the dog began to bark, growling and baying most frighteningly, though, as on the previous occasion, not coming right up to the gate, or attempting to charge at them. If the fact that, a moment before, it seemed not to have seen them, might have been attributed to extreme senility, there was nothing remotely senile about its furious, almost rabid aggression now; and even less, perhaps, about the calculating way it placed itself, whatever might have been the reason. It stood a shapeless, sulphurous mass on its precisely chosen ground, almost like a Chinese demon.

"That is just what it did before," Hilary shouted above the uproar. "Stood like that and came no nearer."

"If you can call it standing," Callcutt shouted back.

He was appalled by the dog, and did not fail to notice that Hilary had turned white, and was clinging to the decorative gatebars. But in the end Callcutt looked upwards for a second. He spoke again, or rather shouted. "There's a wench at one of the upstairs windows. We'd better clear out."

Before Hilary had managed any reply, which the barking of the dog in any case made difficult, there was a further development. The glass-panelled front door of the house opened, and a woman walked out.

Perhaps she had emerged to quiet the dog and apologize, perhaps, on the contrary, to reinforce the dog's antagonism to strangers: to Hilary it was a matter of indifference. The woman was of about his own age, but he knew perfectly well who she was. She was the grown-up Mary Rossiter, who twenty years before had been killed by a dog, probably a mad dog, possibly a dog that had been shot, certainly a most unusual dog, this very present dog, in fact.

Whatever he felt like, Hilary did not pass out. "Do you mind if we go?"

He withdrew his gaze and, without really waiting for Callcutt, began to walk away sharply. Again, it was somewhat as on the previous occasion: veritably, he was behaving exactly as a small boy might behave.

He did not pace out along the rough road, past the houses. Instead, he walked straight into the dilapidated public forest. Callcutt had almost to run after him, in a rather absurd way.

Hilary could not be unaware that while he retreated, the dog had stopped its noise. Perhaps he had even gone far enough to have passed beyond earshot, though it seemed unlikely. None the less, it was quite a chase for Callcutt, and with the most uncomfortable overtones.

Hilary pulled himself together quite quickly, however—once more, as before; and was even able to tell Callcutt exactly what he had apprehended—or, as he put it to Callcutt, fancied.

"I'd have taken to my heels myself, I promise you that," said Callcutt.

"I know it was Mary," said Hilary. "I know it."

They remained silent for some time as they walked over the patchy, tired ground.

Then Callcutt spoke. There was something he could not keep to himself, and Hilary seemed all right now.

"You know how we were laughing about the names of those

houses? Samandjane, and Pasadena, and Happy Hours, and all that; the executive style. Do you know what the doggy house is called?"

Hilary shook his head. "I forgot to look."

"You wouldn't believe it. The name above our heads was Maryland."

7

MEETING MR MILLAR

———————

BEFORE IT IS too late, I set out the events exactly as I recall them.

I seem to recall them very well, and they were not of a kind easily forgotten; but amnesia is, I know, more likely to play a part in my tale than exaggeration. As a matter of policy, I am determined to damp down, to play down, to pipe down. I am a man of the twentieth century as much as anyone else.

Of course when it comes to carrying conviction, I make a bad start by being an author. "After all, he is an author!" I remember my grandmother saying when I anxiously questioned her about a particularly improbable tale Maurice Hewlett had told at her tea party that afternoon. I daresay it is precisely because I have sometimes made small sums of money with my pen that I have not related before now this story that is true.

And really with my pen. With this *very* pen in fact; and I was using the same pen when a year or two after the war (the real war—the first one), I took up my abode at the top of a house in Brandenburg Square. Fountain pens could then be had that were designed, positively, to last at least one lifetime.

I have faintly disguised the address because it is potentially libellous to designate a named house as haunted. I believe mine to be the narrative of a haunted man rather than of a haunted house, but after so many lawsuits, albeit mostly successful, I wish to avoid even a remote risk of another one.

I had the run of three small, dusty rooms, sketchily furnished, on the third floor. Hot in summer, cold in winter, they had been intended for servants' bedrooms. In one of them had lately been installed some inexpensive cooking and washing-up apparatus. In a former cupboard or glory-hole had been lodged an equally inexpensive bath and water-closet; to both of which the supply of water percolated but irregularly.

My father had been killed. My mother had almost no resources beyond the consequent pension. I was an only child and knew myself open to criticism for not taking a job, living at home, and handing over the proceeds. But my mother never did criticize, and I believed that I could at least make enough to pay my small rent and maintain *myself*. I was remarkably sanguine, but so, in the event, it worked out. I was never once in arrears, and never once reduced to living for a week or a month or a year on nothing but bread and margarine, as have been so many poets. That was partly, of course, because I never set up to write poetry: the basic bread and butter of my income was provided by the odd employment of going over other people's porno-graphic manuscripts and turning them into saleable books. As pornography is no longer as badly thought of as it was, I can mention that this work was given me by a man named Major Valentine. In any case, he is now dead; though I maintained touch with him almost until the end, partly because I was grateful to him for having kept me alive and enabled me to go my own way during such a critical period.

Major Valentine had been a comrade of my father's in the trenches. I first met him when he came to visit my mother after it was all over. He turned up one day, still in a "trench coat", and in the course of conversation remarked that the war had changed many people's ideas about the sort of books they wanted to read, and that he was going to put his gratuity into setting up as a publisher. I was eighteen at the time and I was pretty certain that there was an unbridgeable gulf between the amount of a major's gratuity and the topless tower of phan-tom gold needed even by the wariest of publishers. I knew a little about it because already I was set upon being a writer myself, and took the current *Writer's and Artist's Year Book* to bed with me nightly until my bloodstream had absorbed all it had to teach or hint at. But naturally I said nothing, because in those days boys did not venture to carp at mature men, let alone when the mature men were war heroes also; and I was rewarded by being offered an "editor's" job there and then, no doubt in part as tribute to my father's memory and my mother's obvious problems. The American term "editor" was not then commonly used in the context of publishing, and my father's friend was already displaying how modern he intended to be. Before the war he had been a free-lance journalist. He actually so described himself to me, possibly because he claimed also to have made a suc-cess of it, which is most uncommon.

I had been cheaply and indifferently educated in the formal sense, and against a stressful and impecunious home life. Fortunately for me, formal education counts little for most artists (and, according to my experience, less than is commonly supposed for most other people). Though I wanted "to write", I had little idea of how to earn money at it—and a complete mental blank, with unpleasant elements of panic, whenever I thought about trying to earn money at anything else. Valentine made it clear that he was not yet in a position to offer enough to maintain me; but I clutched with joy and relief at the proffered regularity of his pittance, explained myself to my mother that same evening (Major Valentine could not stay to supper, and it was just as well), and was set up within the month in Brandenburg Square.

Valentine was never in a position to pay me much more than he paid me at the outset; but I beavered soberly around, and wrote increasingly persuasive letters, so that other jobs came in, a usefully wide variety of them, perhaps, when I came to writing my own first novel.

Major Valentine's subsequent career may as well be disposed of now: pornography is never—I think I may say *never*—as lucrative as it seems likely to be (I refer to the pornography that is recognized as such), and within three or four years Valentine turned to schoolmastering and then went back to the army as an instructor. In the end, he married. It was rather late in life, by the usual standard: but he married a woman who was older than he was, none the less, and she seemed to make him very happy—or perhaps keep him so, as he always seemed a happy person by nature. I went to visit them on several occasions, and certainly Valentine was living in very much better style than ever before when I had known him. Moreover, he was now a lieutenant-colonel. I suppose he had taken up with the Territorials. He was even fortunate in the manner of his death, which was in a fishing incident, and, they said, instantaneous.

When I took possession of my Brandenburg Square attic, there were two tenants below me.

On the second floor was the office of a political weekly named *Freedom*. Though appearing in English, it seemed to be produced by a staff composed entirely of foreigners, some of whom appeared to have difficulty even with conventionalities about the weather or the staircase cleaning when I chanced to run into them on their landing. A surprisingly large number and variety of them were encountered by me during the six months or so we were in the building together. I wondered how the paper could maintain them all, especially as it was hard to believe it had much sale among the general public. From time to time I used to extract copies from the waste sacks left out at night.

In the basement of the building lived a young man and woman of mildly intellectual aspect. At that time, however, the man worked in the local branch of a well-known provisions chain; and the woman had a part-time job with a credit bookmaker. These dispositions were consequent upon their having four children and, therefore, little margin.

Even the very smallest of the children, none the less, had reached some kind of age for schooling; and the young wife used to flit up to my attic in the afternoon for a cup of coffee and a talk after her return from the bookmaker's establishment and before her departure to collect the child.

At first, I was not too keen. I was scrupulous about her position as a married woman living in the same house. Moreover, her visits soon became more and more frequent, almost daily; while at the same time I noticed that she always refused to commit herself about the day following, which I thought vaguely sinister. I fancied I owed it to myself to object a little to being interrupted in the course of composition (or editorship). Needless to say, none of this reserve availed for much or for long. It was no more than the subjective initial slowness or protest of the youthful male, respectably reared. Soon I was looking forward to this woman's visits so much that my morning's work suffered noticeably; and regretting in an entirely different way her continuing refusal to say whether tomorrow she would be back. "I simply can't tell you," she would reply. "We must make the most of the present." But her putting it like that helped to make it difficult for me to do so. Her name was Maureen. The name of her husband was Gilbert. Once she asked me to visit their place after the evening meal, but it could hardly be expected to be a success. The husband just sat there, worn out after a hot day in the provisions shop, and reading the *New Statesman;* and two or three of the children were old enough to stay up and ask questions and fall about. We never tried it again, I think.

The ground and first floors of the building were originally unlet, but that could not be expected to continue for very long now that the country was getting back on to its feet again. All the doors on to the hall and staircase were kept locked, and Maureen used to complain that it made the house seem depressing. I told her that it made for peace and quiet, but I appreciated that peace and quiet were not what Maureen was principally looking for, despite the hullaballoo of four small children in a not very large flat. One day I observed her in

conversation with the window cleaners who swilled away once a
month at the outsides of the never opened sashes. Of course they were
glad of a few words with a pretty housewife having time on her
hands. "They say there's nothing inside but emptiness," Maureen told
me later. I made no comment, but filled in by kissing her hair or something of the kind. Maureen had at that time rather droopy hair, possibly owing to lack of vitamins during the war; which she kept off her
brow with a big tortoiseshell slide. Her brow was really beautiful, and
so were her eyes. They had that gentle look of being unequal to life,
which, as I later realized, always attracts me in a woman.

One night the numerous office staff of *Freedom* did not depart at
the usual hour; and, as late as ten or eleven o'clock, looking over my
banister, I saw them still heaving and rolling great packages on the
landing below. They were being very quiet about it as far as conversation went: not at all like foreigners, one felt. Obviously, there was a
crisis, but for that very reason I felt it unkind to probe. In bed, I was
kept awake not merely by the stolid thumping downstairs but also by
the likelihood that the crisis was one affecting the whole building and
the harmless, neutral way of life we had all worked out within it. Conceivably it was my first clear apprehension of the truth that is the
foundation of wisdom: the truth that change of its nature is for the
worse, the little finger (or thick gripping thumb) of mortality's cold
paw.

And, duly, the next day the builders moved in. They actually woke
me up with their singing, whistling, jostling, rowing, and other customary noises. They were in for an endless three weeks (though nowadays it would be six or nine); and, as serious work became impossible, I moved back to my mother's cottage for a spell, my first of more
than a night or two since I had gone to London. The day of my departure was the first time also, as I well remember, that I kissed
Maureen full and passionately on the lips. I had feared, if I may be
honest, to commit myself so far: with Maureen's husband and children
in permanent residence just below me, to say nothing of my own narrow circumstances. Now the break in my régime seemed to make it
less of a commitment. It was not a very sympathetic way of seeing
things perhaps, but the options are so greatly fewer than people like
to think.

When I reached the cottage, I found it impossible to work in the little bedroom that was always reserved for me, as the gravel lane outside was being "metalled" and widened. Even in the small sitting-
room facing the other way, the noise was disturbing, and I had to

throw the *Daily Chronicle* over work sent me by Valentine, every time
I heard my mother's step, which was frequently, as she was solicitous
and would have liked to keep me with her. In the end, the rumbling,
indecisive steamroller, the clanking tar-boiler, the roadmenders more
loudly jocund than Michael Fairless, withdrew to agitate other households, to diminish the more distant hedgerow. "Do stop as long as
you can," said my mother.

Maureen had told me, before I left, that our ground, first, and second floors had all been made the subject of a single new letting. She
had a way of picking up such things. She did not know whether the
Freedom people had been actually driven out. It was impossible to
believe that the enterprise could have much future in any case; and,
indeed, I never heard of it again after that late sad night of removal
and retreat, nor saw a copy of the paper on any bookstall or barrow.

In the end, I went to London for the morning in order to prospect.
The whole front of the house had had its woodwork repainted, partly
in blue, partly in white; including my two small square attic windows
that looked on to the street. The early nineteenth-century front door
had been brightly blued, and, to the left of it, at shoulder-height on
the whited jamb, was an unusually large brass plate: *Stallabrass, Hoskins and Cramp. Chartered Accountants.* The plate needed polishing,
possibly because it had only just arrived from elsewhere.

It was the time of day when Maureen was working with her bookmaker. I let myself in and mounted towards my abode. The internal
paintwork had been renewed from top to bottom, though rather
roughly, as was to be expected so soon after the war, and in crude
colours. The staircase walls had been repapered in an assertive mid-
green. There was even a mottled carpet, where before there had been
dark lino and unravelling drugget. It occurred to me that the het-
erogeneous impression might be a consequence of drawing upon
stock-ends sold off (in this moment of world historical renewal) at
bargain prices. There was no one about, and all the doors were closed,
and everything was silent. At least, and at last, the builders were out.

My own front door contained a letter-box, though no postman had
in my time ever ascended to it, all our letters being left on a shaky
shelf in the ground floor passage. Now I found a *billet-doux* marked
"By Hand": the agents were upset because I had not been there to
admit the decorators. Would I please call in at their office as soon as
possible? I never did anything more about that and nor did the
agents. The building belonged to a vague charitable foundation which
supported a school for needy boys. The school had been moved out of

London before my time and the offices of the foundation with it. I had not found the agents to be over-officious. It had been one of the attractions.

My rooms were filled with every kind of grit and dirt owing to the decorating activities outside. They looked almost uninhabitable. I had never thought of affording any kind of professional cleaner; nor, indeed, had I ever noticed such a person in the whole place, though I realized that someone must have brushed the stairs from time to time. Now I wondered whether I should not have to solicit Maureen, or at least Maureen's advice.

It would have to be postponed. I had seen enough to know that in other, more important respects, I could return. Upon a writer unsuccessful and successful also in the degree that I then was, work always waits and presses. I went back to my mother's cottage for another night or two. "You must have found your flat very dusty," said my mother. "You had better let me give it a good spring-clean."

She had not been there before and I was hesitant. But, fortunately, when the time came, she seemed quite to like the attic, despite the disconcerting approach, with all the new colours staring out, and all the doors still locked. I know that at least most of them were locked and not merely shut, because my mother tried many of the handles, and in no uncertain way, which I on my own had not cared to do.

"How do you get on with the people in the basement?" asked my mother.

I told her in some suitable words.

"I'm glad the wife's taken to you. You need a woman around. I'm glad she's pretty too."

It was not until several days after I finally returned that I again saw Maureen. My habits were pretty mousey, and I do not think she had realized that I was there. For my part, I held back from taking the initiative. In the first place, I had never done so hitherto. In the second place, I was more uncertain than ever, after the spell of absence, how things were going to develop, or even how I wanted them to develop. Then, one morning within the first week, as in a column of burning fiery chariots, entered into possession Messrs Stallabrass, Hoskins and Cramp, with all their force, all their mechanism, all their archive. Their arrival was as confident, rowdy, and cheerful as the withdrawal of *Freedom* had been obscure and muted.

On the instant the staircase was alive with short-haired, short-skirted girls running up and down as in Jacob's dream, except that these girls were exchanging backchat with shouting removal men. (Short hair and short skirts were, of course, new at that date, though my mother had already gone in for both, even though she rarely travelled far from her cottage.) Moving through the throng were several men in white shirts, stiff collars, dark trousers, and braces. Could they be partners? Even Stallabrass, Hoskins and Cramp in person? Certainly they were going through motions which might well be a form of giving orders. The total number of persons involved quite eclipsed *Freedom*, even relatively. And that afternoon came Maureen tapping at my door.

"Why didn't you let me know you were back?"

"I hesitated."

She was willing to let it go at that.

"What do you think?" I went on, inclining my head downwards and sideways.

Maureen twitched up a corner of her mouth.

"Do you suppose they'll quieten down?" I asked.

"I don't see why they should. They're a pretty awful lot from what little I've seen."

"I've seen quite enough of them already." Authors always tend to be hasty in their judgments. It is the strain of searching for peace and concentration.

"Have you seen Mr Millar?"

"Not that I know of. Who's Mr Millar?"

"He's the man whose outfit it really is. The names outside don't exist, or are all dead, or something. My guess is that Mr Millar's bumped them all off."

I remember Maureen using that exact expression, which was then as new as short hair and short skirts.

"Not necessarily," I said. "You often find these firms with lots of names and none of the people really existing."

"*You* haven't seen Mr Millar," replied Maureen.

"Not that I know of. There seemed to be about a hundred of them. Is there anything special about Mr Millar's appearance?"

"Yes," said Maureen. "He looks like Cordoba the Sex Vampire." This, I should observe, was a silent film that made a mark at the time, though I was a little surprised to find Maureen citing it.

"Then you'd better rub yourself all over with garlic before you go to bed," I replied; and this helped to make things go more easily between Maureen and me after our separation.

I cannot say that Maureen's description of our new neighbour even stimulated my curiosity. As will have been gathered by now, I was an anxious and cautious youth, walking his own tight-rope, and rather afraid than otherwise of new company, of becoming involved. Possibly the frightful stuff that Major Valentine sent up to me contributed to my social timidity. I am sure I thought that the longer I could keep entirely out of contact with Maureen's Mr Millar, the better. I had very little idea of "gathering experience", and never doubted that I could spin books from inside me. For me the matter did not even need thinking about.

It was bad enough that the new tenants were all over the stairs and landings, with endless giggling, shouting, and banging of doors. Even during the first two or three days I noticed that they had a way of banging ordinary room doors several times in succession, as people do nowadays to doors of motor cars. None of it was at all the way I had supposed chartered accountants to behave.

"I wonder how they get any work done at all," Maureen was soon exclaiming. It was indeed on the next occasion I saw her.

I agreed with her: being one who needed complete silence and total absence of distraction before I could work at all. Or so I then thought. Indeed, I elaborated a little to Maureen.

"It's different for you," Maureen observed amiably. One of Maureen's many good points had always been her apparently sincere respect for an artist. It is probably grudging of me to term it "apparently sincere", but it is a thing one never really knows.

"You're welcome to use our living room at any time," Maureen continued.

"Thank you very much."

"If Mr Millar makes himself at home there, I don't see why you shouldn't. I like you much better," Maureen added coquettishly.

"Mr Millar! How did he get in?"

"He rang our bell the afternoon he arrived. The day I told you about him. You'll find he does the same to you soon. I rather fancy it's the way he goes about things."

"But what does he do in your flat?" I enquired feebly. I was astounded by what Maureen had said. The new people had been with us for only a few days.

"He lies down. In a darkened room, as he puts it. Though, as a matter of fact, our flat's not at all easy to darken properly. I once tried. Mr Millar says that he has to have what he calls intermissions. You can see what he means when you think about the din they all make."

"They're his staff, after all. Why can't he make them shut up?"

"I can't tell you, Roy."

"But what are *you* doing when he's there?"

"So far I've not been there. After all, it's only happened about three times. I suppose I can always keep the kids in the kitchen or put them in their bedroom."

"You'd better charge him something," I said sourly.

"Are you jealous, Roy?" asked Maureen.

"Yes," I said; though it was not entirely the truth.

"Oh, good," said Maureen. "We progress."

I had to admit to myself that I had probably invited remarks of that kind.

I had also to admit that, in the matter of meeting Mr Millar, to general distaste had now been added specific embarrassment.

I began to be upset by another irritating habit: the people downstairs had a way of letting their telephones (undoubtedly several of them—commoner now than then) ring and ring and ring before lifting the receiver. As they almost always left all their doors open, the trick contributed greatly to the distant uproar that ascended to my attic.

Sometimes I could not but overhear one end of these delayed telephone conversations; when I was passing through the house, I mean: I do not imply that actual definable words penetrated my floor or walls.

Whatever I did hear was always of unbelievable commonplaceness or banality. It never seemed to be business in any sense; only a flow of vapourings, mixed with giggles. It is obvious that I judged with prejudice, but, as time passed, and I heard more and more of these vapid utterances, and never anything else, prejudice began to be mixed with a certain wonder, and then with a certain concern. Yes, I am almost sure that it was these overheard inanities, in no way my business and not even overheard all that frequently, because I passed through the house during business hours as rarely as I could, that *first* made me feel disturbed . . . feel that about the new tenants was something that as well as continually irritating me also frightened me. I had, of course, come upon jokes about typists talking on the telephone to their boy friends, but here was something that seemed to go much further. I think I might put it that a conversation as reasonable as a chat with a boy friend would have been positively welcome to my long ears, and explicable. Everything I heard or overheard was merely *empty*. For that reason nothing of it can be remembered. I doubt if I could have written down immediately what I had just heard as I climbed up to my third floor. Apart from anything else, I should have been *ashamed* to harbour such futilities in my thoughts or memory.

When I met them in the hall or on the stairs, the little girls leered at me forthcomingly, or smirked at me contemptuously, or sometimes manifested real hostility. Some of these words seem absurd; but they describe how the girls made me feel. All of them were very young. Many people would say that the fault must have been largely mine. No doubt in a sense it was. I admit that I could find no way of dealing with the girls. Conventional greetings seemed absurd. Moreover, the girls were always new: I suppose there might have been five or six working there (if that was the word) at a time, but faces that I had come to know soon disappeared, and were apparently replaced by complete strangers. It was not possible to think in terms of getting to know individuals; even if that had been what I wanted to do.

As for the men in the firm, who did not change (and were, needless to say, older), the custom was to stare me up and down, while, perhaps, I descended the stair or came in through the front door; to stare me up and down as if I were a stranger and an intruder off the street; and then sometimes, but not always, though always at the last moment, to utter an over-bland Good Morning or Good Evening.

The men never seemed to be fully dressed. Their clothes were always formal, the garments of the properly dressed professional man, but never (when I observed them) did the men seem to have them all on. It was always as if they were frightfully busy, or much too hot: even in winter, though, there, it is true that the offices were remarkably well heated. I would hardly have gazed in at the gas stoves or whatever they were, but from every open door, it might be in December or January, would come a positive and noticeable wave of hot air as one passed. The girls would wear summery dresses even in winter and then, necessarily, depart in heavy coats. But, of course, most people prefer to live and work in great heat; and I do not. I have to add that while the men always performed as if they were weighed down with work, I have no more recollection of seeing them doing any than I have in the case of the girls. But possibly I was and am influenced here by my own personal inability to work in an uproar. I did not know the names of the men (or, of course, of the girls); and though the girls chattered on through the open doors and all around me as if I were not present or were invisible, the shirt-sleeved men tended in the opposite direction, to fall silent and stand motionless until I had altogether passed and was out of earshot. Nor, now I come to think of it, did I notice any of the usual office horseplay between the men and the girls; though most of the girls might have been thought ready enough for it.

And then there was the mystery of the firm's clients. The mystery was that one never seemed to see one: only the internal staff seething up and down.

"Have you ever seen any?" I asked Maureen.

"Mr Millar says there are a lot of people who've been with them a long time."

"I wouldn't care to be among them."

"How can we tell?" responded Maureen vaguely.

I noticed that Maureen had ceased asking me whether I had met Mr Millar.

I suppose the number of letters arriving each morning might have given some idea of how much genuine business there was. But here I was at a disadvantage. Authors are not normally early risers. In the old days I had put on my dressing gown (quite faded and stained—even torn, I believe) and descended to the shelf in the hall without giving a thought to what the *Freedom* people might think about me, numerous though they were (as I then considered). Now it seemed quite impossible: partly because of the girls, of course, but not entirely. So my slender morning post, even the ill-made packages from Major Valentine, had to await my being shaved and fully dressed; and by then any post there might have been for the people below had been long "taken in", as the expression is. This was all the more unavoidable in that usually I made my simple breakfast before shaving and dressing, and could see no reason why I should change my ways because of Mr Millar and his merry men. But I think also that I had very little *wish* to know more of what went on below me. I have just spoken of "genuine" business. I found it hard to believe there was much of it, though I could not even surmise what went on all the rest of the time. It is true that I found odd letters for the firm at other times of the day: almost all of them impersonal emanations on his Majesty's service. They did, I realized, suggest there might be *some* accountancy in hand. I recollected an uncle of my mother's once observing that figures, my boy, are only a very small part of what a successful accountant does. And, indeed, I still do not know what did go on in that office. I have related my impressions as clearly as I can; but new developments began to seem of more importance.

I think it must have been at least a month before I even set eyes upon Mr Millar. For obscure reasons, Maureen and I had altogether ceased referring to him. Then, all at once, I not only saw him but had to talk to him, with very little warning or preparation; and *à deux*.

One Friday, in the late afternoon, at half past five perhaps, my own rather noisy doorbell suddenly rang. I say "suddenly" because I had heard no steps coming up my staircase, which remained uncarpeted. Swearing, I threw my raincoat over the current material from Valentine, and went to see who it was. A man stood there.

"I'm Millar." But he did not offer to shake hands, as one usually did in those days, and his eyes wandered about, never once looking into mine, but not, as I thought, examining my humble environment either. "Won't you come in for a drink?" he said. "Just on the floor below. And of course bring anyone with you."

I need hardly say I did not want to, but I could think of no way to refuse, and it would be no doubt unwise to make an enemy. So I got out something affirmative.

"Come when you're ready. Second floor."

It seemed a slightly odd way of putting it; but, for that matter, it was perfectly obvious that there was no one "with me", not even a girl pushed into a cupboard. Without another word, Mr Millar descended. I saw that he was wearing beige suède shoes, doubtless with crêpe rubber soles. And of course he was in his braces, like the rest of them.

I was glad to have a few minutes for rehabilitation. One does not wear one's best clothes for editing a pornographic manuscript alone in an attic; and also I had in those days a habit of unconsciously running my right hand (I am left-handed) through my hair as I wrote, wrecking whatever parting there might have been, and making myself look like the picture in the German book for children, my hair being then unusually thick and wiry. I changed my shirt, put on my old school tie (such as it was), and tried my luck with the comb.

Then, striving to think about nothing, I plunged through the door on the second floor landing. I had been in there several times during the *Freedom* period, but everything was now very different. The walls of the outer room had been newly papered in pink with a cornice of flowers, and were decorated with what appeared to be small English landscape paintings, probably by an amateur, and framed in nothing more permanent than *passe-partout*. There were a surprising number of them, not all exactly on a level from the floor. In the middle of the room was a desk, obviously new; but with nothing on it, not even a cloaked typewriter, or a rubber-out. Also I was alone. But the door into the further room was ajar. I went up to it. "Anyone at home?" I said.

Mr Millar drew the door fully open. "Come in," he said, still neither looking me in the eye nor offering his hand. Also he was still without his jacket.

"No one with you?" He seemed disappointed, though, as I have said, it was absurd.

"No," I said. "Only me."

"Working?" He said it not in the way of apology for interrupting me, or even in the way of making conversation, but rather as if he referred to some unusual hobby he had heard I went in for.

"Yes. But it doesn't matter. I'm glad of a break." That, of course, was not the exact truth.

"Sherry?"

The bottle indicated that it came from one of the colonies, and the three glasses on Mr Millar's desk were from the threepenny and sixpenny store. One is not supposed to say such things so plainly, but on this occasion I think they are of significance. Conclusive perhaps was that the bottle had to be opened, and some small shavings or chippings brushed out of two glasses with the back of a carbon paper, before they could be used. It seemed clear that the feast had been assembled especially for me.

"Thank you very much."

It was not a matter of an alternative to sherry. Obviously there was none.

Mr Millar fumbled away with a not very good corkscrew; one (as I knew even then) with too small a radius to the screw and too slender and cutting a handle. I almost felt that I should offer to help. I was quite sure that at least I should say something, as time was passing in silence while the cork split off and refused to come out; but I could think of nothing to the purpose.

I had not been offered a seat, though there were two new office chairs, as well as the one behind Mr Millar's equally new desk. Mr Millar's desk was in imitation mahogany, where the desk outside imitated some much lighter and yellower wood. The sanctum was papered in light purple, or perhaps deep mauve: I can see it now, even though I never saw it again after this one visit, and quite a brief visit too, as will be seen. There was also some purple stuff on the centre part of the floor, where the desk stood; though the purple was not the same. There were four or five old portraits of the kind one can buy twice a week at certain auction-rooms. Normally such portraits are genuinely ancient, but of limited artistic value. They are like the "old books" which so many people believe to be of great value but which, though quite truly old, prove almost impossible to sell at all in the hour of need. These specimens were of seventeenth- and eighteenth-century gentry in lace and wigs, four men and one woman; and they were in battered, discoloured frames. The one woman was elderly and unexceptional. Somehow it could not occur to one that these could be likenesses of Mr Millar's own ancestors.

"Pity there was no one with you," said Mr Millar, pouring out. He fished out from one glass a scrap of tinfoil dropped off the bottle. That was quite a job too, as only a paperknife was available to do it.

"My home is not in London," I said. "I don't know many people here yet."

Mr Millar seemed uninterested, and one could hardly blame him.

"I wonder how long Lloyd George will last?"

This was, almost aggressively, "making conversation." Plainly I had failed badly in having no one with me. But at last the glass of sherry had reached me. As I was still not offered a seat, I sat down on one for myself. Immediately Mr Millar sat down also. I could think of nothing intelligent to say about Lloyd George, but I suppose I said something.

"Santé!" said Mr Millar, still not looking at me—or at anything else, as it seemed to me. He was like a man with two glass eyes. I took a strong pull at the sherry glass, fortunately quite large.

"Thundery weather," said Mr Millar. "How long before it breaks?"

"Not just yet I should say."

"You're a countryman?"

"More an outer suburban, I'm afraid. At least it's become that."

"Rather good sherry, don't you think?"

"Frightfully good."

"Do you take the *Post* or the *Telegraph*?"

"I take *The Times*."

"Bit young for that, aren't you?"

"I grew up with it."

"Really?"

"Never another paper in our house."

"Good Lord! You'd better write and tell them so." Mr Millar laughed metallically.

It seemed that there was positively nothing to me without that missing person "with me". Really we could hardly continue.

"Let me fill you up." He said it as perfunctorily as he had said everything else; but I accepted with some relief. I much needed daredevilry. I could hardly escape for a few more minutes.

I could think of nothing to say which would continue the conversation. I doubted very much whether anything I could possibly say, would continue it. The central fact about Mr Millar was that his thoughts were elsewhere: were, I felt all the time I was with him, elsewhere permanently. His glass eyes and wandering hands spoke truth of a kind, where his lips spoke only cotton wool.

"Fancy anything for the Cambridgeshire?"

I could but shake my head. From one point of view, I could see that Mr Millar might hope for more lively company.

"What about the tennis this summer? Good to have it back, don't you think?"

"Good to have a lot of things back."

"But there's a lot that won't come back so soon."

"Yes," I said. "That's true."

"I shouldn't wonder if there's never proper polo to watch again. Not polo worth watching."

He was sitting sideways at his desk, showing me his left profile. I have said little—indeed, as I see, virtually nothing—about Mr Millar's appearance. Perhaps it is because there is so little to say. As far as I recall, he was a slender, dark man of medium height. He was clean-shaven, always a trifle black in the jowl—but only a trifle. I suppose he was 40; maybe a well-preserved 50. He had a wad of blackish hair, carefully trimmed round the edges, so that it seemed to fit his head like a cap, and always honeyed with brilliantine. He was at all times well dressed; at all times noticeably so, but not in a pejorative sense, except, conceivably, for such details as the suède shoes I have mentioned (he was wearing a townsman's country suit with them, it being the eve of the weekend). His counterparts are to be seen everywhere, at all times . . .

I think I might even say that Mr Millar belonged to a *type* whose members tend to make one feel that their thoughts are elsewhere. But few of them carry this impression as far as Mr Millar carried it. Even at that first (but almost only) meeting, I sensed that Mr Millar's thoughts were as far away as those of Boris Godunov, who had, some said, made away with the rightful heir; or even of our own misled Macbeth.

"While you're here," said Mr Millar, "there's something I'd like to explain. It seems a good opportunity."

"Oh yes," I said, slanting my sherry glass, now once more less than half full.

"We're very busy just now. I often have to stay on. So don't be surprised if you hear sounds."

"I'm glad you've mentioned it."

"I didn't want you to think we'd got the burglars in." Mr Millar laughed his metallic laugh. "I supposed at first I could come to an arrangement with the girl in the basement. Rather a sweet person, don't you think?"

"From what I've seen of her," I said.

"But of course she has her family to think about and all that sort of thing. So I've decided to shake down up here. After all, why not?" Mr Millar's colourless eyes roamed uneasily round the room, almost, it seemed, as if he thought his question might be answered. His gaze then proceeded to traverse the ceiling. To me his news was so unwelcome that again I could find nothing whatever to say.

"You're one of these famous authors, I'm told?"

"I aim to be," I replied.

"I once thought I'd write a book myself."

"Had you a subject in mind?" I enquired without a trace of sarcasm.

"I'm sure I had," said Mr Millar. "God knows what it was!" He laughed again. "Let me fill you up."

"I really ought to be on my way."

"Just one more before you go," said Mr Millar, making a discernibly minimal effort to retain me. He was waving the bottle about nervously, but managed to concentrate enough to refill my glass. "Yes, a sweet little person that!"

I smiled as man to man; or rather that was how it would have been if both of us had been men, instead of one of us an adolescent and the other a simulacrum.

"Man was not meant to live alone. Don't you agree?"

"There are arguments on both sides," I replied.

"You wait till you're older," said Mr Millar, and laughed his laugh. "You can't talk till then."

"I live a long way away, you know," he continued. "I couldn't possibly go home every night when we're so infernally busy. Couldn't stand the fag of it."

"I suppose it's a good thing accountancy's so prosperous." But I was quite surprised that Mr Millar claimed to have a "home", however distant.

"Yes, I suppose it is if you care to see it like that."

I rose. "Anyway, I must leave you to it."

"Glad you were able to come."

He saw me only to the door of his sanctum; then turned back, his mind concentrated upon someone or something else, one shrank from thinking what.

From then on, as I might have known, Mr Millar seemed to remain in his office almost every night. The rest of them disappeared at more or less the usual hour, but Mr Millar would continue pottering up and down stairs, locking and unlocking doors, carting small objects from place to place, making and answering late telephone calls, sometimes talking to himself as he roamed. When his shuffling about stopped me working (which, I have to acknowledge, was only occasionally), I would quietly open my door and shamelessly eavesdrop down my dark stair. But Mr Millar's activities seemed so trivial and futile as to be hardly worth spying on for long, and the chatter he addressed to himself (quite loudly and clearly) was not so much obsessive as escapist. The burden of his thoughts had long ago driven him out of his own personality, even when he was by himself. He had become a walking shell from which the babble of the world re-echoed.

Did he ever really sleep? And, if so, on what? His sanctum had offered nothing but the floor when I had been in it; but, as I have said, I never entered it again. I suppose a sofa could have been introduced without my meeting it coming upstairs or hearing it bruise the new paintwork. I did not know whether Mr Millar locked his door, the outer one or the inner one, when finally he ceased to travail on the staircase and from room to room. Assuredly, I never heard him snore through the ceiling; although his bleak sanctum was immediately below my bedroom. But snoring is always absurd, and absurd was never quite the word for Mr Millar.

That was how it was in the early days of Mr Millar's virtual residence beneath me. (I often wondered about the terms of his lease. It was as well that the agents we had to deal with were so easy-going.) But before long Mr Millar began to receive visitors.

I had observed that rather late in the evening he seemed often to be out of the building. I would wander downstairs for some reason, or come back from the gallery of a theatre or the front rows of a cinema (my mother warned me about the effect on my eyesight). At any time between, perhaps, nine o'clock and two o'clock, I would find the lights on, and some of the doors still open, but no sight or sound of Mr Millar. I supposed that even he had had to seek a bite of food. I never looked into any of the open rooms, because I feared that Mr Millar

would spring from behind the door, cry Peep-bo, and do me a hideous
mischief; but I think I was right in supposing him out of the office at
these times, and this was confirmed when he got into the way of not
returning alone.

Normally I only heard voices; voices and trudging steps, coming up
the stairs, often very slowly, and then interminable talk on the floor
below me, though sometimes there were other noises less easily
definable, or explicable. More often than not, the voices were female;
and, more often than not, very common voices, even strident, though I
could seldom hear precise words. Up to a point the explanation was
obvious enough: in those days, and before Mr R. A. Butler's famous
Act, there were streets in the immediate area where it was far easier
to pick up a woman and do what you liked to her than to pick up a
taxi. On other evenings, Mr Millar's late callers were men, and several
of them at a time, and as rough-spoken as the women. But the women
also usually came several at a time: several at a time and apparently
all friends together.

I really had no will to investigate closely: Mr Millar both bored me
and alarmed me, in oddly equal measure. But the noise that he and
the late callers made together was sometimes a serious nuisance,
though the things I have described did not happen every night.

An unfortunate development was that I felt inhibited from bringing
in my own few friends, especially my few but precious girl friends.
One never quite knew what would happen, and explanations were at
once ridiculous, unconvincing, and sinister. It was impossible to devise
even an invented explanation that meant anything. A very young man
who can bring no one home is at a major disadvantage. I found myself
spending far longer periods as a hermit than I cared for. I perceived
that I was being handicapped by circumstances even more than by
temperament in making new approaches. Moreover, Mr Millar had
not only altered the atmosphere in the house, but had already brought
about an indefinable change in me.

It first struck me in the matter of Maureen. Maureen had ceased to
visit me, and when we met by chance, we were strangers. We stared
into one another's eyes coldly, as if divided by incommunicable experiences. What horrified me, when I thought about it, was that I realized I did not care. And I had previously become far fonder of
Maureen than I had ever been able to make real to her. Nor was it
that another had taken her place. Far from it. It had somehow diminished.

In the end, and inevitably, I met, or at least encountered some of

Mr Millar's late visitors; on the doorstep, or surging upwards with Mr Millar in the midst, or, once or twice, standing silently on the staircase waiting for something to happen. It was especially odd to come upon these complete strangers standing about one's own staircase late at night. Never did they think of speaking to me; but then the persons actually accompanying Mr Millar, sometimes arm in arm with him, never spoke to me either, though often plainly embarrassed, even startled, to see me. Least of all at these times did Mr Millar himself speak to me. He kept his eyes away from me in his usual way; apprehending me and making way for me, drawing the others back, all as if with his pineal gland.

Mr Millar's callers looked as they sounded, only sometimes still rougher. Hogarthian groups can be entertaining in a picture but seem less so when encountered going the other way on a narrow stair. The men callers looked like small-size professional criminals; with violence taken for granted, and a bad end also. I noticed that the sexes were seldom mixed among Mr Millar's callers, though once I did encounter a very pregnant girl, horribly white, being dragged upstairs by a man with gashes all over his face. Men and women alike tended to become silent even among themselves when they saw me; and when I did catch things they said, the things were always banalities worthy of Mr Millar himself. Never was there any question of a "revelation". But then about Mr Millar, though everything was in a sense wide open, nothing was revealed from first to last.

An almost ludicrously flat explanation of the late callers occurred to me at one time. Was it not possible that these people, or some of them, really were clients; concerned with small enterprises, cafés for example, which, though doubtless shady, still needed to keep accounts of a kind, perhaps several sets of them (as my great-uncle would have said)? The people might have reasons for not calling during the daytime. They might even have good and honest reasons: the demands made by one-man and one-woman businesses. Thus, further, might be explained, or partly explained, Mr Millar's policy of sleeping in the office, and his claim that business required it. And indeed that explanation may have been a true one as far as it went; whatever else may be said or surmised about the late callers. It struck me also, however, that at no time did I seem to see any other persons who could be thought of as friends of Mr Millar. One would suppose that these late callers *were* his friends; even his only friends. Certainly he treated them as friends: with uneasy shoves in the ribs, and sidelong jocularities, and teeth-flashing After-yous.

Looking back on it all, it seems to me that it slowly worked up. There appeared to be nothing stable about Mr Millar's life in any of its aspects: one doubted whether he slept regularly, ate regularly, ever saw the same friend twice; had any underlying framework of habit and routine. None the less, there was a perceptibly advancing intensification as the pageant of his life with us flowed on; at once ludicrous and alarming, as everything else about Mr Millar—and steadily more embarrassing for me, in every sense of that epithet.

Indeed, I suppose I should try to say a word about why I did not myself soon move out; or at least *seek* some other abode sooner than I did.

About this I could rationalize unanswerably. With truth I could say that three rooms at a low rent in central London were exceedingly hard to find, and that everyone I knew told me I was very lucky and should sit tight at all costs—not that any of them knew in the least what the costs were. I could stress how notional was my cash basis, so that almost any change, not absolutely compelled, would indeed on balance be almost certainly for the worse. I could point out that the inconvenience (or menace) linked with Mr Millar was by no means continuous. Even towards the end, or apparent end, of his sojourn, there would be several evenings in each week when there was no trouble at all except the marginal one connected with his own, solitary fumblings and mumblings. And then there was the important problem, one which I could never forget, presented by my mother's strong, though mainly silent, wish to have me back with her at the cottage. Any weakening on my part would probably lead to my giving up my London life completely, and the new friends I had made. They were few, but I felt that they were nearly a matter of life or death to me, even though Mr Millar was a problem there too.

All these things were entirely enough to settle the matter. But what really settled it was, I think, something quite different. It was as if Mr Millar had injected me with a lightly paralysing fluid, cocooned me in an almost indetectable glaze or fixative; diminishing my power of choice, weakening my rational judgment, to say nothing of the super-refinement that had been put upon it by the super-refinement of the way I had been brought up. Though, when I thought about it, I was antagonized by almost everything to do with Mr Millar, yet I realized that he was an experience (or ordeal) I might be unwise to avoid. I could not live for ever as a child, free and light as air. As we acquire weight in the world, we lose it within ourselves. Maturity is always in part a matter of emptying and contracting. By that standard, Mr

Millar, almost weightless, almost adrift, almost without habits (where a baby has nothing else), had passed beyond mere maturity; but contact with him amounted to a compressed and simplified course in growing up. Mine was similar to the real reason why a schoolboy does not run away from the school he hates.

One evening—it was perhaps seven o'clock—came Maureen, once more tapping gently at my door.

"How are *you* getting on?" she asked. It was the first time in months that actual spoken words had passed between us; and never before had she been able to visit me except in the afternoon, between her job and collecting the youngest child.

She was wearing a short, sleeveless grey dress, with a scooped out neck: very little of it altogether in fact; and with several stains on the front, left there by cooking, or the children. She wore no stockings and a pair of high-heeled shoes that more or less matched her dress. She had left off her slide, and her hair was drooping over her eyes, so that she had to look up from under it. Her hands were in need of a wash, and there was even a small grimy patch on her face.

It was summer, and I was wearing simply a shirt and trousers.

I stepped up to her and held her tightly and kissed her as if it were for ever.

"Stranger!" said Maureen affectionately.

I took off her dress, quite gently; and then wriggled her out of her underclothes, which were charming.

We lay down together on my cheap bed, neither glamorous nor particularly comfortable.

"What about you?" asked Maureen.

So I removed my own clothes, which I had quite forgotten about; and I put her shoes neatly alongside one another.

We were together for three or four hours, until long after it was dark, listening to our hearts, and, intermittently, to the sounds of London.

I did not ask her about her husband and family, nor did she expound; and when suddenly she said, "I'm going now," my luck was in, or ours, because Mr Millar was not even walking from room to room with bits of paper in his hands, let alone entertaining the visitors. I should have hated Mr Millar to have seen me kissing Maureen goodbye.

"When can I see you again?"

"I simply can't tell you. We must make the best of the present."

Talk about maturity! I still had far to go, and perhaps had even experienced a setback, a reversion to happy childhood.

I have said that the pageant (or mirage) of Mr Millar's life seemed steadily to work up, to intensify.

One thing that was a new embarrassment as far as I was concerned was that Mr Millar was drinking. The ludicrous side of it, if one saw it like that, was that large crates of cheap spirits were continually being delivered to the house by men in peaked caps. Remarkably often they rang my outside bell instead of the one appertaining to Messrs Stallabrass, Hoskins and Cramp. I would toil down, with all the men in their braces staring at me as if they had never seen me before, and all the girls giggling, and then have to toil up again; the booby who had fallen into the trap. (Mr Millar himself continued almost invisible during working hours, at least as far as I was concerned. For a time I wondered whether he did not use the day for sleeping.) I have described the spirits that were ceaselessly delivered as "cheap": they were gins made by brewers, and whiskies not made in Scotland or in Ireland; both with jazzy labels on the bottles.

The alarming side of Mr Millar's new propensity was that now when I returned home, I would sometimes find him not wandering about, but sprawling or huddled on the staircase, very white and dishevelled, breathing hard, and once or twice with the pupils of his eyes unnaturally turned upwards. The stairs would smell of drink, sometimes the whole house, though I do not think I ever actually saw Mr Millar with a glass in his hand or a bottle (after that first uneasy party with him, of course). None the less, he must have been drinking heavily, if one might judge by the deliveries; and I began to fear worse consequences, such as delirium tremens, concerning which I felt the apprehension that arises from total ignorance. My great-uncle, again, had been terrifying on the subject without going much into detail, "while your mother's in the room", as he had said. Nor did the possibility of finding Mr Millar lying dead on the stairs rather than merely insensible at all attract me.

In the meantime, the aspect of the matter, not necessarily either funny or frightening, which none the less gave me the most trouble was that Mr Millar, instead of merely talking to himself, had begun to warble and carol, to bawl and bellow. He seemed capable of keeping it up, at least intermittently, for hours on end, as he fussed around.

When he was japing his late-night friends, the noise could be appalling. The urban sons of toil, even when the nature of their toil is probably criminal, are seldom slow in striking up, nor, traditionally, are the daughters of joy, who seemed to constitute the larger part of Mr Millar's acquaintanceship. Indeed, the police came ringing in protest: at *my* bell of course. And, on another occasion, banging and thumping at the outer door; a small posse of them, to judge by the sound; and by the stamping when once they had got in.

As far as I was concerned, there was occasionally another kind of interruption. I would hear hysterical shouting in the room below me and then steps running up my own uncarpeted stair. There would be frantic pounding at my attic door, and when I opened it, a dishevelled girl too distraught to say what was the matter. I would glance over her shoulder as she stood there crying and raving and beating at me to let her in; and there would be Mr Millar at the bottom of the stair, comparatively calm, though not always entirely steady. He never spoke a word at these times, but seemed merely an uneasy spectator, collapsed against the banister. One might have thought him genuinely embarrassed and baffled by what had happened: resolved not to take the risk of saying a word when someone else was dealing with the situation.

In all the circumstances, I could not possibly admit the girl, so I would edge her downstairs again, saying that I would see her safely out into the street, and of course trying to buck her up, though I had no idea how best to do that. We would creep past Mr Millar, sometimes with my arm round the girl's shoulders; and he would never say a word of any kind, or make a move.

On one of these occasions, out of the four or five that I suppose there were in all, I was much frightened. It was bad enough to have to drag the girl past Mr Millar himself standing there watching; but on the occasion I refer to, when I reached the bottom of my stair, which ran straight up between two walls, I found that standing beside Mr Millar, and previously hidden from me, were two huge louts in cloth caps. They looked like chuckers-out or unsuccessful bruisers, but now they were as still and silent as Mr Millar. I did not find it easy to continue downwards with the shrinking girl at my other side, pressing herself against the wall; but I managed it and, as usual, nothing further happened. When I came up again after these incidents, Mr Millar had usually withdrawn into his room and shut the landing door. This time all three of them had disappeared. I expected some kind of rumpus to resound from below me; but none did.

On another occasion, I remember that the girl was of a different type from the usual: standing ashake on my dingy doorstep, she told me that she had met Mr Millar at Wimbledon, but, though she knew she had been a fool, she had no idea it would be like this. "I had no idea it *could* be," she said, her eyes boring into me. She very much wanted me to telephone the police but I thought it would solve nothing and end nothing. Moreover, I should have had to borrow Mr Millar's telephone. So I just manoeuvred her out in the usual way, and in the street she recovered remarkably. "I'm most awfully sorry to have been so silly," she said. Then she added, "Curse it, I've left my coat behind and it's a new, summer one."

Going down for my post a day or two later, I found Mr Millar's male staff chucking a girl's coat from one to another in the big ground floor room; snatching at it and yelling at each other in mock antagonism. I supposed it was the same coat. I remember the colour still; a rather unusual greenish yellow, like yerba de maté.

Nor, very evidently, were lawn tennis and improvised office throwabouts and kickabouts (more usually with a waste-paper basket) the only sporting interests of the firm. Every day I noticed communications from bookmakers; and others with continental stamps that I identified as coming from operators of casino systems. (My great-uncle yet again, I fancy.) I suppose now that the bookmakers' letters can only have arrived during the racing season, and that I must tend to exaggerate their continuity. But I truly remember a very large number of them. I suppose there is a possible link between accountancy and the computation of odds; and even more, one would think, on the tables than on the turf. I came to modify my speculations about what Mr Millar did during the day: since he went to Wimbledon, he might well go to race meetings also, as well as on occasion simply sleeping.

Certainly there were sometimes "sporting types" about the building during the day. I do not refer here to the evening bashers and barrow boys, but to men in tweeds, with rolled umbrellas and public-school idioms. They would exchange loud badinage with the firm's staff, slap the bottoms of the girls (remarkably hard, I thought), and be gone in fast, popping cars almost as soon as they had come. One of them is associated with a development that was particularly upsetting; and thus with my decision to move out.

Up to a point, I could not mistake this particular man. The noise of his car was both doubly loud and very distinctive. I could always hear him approaching from afar. And when he had arrived, he immediately clumped upstairs with a quite particular firmness. He always climbed right up to Mr Millar's own second floor, and there, with clatter and circumstance, he would open Mr Millar's outer door, using, apparently, a key on his own ring. He would go inside, be heard loudly tumbling things about for a minute or two, and then emerge, relock the door, and clump off again. The whole performance was regularly audible through my window, door, and floor; right through to the long withdrawing thunder of the man's machine.

Originally, I supposed that it was Mr Millar himself arriving and departing; Mr Millar who had left something behind, or wanted to see how things were getting on. But one day I met the stranger. His car roared up just as I was about to go out. In came a round, red-faced, stocky man in a green suit and a green pork-pie hat. He threw back the front door and gave me a really heavy push against the wall—in fact, seriously bruising my elbow, as I later found, so that for several days I had some difficulty in writing. Before I could say a word (if I could have thought of one) he was well upstairs with his familiar clump. I knew that from those around I could expect laughter rather than sympathy, so I continued on my way.

All the time I was in Brandenburg Square, I spent nearly every weekend with my mother. On the few occasions when I did not, but stayed up in London, either to complete some work or to spend time with a friend, I thought I had established that Mr Millar took himself off; as, of course, one would expect. I assumed that he withdrew to the home he had mentioned to me over the sherry; difficult though I had found it to imagine.

Some time (I cannot remember how long) after my direct encounter with the sporting man in the green suit came one of these London weekends. I think my mother had departed to stay with my father's stepsister in Frinton, as, since my father's death, she had grown into the way of doing several times each year. By now I had ceased inviting people round to see me even at these rare weekends, so disconcerting was the atmosphere in my house. And, at that particular weekend, it was possibly as well that I had.

Everything remained silent and as usual on the Saturday night, while I worked away on some rubbish from Major Valentine; but after I had gone to bed, quite late, I was awakened by the noise of somebody moving about downstairs.

Almost my first conscious thought was that the noise was nothing like loud enough to have actually awakened me. Then I remembered that it was a Saturday-Sunday night when there should (as I thought) have been no noise inside the building at all. I realized that my unconscious mind might have taken stock of this fact and sent out an alarm. I was frightened already, but that thought made me more frightened.

The noise was totally unlike the usual stamping and banging. I could hardly hear it at all; and was soon wondering whether the whole thing was not fancy, a disturbance inside my own ears and head. But I could not quite convince myself of this as I lay there rigid with listening, while the gleam from the street lamp far below seemed to isolate my small bedroom from the blackness of so much around me. I began to wonder if this might not be purely a conventional burglary. I could just see the time by my watch. It was ten minutes past three.

It was my duty to take action.

I made my muscles relax, and with a big effort jumped out of bed. In the most banal way, I seized the bedroom poker. (At that time, even central London attics still had fireplaces.) I opened the door into my sitting-room, darker than the bedroom, but not so dark that I could not cross with certitude to the outer door, where the light-switch was. Without turning on the light, I opened the outer door. I looked down my pitch-dark flight of stairs. When a light was on further down I could from this point always see the glow. Now there was no light.

I became aware that a smell was wafting up. It was quite faint, at least where I was, but, none the less, extremely pungent and pene-trating. I must admit that the expression "a graveyard smell" leapt into my mind at the first whiff of it. Even a faint whiff was quite enough to make me feel sick in a moment. But I managed to hang on, even to listen with all the intentness I could muster.

There could be no doubt about the reality of the sounds beneath me; but every doubt about what caused them. Something or someone was shuffling and rubbing about in the almost total darkness: I found it impossible to decide on which landing or on which part of the stair-case. In a flight of rather absurd logic, the thought of a blind person came to me. But, truly, the sounds hardly seemed human at all: more like a heavy sack wearily dragging about on its own volition, not able to manage very well, and perhaps anxious not to disturb the wrong person.

As well as feeling sick—really sick, as if about to *be* sick—I was trembling so much that no difficult further decision was needed: in-vestigation was just physically impossible. I withdrew into my own territory, and locked my door as quietly as I could. By conventional standards, I suppose I had heard enough to justify a robbery call to the police, but I do not think it was only the lack of a telephone that deterred me. I sat there in the dark, with my handkerchief held tightly to my nose. Soon I began to feel chilled, and crept back to the comfort of my blankets.

Mercifully the smell did not seem strong enough to penetrate, but I pressed my face hard into the pillow, and lay listening, stretching my ears hard for sounds I dreaded to hear, eager above all to draw no attention to myself. And thus, in the end, despite all discomforts, I fell asleep.

And on the Sunday morning, while I was still trying to eat my breakfast, I heard the first, distant roar of the green man's noisy car. I heard him throw open the street door with a bang and come clumping up the many flights of stairs. Neither he nor anyone else connected with the firm downstairs had ever before entered the building on a Sunday when I had been there. The man did not even pause at Mr Millar's level, as he usually did, but came straight up to the attic. I could feel my flesh creep obscurely as I heard him. Horrors often come in pairs. Instead of ringing my bell, he waited silently for a moment. Perhaps he assumed that his advent was sufficiently apparent already, as indeed it was. However, since I did nothing, he delivered an immense kick at the lower rail of the door.

I opened up with as much as I could manage of dignity. At least the faint smell seemed gone.

"Thought you would have heard me," said the man, in a thick but (as we said in those days) educated voice.

"I did."

"Well then," said the man; but as if he were offhandedly agreeing to take no exception to a slight. He stared at me hard: his manner was most unlike Mr Millar's. Nor was he wearing or carrying his pork-pie hat.

"Seen anyone about?"

"Since when?" I asked.

"Yesterday or today," said the man, as if it hardly needed saying, which of course it did not.

"No," I said truthfully. "No, I don't think so."

"Or heard?" asked the man, staring at me still harder, consciously breaking me down.

"What should I have heard?"

"People or things," said the man. "Have you?"

"Out of the ordinary, I suppose you mean?"

I was merely gaining time, but the vigour of the man's affirmation shook me.

"If you like."

I was, in fact, so shaken that I hesitated.

"What happened?" asked the man. It was the tone the prefects used to learn in public schools for interrogating the juniors.

"I don't know what it was," I replied with extreme weakness of spirit. Doubtless I should have played my part as new boy and asked what business it was of his.

"So they've arrived," said the man, much more thoughtfully. One might almost have supposed him awed, if such a man had been capable of awe.

I felt a little stronger; as if life had passed from him to me.

"Who do you mean by *they?*" I asked.

"I'm not telling you *that,* my boy," said the man; now within distant sight of equal terms. "What I'm telling you is that you'll never see *me* again for dust. There's an end to all things. Thanks for the tip-off."

And he clumped off. In a moment, I heard his reverberant car explode into life and charge away as if unscorchable entities would any moment be clutching at the exhaust-pipe.

"There's an end to all things," the man had said; and clearly this was the end for me also, and in a sense far past it: an end to setting my teeth in order to face life, putting up with injurious incidentals for the supposed sake of a higher settled purpose; an end, at almost any cost, to my Brandenburg Square tenancy.

I managed to finish my breakfast ("No breakfast, no man," my father had always said), and then went down to have a word with Maureen.

After that marvellous evening when Maureen had worn the grey dress, she had reappeared a number of times, unpredictably as before; and things had continued to be marvellous, though, naturally, not so marvellous as the first time, because things seldom are. I realized very clearly that, situated as I was, I was fortunate in Maureen, though it was a disadvantage that I had virtually no voice in our arrangements, however unavoidable that might be. Very much had Maureen been a further reason for my not moving out.

Now that I had made up my mind, I took the initiative with her, even though I realized that her husband, Gilbert, would almost certainly be there too, let alone the children. It was almost the first time I had been down there since my visit soon after my arrival.

I rang, and the husband answered the door. He was in very old clothes, I could hear the children screaming in the room behind him. I hardly knew him, and, in any case, the conversation I am about to report was the only serious one I ever had with him.

"Maureen is away," he said, as if there could be no doubt why I had called. "She's in hospital. A breakdown. I'll give you the name of the hospital, if you like. Though it'll probably be some time before you'll be able to see her."

"I'm sorry to hear that," I said. "But not altogether surprised."

I realized by his look that he completely misunderstood me.

"It's this house," I elucidated. "I've decided to move."

"If you can find anywhere else."

"Quite," I said. "I suggest you should think about moving too."

"All together, in fact?" He was not hostile, I thought, but he had again misunderstood me. It would indeed have been nice to continue living in the same building as Maureen, but I had taken for granted that it was too much to hope for, with accommodation of any kind as short as it was then; and has been ever since, needless to say.

"Splendid, if we could find anywhere. But I suggest that you and Maureen should move too in any case. This house is all wrong."

He glanced at me. "Will you come in and have a coffee? I've become quite good at pigging it since Maureen left."

"Thanks very much," I said. The situation was not what I had had in mind, but I was willing to talk about recent events to anyone remotely suitable.

"Sorry I'm not togged up." He pushed back the door for me to go in first.

The din and dust inside were duly frightful, but Maureen's husband set about making the coffee as if we had been alone in the flat, and the children stared at me for only a minute or two, then started running up and down again. I picked up the *Observer*.

"What exactly do you mean by wrong?" asked Gilbert in due course. "Milk and sugar?"

The coffee really was good, and thoroughly welcome, even though so shortly after my own small breakfast.

"The people on the floors above don't run a normal business."

His brow creased slightly. "I agree with you."

"I don't know what they do."

"Maureen doesn't either. You know we used to have that cove, Millar, *in* here from time to time. He paid a small *pourboire,* and I admit we were damned glad to have it. I find life a struggle, as I don't mind telling you. But Maureen never discovered very much about him. I never met Millar myself. I take it you know him quite well?"

"Not really."

I thought I could tell him exactly how much I did know of Mr Millar, even though I had to speak more loudly than I should have wished, because of the din in the room.

Gilbert listened very carefully, and then, after a moment's thought, shouted out: "Children! Go *outside* and play." I was surprised by the way they instantly departed and climbed up to the street: in those days, safe and almost silent on the Sabbath. "And I take it that there've been developments since?" he continued.

"In that connection I'm rather glad the children have gone," I said.

"Sex or spooks?" asked Gilbert. "Have some more coffee?" he went on before I could answer. "Sorry, I forgot."

"Thank you very much. I'm the better for it."

"I'm sorry Maureen's not here."

"I hope it'll not be too long," I said.

We paused a moment, lapping coffee.

"Are you clairvoyant?" he asked.

"Not that I know of. I'm probably too young." He was perhaps six or seven years older, despite all those children. "Why? Do you think I've imagined it all?" I put it quite amiably.

"It just struck me for one moment that you might have seen into the future. All these people slavishly doing nothing. It'll be exactly like that one day, you know, if we go on as we are. For a moment it all sounded to me like a vision of 40 years on—if as much."

And indeed I had to take a moment to consider.

"But they're doing it all the time," I objected. "Now. Well, not this moment. I *think* not this moment. But you can go up and look tomorrow. See for yourself."

"It's not something I particularly *want* to see. Forty years on. Though I *was* at Harrow, strange as it seems."

I admit that I was surprised. I doubt whether I had then knowingly met another Harrovian, though I knew the song he had quoted.

"I was sacked, of course."

I attempted an appropriately expressive look before returning to the matter in hand.

"Maureen must have seen," I continued. "Isn't that why she's not here? Wasn't it all too much for her?"

He eyed me a little; then said nothing. I suddenly apprehended the possibility that he might attribute Maureen's breakdown simply to me.

I pressed my point about the people upstairs. "Do you know how much Maureen knows? Some of what there is to know is pretty shattering."

"I really don't doubt it. I agree with all you say. I told you so."

"There's a bit more. Something rather different."

"Do you want to talk about it?"

"I think I should."

"Sorry the coffee's finished."

"It was good."

"Well?"

So I told him about the even odder events of that morning and of the night before. After all, I had to tell someone.

"So we've got the Un-Dead in too?" he commented.

I stared at him.

"What's the matter?" he asked. "Isn't that more or less what you were implying?"

I must have continued to stare at him.

"Or did you mean something quite different?"

"On the contrary," I replied, "I think you've got it. It's just that it never occurred to me."

"That you were visited by a creature from another world than this? Or supposed you were. I thought that was your point?"

"What never occurred to me was——" I couldn't quite say it. "I've told you," I went on, "that Mr Millar gave me the impression of having something very much on his mind."

"A haunted man, in fact. Yes, I got that," said Gilbert.

I cannot pretend that my voice did not sink a little foolishly.

"This house might be haunted by the ghost of his victim."

Maureen's husband looked straight at me. "Victims. Didn't your friend in green put it in the plural?"

"Mr Millar might be always on the move, always running away. And going through the hoops in the attempt to forget. Through all the hoops he can find. Even asking me down for a drink."

"Still like 40 years on," said Maureen's husband. "But you mustn't let me philosophize. It's probably only that I'm not being a wild success myself. Why do you call him *Mr* Millar?"

I could see that it might irritate an Harrovian. But my answer, though a mere inspiration of the moment, I rather liked. "To link him with the rest of the world. He's one who needs it."

"I see," said Maureen's husband. "I'll think about what you've told me. I've never doubted that old Millar was a dead loss. I suppose I've kept away from him for that reason. Of course we're not in a position to move just at the moment. You might say that the tangible factors outweigh the intangible. So forgive me if I don't offer to sit up with you waiting for the line of nameless horrors." His expression changed. "You will forgive me? To start with, I can't leave the kids and I can hardly bring them with me."

"I never even thought of it," I replied; which was true.

"If you come screaming down the stairs at any time, don't hesitate to knock me up. Knock hard, because I sleep hard after slogging all day at the filthy shop. Besides it might scare away the apparitions."

I should perhaps have been grateful for a slightly different attitude, but one had to take the man as he obviously was. I attempted one more word.

"I see it's no business of mine, but I do sincerely advise against staying long in the same house with those people upstairs. If they were to go, of course it would be different."

"It might not, of course, from what you say. But the real trouble is that there's always something. Not just something wrong, but something badly wrong. I can see that Millar's got on your nerves and I don't blame you either. But if you'd ever lived in some of the places that Maureen and I have lived in since I was invalided out . . . Believe me, my friend, there's always something that's bloody about living among the toiling masses. From my point of view this place is a real oasis. You may see what I mean when you start looking for somewhere else. Mind if I get the kids down again?"

"I'll go," I said. "Thank you for listening."

"Any time," he said. "Always a friendly bosom on which to lay the troubled head. I'll tell Maureen you looked in. When she's more compos, that is."

Needless to say, Maureen's husband proved to be almost gruesomely in the right of it. I could find nowhere else to live that was even possible; and I found much on offer that was quite horrible. That was after spending almost the whole of the next week in the search; regardless of my duties to Major Valentine. A week does not sound very long, but it is surprising how many small, dark cavities six days can unearth.

In any case, the unit of a week was critical. I should have liked at least to be sure of having somewhere else to go before having to face another Saturday and Sunday.

Messrs Stallabrass, Hoskins and Cramp seemed to be carrying on as usual, though as I was out of the house for the greater part of each day, it was impossible for me to be sure. On the Thursday night, Mr Millar was beating it up with three noisy girls until the dawn was filtering through my windows, grey as Maureen's dress.

I decided that I could not face the Saturday and Sunday nights. On the Saturday evening, I retreated to my mother, after spending a long day visiting a list of impossible addresses (many of them stated to be accessible on a Saturday only—often on a Saturday afternoon only, perhaps between two and four).

"What a surprise!" exclaimed my mother. "I wasn't sure I should ever see you again."

And when, against some reluctance on my part as well as against the usual resistance on my mother's, I returned to Brandenburg Square in the later part of the Monday morning, I found a transformation.

In the first place, I had to open the street door with my key. This was unknown during "business hours": the staff of Messrs Stallabrass, Hoskins and Cramp, and their sporting friends, pushed in and out so incessantly that a locked front door would have been ludicrous. It would have been entirely out of harmony with the firm's way of life and what would now be called "image".

Within all was quiet. All the room doors were shut, which was also quite unknown. This time I applied myself to several of the handles with confidence. Every door I tried was locked.

I put down my canvas bag and went outside again, the front door swinging shut behind me on its heavy spring.

The firm's unusually large brass plate had gone. Even the phantom shape of it was fainter than usual in these cases; the firm having been with us for so much less than the customary (or then customary) 40 or 80 years. I picked a bit at the screwholes, but nothing peeped out. I stood back and looked up at the windows of the house. All were shut, but there was nothing unusual about that. I had never noticed an open window on the floors occupied by Messrs Stallabrass, Hoskins and Cramp. I reflected that it would be no use enquiring in the basement, as Maureen's husband would be at the provisions shop. (I wondered for the first time who was nowadays collecting the children from school.) As people were now staring at me, I gave the front door a push and re-entered.

Maureen stood halfway up the first flight of stairs, as if awaiting me.

She wore a white blouse that some of my mother's generation would have called "skimpy", and a bright red skirt, and equally bright red shoes. Her stockings gently gleamed, her hair positively shone, and her face was nothing less than radiant.

"All silent as the tomb," she said.

"Maureen!" I cried and hugged her and kissed her. It was impossible to do anything else.

"Suddenly," she said. "Quite suddenly. During the weekend. I was very ill, you know, Roy, and then almost at once I was all right. It was yesterday, and I've been in a bit of a trance ever since. I've spent this morning buying clothes that we really can't afford, and having my hair done, and just sitting in the square, and smiling at everything."

I kissed her again.

"How long have this lot been gone?" she went on. "Gilbert's departed for the weekend and taken the children. Thought I was safely shut away. What's he up to, I wonder?"

"This lot were here when I left on Saturday. Come upstairs, Maureen."

We went up arm in arm, even though I was carrying my canvas bag.

At Mr Millar's own floor, we stopped, and, for the hell of it, I tried the handle of Mr Millar's own outer door, the door into the pink room with the cornice of flowers. This time, the door opened.

I tried to push Maureen out, but I failed. Mr Millar was hanging there, in the outer office for all to see; and from a large hook, meant for hanging overcoats on a wall, which he, or someone, must have spent much time screwing into the plaster of the ceiling, or rather, I imagine, through the ceiling into one of the wooden joists of my floor above. The most curious thing was that though there was no detectable movement of air in the room, the body swung back and forth quite perceptibly, as if it had been made of *papier mâché*, or some other featherweight expendable. Even the clothes looked papery and insubstantial. Was it the real Mr Millar at all who dangled there? It was remarkably hard to be sure.

A curious thing of another kind was that though, for a long time, I had been scared out of my wits by events in the house (and Maureen perhaps literally so), yet from quite soon after that climactic Sunday, I began to feel reasonably happy there almost all the time, indeed very happy indeed when I thought about Maureen or covered her sweet hair with kisses; and entirely forgot the idea of moving, or as entirely as life ever permits one to forget anything.

8

THE CLOCK WATCHER

Now THAT IT has all come to an end, so that even the police are "making enquiries", I am trying to keep myself occupied for a little by writing out a story that no one will ever believe. Or no one just yet. Possibly some new Einstein will come to my rescue, sooner or later; and prove by theory what I have learned by experience. That sort of theory is thought up about every second year nowadays, though none of the theories make much difference to ordinary people's lives.

Perhaps I never was quite an ordinary person, after all. Perhaps I ceased being ordinary when I married Ursula. Certainly they all said so; said I hadn't thought what it implied, even that I had gone a bit round the bend during the last part of the war. But, when it comes to the point, not many people bother very much about who a *man* marries; though it can still be different when it is the case of a girl. And of course I had no parents by then.

Will anyone ever read this but me? Well, yes, perhaps they may. So I had better mention what happened to my parents, and remember to put in a word or two about other things like that. My father fell from the top of one of his buildings when I was four years old. Of course it was a dreadful thing to happen, but I was never what is called close to my father, or so it has seemed to me since, and my mother would not let me even go to the funeral, said it would be too morbid an experience for a young child, and left me locked in the bedroom when the procession left the house. Not that you could really call it a procession, I imagine. Especially as it was simply teeming with rain. But possibly I exaggerate that aspect of it as children are apt to do. My mother died during the war I was engaged in fighting. There was nothing unusual about her death. Every second person seems to die as she did, I regret to say.

So, despite a certain amount of chat, some of it fairly hostile, I was pretty much on my own at the time of my marriage, though I had managed to struggle back into my profession, and had a very fair job, all things considered, as a draughtsman with Rosenberg and Newton. I had better explain that too.

Old Jacob Rosenberg had been a friend of my father's: so much so that he went on keeping an eye on my mother until his own death about a year before hers. (He dropped dead on one of the platforms at Green Park underground station, which is just the way that I myself should choose to go.) His son, young Jacob, gave me a place in the office after I came back from destroying the Nazis. Of course, the Jews are like that: once a friend, always a friend, if you go on treating them properly. I cannot help saying it was where the Nazis went wrong. There was a great deal to be said in favour of the Nazis, of course, in many other ways. The Germans wouldn't have fought so hard and long, if it hadn't been so, quite unbelievable actually.

Rosenberg and Newton called themselves architects, but they were really something more speculative than that: more like business men with a good knowledge of construction. Not that they were not on the architectural register. Of course they were. Nor that their methods were not completely clean and honest. I saw enough of what went on to be quite sure about that, or I should not have stayed, however badly I needed a job, as I certainly did when mother proved to have left almost nothing. I think she had expected something appreciable from Mr Rosenberg's will, but all she got was—of all things—a clock. A *clock*. Well, the police will find the pieces of it buried in the garden, if they care to dig . . .

I had learned a lot from Rosenberg and Newton before I left them to set up in a similar line of business on my own, though far more modestly, needless to say. I have been on my own for nearly three years, not very long, but my name has become quite well thought of in this extremely prosperous suburb where so many appalling, unbelievable things have been happening to me, without anyone really knowing, though not without some observing—what there was to be observed. And, even there, it is not altogether a case of so *many* things happening. There is only *one* thing really; *one* thing that is capable of indefinite extension.

I am a quiet sort of person really. They say that you won't succeed in business unless you make friends fairly readily; especially in the property business. Myself, I don't know about that. I have acquaintances, of course, many of them; but Ursula and I hardly went in for friends at all. We didn't need them. I had always been rather like that, and now we were wrapped up in one another and thought that third parties would only spoil things. I know that was how I felt; and, as a matter of fact, I *know* it was how she felt also. And it never seemed to stand in the way of business success: well, quite enough success to satisfy *me*. I never wanted to be so successful that I should see less of Ursula, and I simply cannot understand all those Rotary Clubs and Round Tables and Elks and Optimists, though I might have felt it right to join the British Legion, if the British Legion had been what it was after the first war. All the same, I like to dress smartly, and that *is* good for business, whatever they say. I hated the state one got into during the war. But then, though I have certain views of my own, I hated the war altogether. God, it was ghastly!

I first set eyes on Ursula when she was sitting on a bank by the roadside, somewhere near Mönchen-Gladbach. I cannot say *exactly* where it was. As a matter of fact, we actually went back some years later to look for the place, and could not find it at all. Not that I wish to suggest there was anything peculiar about that, or anything related to what was already very much happening—elsewhere. It was simply that the whole face of Germany had changed by that time, and thank God for it.

When I originally spotted Ursula, there was no traffic on the roads, first, because all the vehicles had been destroyed or commandeered; second, because in that area there were no roads that remained passable except by military stuff, tanks and jeeps. There were no people about either: local people, I mean. Of course it was nothing like the Somme and the Aisne twenty years earlier, nothing at all. It was perhaps more depressing than horrifying; anyway at a first look. The second world war was just over, and some of those whom I knew—not well, as I say—had the pleasant job of routing out the local concentration camp.

Ursula, mercifully, had nothing to do with that. She came from the Black Forest, hundreds of miles to the south. She was an only child and had lost both her parents when Freudenstadt was removed from the face of the earth. She herself had been working nearby as a domestic servant right through the latter part of the war. This seems strange to us, but Germany never really got round to "total war" and all that, although people here think that she did. Of course, Ursula was not properly a domestic servant. She was simply allowed to masquerade as one by the people who lived in one of the big houses, and who, like many of their kind, didn't care for the Nazis. Ursula's father was a manufacturer of Black Forest souvenirs, and, Ursula told me, no one interfered very much with that either, until the very last months of the war. I describe him as a "manufacturer", because he seems to have been in a quite big way of business, with many employees, and an agreeable income. Certainly, Ursula went to a costlier school than I did, and she also emerged better educated, Nazis or no Nazis. Though I went to a public school, and a quite well-known one, it was not Eton, and the field is one where the descent from the best is steep. More than anything else, Ursula's father manufactured clocks; cuckoo clocks, painted clocks, and huge clocks in dark spiky wood or in polished spiky metal that chimed and struck and kept tabs on the phases of the moon, not to say the zodiac. I can be specific because Ursula brought many such clocks into our home; in memory of her father, or otherwise. It was the downfall and ruin of her beauty and of our love.

And how beautiful she was when my eyes first lighted upon her! Her parents being Catholics, she had been named after St Ursula of Cologne, who went on the long voyage and was ultimately martyred with all her virgins, hundreds of them, I believe; and a saint is precisely what my girl looked like—then and for a long time afterwards. She had a gentle, trusting gaze, despite everything that had happened to her; and a mouth like a soft flower at the most perfect moment of its blooming. She was still wearing the maid's black dress which had been part of her disguise, so to speak; and, again, many people will be surprised to hear that it was made of real silk. Even the fact that this dress was slightly torn and slightly dirty, added to the effect she gave of having something to do with religion. She had no property of any kind, apart from a handkerchief. That was made of silk too, but this time it was a survival from her first communion. It was very small, but it had a wide edging of lace, made—yes—by the Black Forest nuns. Later, she gave me the handkerchief as a treasure to keep. I kissed it and hid it away, but, though it seems incredible, especially to me, I realized in no time that I had managed to lose it. Of course it must be somewhere in the house now, and I never mentioned the loss to Ursula. At the time I first saw Ursula, she was weeping into this tiny handkerchief, and I lent her a much larger one, just as the kind man does in a novel or a show. I was awaiting "repatriation" at the time, and had managed to evade any particular duties now that the destruction was over. No one who missed seeing what we did to Germany can have any idea, and the Germans put it all back in no time; Freudenstadt, as it happens, first of all, or just about.

I took Ursula under my wing at once, right close under it. It was what one did at that time, but, from the very first, I meant more by it than did most of the others, and when difficulty arose about Ursula coming to England, I had no doubt in my heart about assuring the authorities in writing that she was coming to marry me.

I hadn't seen her for more than three months and I went to Harwich to meet her. Little Attlee had come into power by then, and many of my acquaintance had voted for him, especially, as we all know, those who had been fighting under Churchill. England had started on her long soft greyness, but when Ursula emerged from her grilling by the Aliens Department, she was startlingly well turned out and accompanied by an unexpected quantity of brand new luggage. She told me that she had managed to avoid "relief agencies" of all kinds, and had always been in a real job of some sort. Ironically, it was a bit different here. Though we all know how run down England was at that time, Ursula was not permitted to take a job at all until after we were married and she had become a British citizen; so that at first she was reduced to working free of charge for a charity. It sent bundles somewhere or other; and, as in Germany, it was amazing how much had remained in back rooms with which to stuff them.

When Ursula arrived, I was back to living in my mother's and father's old house, and there was nothing to do but take her there. I was with Rosenberg and Newton by then, and young Jacob Rosenberg knew all about it, and was very kind and decent. Certain others were not; and, oddly enough, when I made it clear that I was about to marry Ursula, seemed not in the least reassured, but rather the contrary, as I have said. There was even talk of my having brought over a foreign mouth to feed. No doubt it was called a Nazi mouth when I was not actually listening. Of course it is unconventional for the bridegroom to lead the bride from his own front door.

In my mother's house, Ursula set up the first of her clocks. I had noticed that her shiny baggage at Harwich included a black, oblong box in what looked like leather but was, in fact, a good imitation of leather. The clock inside was a cuckoo, fairly large and in plain dark wood. The bird, which was paler, emitted a sharp, strident shriek, which could be heard at the hour all over the house. At the quarters, including the half, the bird was silent, so at first I reflected that things might be worse. I was working hard both with Rosenberg and Newton (I abominate those who take money without even attempting to give a proper return for it) and also with finishing off the house before putting it up for sale; so that I could sleep like a log even with the cuckoo clock in the same room with me.

But before long the woman next door came in with a complaint about it. She refused to "discuss the matter" with Ursula and insisted upon seeing me. She was quite young, with blonde shoulder-length hair turned outward at the ends, and nice legs. Indeed, she was a nice person altogether, I thought. She said, quite agreeably, that the cuckoo kept her three little boys awake all night. "It doesn't sound like a *cuckoo*, at all," I remember her saying. I couldn't disagree, but replied that clock cuckoos seldom do; which is, surely, true enough? I said I would speak to Ursula about it, and even, at that early stage, so to say, I thought I detected a gleam of scepticism in the woman's eye, though a scepticism that was not unfriendly to *me*. "I'll do what I can," I concluded, and the woman smiled very nicely, and attempted no further argument. I was rather shocked to realize that the wretched cuckoo could be heard at all outside the house.

Ursula did not enter into the spirit of what was, after all, a typically British situation. On the contrary, when I raised the question, in as offhand a manner as I could manage, she became tense, which with her was unusual; and when I suggested that the cuckoo might be silenced at least during the night, bedded down in the nest, as it were, she cried out, "That would be fatal."

I was at the same time astonished—and yet not astonished. I have to leave it at that.

"We could easily have someone in to make the necessary adjustment," I said mildly, though, I suppose, with some pressure behind the words.

"No one may touch my clocks except the person I bring," she replied. Those were her exact words, very faintly foreign in form, though by now Ursula spoke English pretty well, having improved her knowledge of it with a speed that amazed me.

"Your *clocks*, darling?" I queried, smiling at her. Of course I knew of only one.

She did not answer me but said, "That woman with her hair and legs! What business of hers is our life?" It was curious how Ursula specified the very points that I myself, as a man, had noticed about our neighbour. I was often aware of Ursula's extraordinary insight; sometimes it was almost telepathic.

Even then, however, it seemed to me that Ursula was more frightened than aggressive, let alone jealous, as other women would have been. I reflected that a foreigner might well be upset by a complaint from a neighbour and uncertain how to deal with it. Already, Ursula was smiling through her sulkiness and telling me that even the sulks were assumed. All the same, it was obvious that there was a reality somewhere in all this.

Ursula duly did precisely nothing about the shrieking, nocturnal cuckoo. But shortly after the approach by our glamorous neighbour, Ursula and I married and moved on.

The wedding took place, of necessity, in the local Catholic church, and I admit that it was one of the most unnerving experiences I had by then been through, war or no war. The keen young priest was bitterly antagonistic and, at the actual ceremony, kept his burning eyes fixed upon me at every moment the ritual left possible, as if he hoped to sear me into "conversion" there and then, or, alternatively, to scorch and dissolve me from the backbone outwards. And, of course, in those days I had to sign a declaration that all our children would be raised in the Catholic faith. (And quite right too from the Catholic point of view.)

Ursula, moreover, seemed different—very different. This was territory that was hers, and not mine: and more, of course, than just territory. I am sure she tried to bring me in too, but there was nothing really possible for her to do about that. Earlier she had been upset when I refused in advance to wear a wedding ring in ordinary life, as it were, in the way the continentals do. But there was nothing for me to do about that either.

Most weddings are matters of equal gain and loss. It is not the wedding that counts, though so many girls think it is. Weddings are, at the best, neutral. Seldom are they even fully volitional.

But I should say at once, very clearly, that Ursula and I were happy, incredibly happy. It would not be sensible to expect happiness like that to last, and I now see that I stopped expecting any such thing a long time ago. Our happiness was not of this adult world, where happiness is only a theory. Ursula and I were happy in the way of happy children. What could we expect, then? But other kinds of happiness are merely resignation; and often abject defeat.

People couldn't at that period go abroad for their honeymoons, so Ursula and I went to Windermere and Ullswater. They seemed more suitable than Bournemouth or than even Kipling's South Downs, by now under crops. Ursula excelled me without difficulty in swimming, sailing, and fell-walking alike. Marriage had sheered off the first edge of romance from our actual caresses, but there was a sweet affection between us, as between a devoted brother and a devoted sister, though I suppose that is not an approved way of putting it. I always wanted a sister, and never more than at this present moment.

Our nights were certainly quieter without the noisy clock, though Ursula had brought with her a small substitute. It did not work on the cuckoo principle, and indeed neither chimed nor struck in any way. Even its tick was so muted as to be inaudible. None the less, it was in appearance a pleasant object, brightly painted; in the modern world, still very much a souvenir. Ursula said that she had merely seen it in a shop window and "been unable to resist it". I wondered at the time from whom she had learned that always slightly sinister phrase; and I fear that I also wondered, even at the time, whether her story was strictly true. This sounds a horrible thing to say, but later it emerged that something horrible indeed was all around us, however difficult to define. I imagine that the little clock that accompanied us on our honeymoon had been constructed by the insertion of a very subtle and sophisticated mechanism into a more or less intentionally crude and commercial case. It purred like a slinky pussy, and when, later, I clubbed it to shards, I daresay I destroyed more than £100 of purchase money.

One curious thing I noticed on the honeymoon. I may perhaps have *noticed* it earlier, but I am very sure that it was on our honeymoon that I spoke about it. This was that for all her obvious interest in clocks, Ursula never had the least idea of the time.

We were sitting by the water near Lowwood, and dusk was coming on.

"It's growing very dark," said my Ursula, in her precise way. "Is there a storm coming?"

"It's getting dark because it's nearly seven o'clock," I replied. This was in April.

She turned quite panicky. "I thought it was only about three."

This was absurd, because we had not even reached the waterside until well after that. But we had been much occupied while we had been sitting and lying there, so that, after thinking for a moment, all I said was "You need a watch, my darling. I'll buy you one for your birthday."

She answered not a word, but now looked angry as well as frightened. I remembered at once that I had made a mistake. I had learned the previous year that Ursula disliked her birthday being even mentioned, young though she was; let alone being celebrated, however quietly. I had, of course, without thinking used a form of words common when the idea of a present arises.

"Sorry, darling," I said. "I'll give you a watch some other time." Oh, that word "time".

"I don't want a watch." She spoke so low that I could hardly hear her. "I can't wear a watch."

I *think* that was what she said, but she might have said, "I can't bear a watch". I was uncertain at the time, but I made no enquiry. If it was a matter of *wearing* a watch, we all know that there are people who cannot. My own father's elder brother, my Uncle Allardyce, is one of them, for example.

In any case, the whole thing was getting out of proportion, not to say out of control. Endeavouring to make the best of my mistake, I kept my mouth shut, tried to smile, and gently took Ursula's hand.

Her hands were particularly small and soft. They always fascinated and delighted me. But now the hand that I took hold of was not merely cold, but like a tight bag of wet ice.

"Darling!"

I could not help almost crying out; nor, I fear, could I help dropping her hand. I was completely at a loss for the proper thing to do next; as if something altogether unprecedented had happened.

She sat there, rather huddled; and then she gazed up at me, so sweetly, so lovingly, and so helplessly.

I sprang to my feet. "Get up," I cried, in my brotherly way—or the way I always thought of as brotherly. I lifted her on to her legs, pulling her not by the hands but by the shoulders, which was always easy, as she was so petite in every way. "Get up, get up. We must run back. We must run."

And run we did, without a word of comment or argument from her; though not all the way, or anything like it, because we were staying about a couple of miles off in a sort of apartment house owned by a retired school-teacher named Mrs Ardale.

In theory, I could have afforded something rather better, but the big hotels were either out of action just then or in some way unsuitable. In the end, I had just gone to the Post Office and enquired, and they had told me about Mrs Ardale at once. It seemed a queer way to organize a honeymoon, especially when we are supposed to have only one honeymoon in each lifetime, but Ursula and I were like that from the first—and for some time still lying ahead. In any case, between us the idea of a honeymoon was a bit of a joke, as it often is in these times; but, for Ursula and me, a tender joke, which is perhaps *not* so usual. Mrs Ardale, by the way, was a divorcée, unlikely though that seems. She never stopped mentioning the fact. She also wore a very obvious chestnutty wig, though Ursula said her own hair was perfectly all right when one was permitted to catch a glimpse of it. I never took to Mrs Ardale, but she certainly kept the place very clean, which was important to Ursula, and food at that time was much of a muchness everywhere, or, rather, little of a littleness. Mrs Ardale used to serve us crabs caught in the lake. Not every day, of course.

Later, we moved on to a less satisfactory place, high above Ullswater. It was a bit of a shack in every way, but, fortunately, Ursula seemed not to mind much, possibly because she was now really getting into her athletic stride, small though she was. She was often a long way ahead of me at the crest of the fell, and she could swim like one of those slender, swift fish that never seem to undulate (or are they really fish?). But it was when we hired a dinghy and went sailing that I felt almost embarrassed by my uselessness and general ineptitude. Ursula always *looked* so competent, and she always seemed to have exactly the right clothes for whatever we were doing, simple though they were. I myself both look and feel better in business clothes—clothes for ordinary life in town. But I reflected that the hire-dinghies could hardly be at their best from a handling point of view after five years of total war and with no tackle yet available for repairing them; and, in any case, I have never seen myself as any kind of sportsman, nor has my health seemed to suffer from it. I liked my darling to be so spry and agile when we were on holiday together. I never minded in the least being shown up by her, though many would have said it would be bad from a business point of view. But at that time it could hardly have mattered, as I was still with Rosenberg and Newton, and not yet self-employed.

Which, needless to say, was why, when we settled down again, we started buying a house in the same suburb, the place where I had always lived. Also, old Newton, young Jacob's partner from his father's time, was able to help us a lot there: not only with getting a really good mortgage, but with getting a really good house too, and quite reasonably cheap, as he was in a position to put a little quiet pressure on the man who was selling. The property business is full of aspects like that, and it is useless to deny it. It always has been, and doubtless it always will be, until we mostly become cave-dwellers again, which may be soon. It was a remarkably good thing to have old Newton

behind one when one was looking for a suburban house about twelve
months after the second world war, especially as he was in local politics, which the Rosenbergs, father and son, always made a point of
avoiding.

But Ursula would have done well in one of those caves. I could
imagine her, small though she was, in a bearskin, and nothing much
else; and coping with all that might arise far better than I can cope
with even a luxury hotel, and terribly sweet and attractive all the
time, often unbearably so. As it was, she settled down as if she had
lived in this steady-as-she-goes suburb all her life. *This* suburb. *This*
house. We had given more than three weeks to our honeymoon, world
scarcity or no world scarcity. Speaking for myself, I could have gone
on like that with Ursula for ever. I have a conscience, but few strong
ambitions, as I have said. Oh, I can see Ursula's deep blue eyes now—
as they were then—on our honeymoon—and afterwards.

But as soon as we were well and truly in, Ursula brought out no
fewer than three more clocks. They were additional to the original
cuckoo clock, and, I suppose, to the soft-speaking traveler's clock also.
As it happens, I was never told at the time what became of that one.
When I enquired, putting in a good word for the quietness, Ursula
simply replied that "it was a once-for-all clock for a once-for-all purpose, darling," and smiled at me knowingly, or mock-knowingly.

"That was a clock I really liked, darling," I replied, but she said
nothing in return, knowing perfectly well that, even then, I did not really like any of the others.

The truth was, from first to last, that one could not *talk* at all to
Ursula about the clocks. About many other things, including some that
were beyond my own scope, as I am no intellectual; and at almost any
time: but never about *them*—about the clocks. One's words seemed to
slip off her pretty, perfect body, her prettily chosen, freshly ironed
dress, and then to dissolve on the carpet around her pink or yellow
high-heeled shoes. I have in mind the grey carpet with the big, bold
chains of flowers on which I last saw her standing and saying her list-
less goodbye when I set out to consult Dr Tweed.

I have said that *one* could not talk on the subject to Ursula. I suppose it would be truer to say that *I* could not. That, before long, was
just the point. Perhaps there was another who could.

But, then, what normal, ordinary person—English person, anyway—
could like those particular clocks; or at least so many of them? A single decorated clock, possibly—if the person cared for things of that
general type—as I admit many seem to—though fewer perhaps than

formerly. I am fairly sure that, at the best, the quantity of souvenirs brought back to Britain from the Black Forest by the public at large is nothing like what it was when the Prince Consort was alive and setting the vogue, with real trees at Christmas as well. And now it is years after the end of the second world war.

The clocks that Ursula brought into the house were not all grotesque in themselves: not all of them were carved into grinning gnomes, or giants with long teeth, or bats with wings that seemed to have altered their positions from time to time, though never when one was looking (or, once more, never when *I* was looking)—though *some* of them were, indeed, carved in those ways. It was more the overall uncouth monotony of the clocks that palled: *that*, more than the detail work applied to any one of them. As time passed, Ursula brought in more and more clocks, until, long before the end, I was almost afraid to count how many. I own it. I am not in the least ashamed of it, and what went on to happen, showed that I had no reason to be.

The clocks were so evenly brown—dark brown. When there was coloured detail, and often there was a mass of it, the colours were never bright colours. Or rather they were, and, at the same time, they weren't. I have often thought that the sense of colour is not strong in Germany. Of course, no one country can expect to have everything, and the last thing I wish to do is introduce an element of rivalry. I detest all things like that.

The coloured decoration of the clocks reminded me of fungus on a woodland tree, and there are many who find fungi not only fascinating but actually beautiful. One can eat many of them, if one has to, and sometimes I felt exactly that about the coloured clock decorations. They looked *edible*—upon compulsion. I imagine that the people who thought up the style in the first place based it upon what they saw in the vast, dark forests around them. The fungi, the teeth, the wings, the dark or shiny brownness. Even the shrieking and calling of the hours and the quarters might have been imitated from the crying of extinct, forest fowl. When there was a chorus of it in the same house, the effect was very much of a dark glade in which some unfortunate traveller had been deserted—or had merely lost his way.

This house is a fair-sized structure for these times, and the clocks were distributed about it very evenly, there being seldom more than three in any single room, and often only one. I fancy (or perhaps I know) that Ursula wanted there to be no room in our house without *one* of her clocks in it. Distribution was important. It is true that it dispersed the quarterly chorus, but, on the other hand, it positively enhanced the forest glade impression, especially if one were alone in any of the rooms. First, one creature would shrill out, and then, almost instantly, another and another, all at different distances in the house, and with very different cries, and another and another and another; some, one was aware, made of wood, usually carved crudely but elaborately, others made of tin or sheet steel, some made even of plastic. Of course we in the construction business have good reason to be grateful for the coming of plastic, but I like it to keep its proper place, and not set about devouring every other material in the home, as it is very apt to do.

As will be imagined, clocks often spoke simultaneously, but what I found particularly eerie was the sequence of sound that arose when two or more of them not so much coincided as overlapped. This effect, in the nature of things, was seldom repeated in precisely the same form. Clocks only harmonize to *that* degree when a team of scientists has been at work on the design and setting up (if even then). In this house, the normal tiny variations in the time-keeping led to sounds that were unpredictable and often quite disturbing. And this was true even though most of our clocks spoke but once, however frequently they did it. Not all, however: Ursula had found some expensive pieces in which the bird sang a whole song. One of these vocalists was golden all over, from tail to beak; and lived in a golden schloss with a tiny golden deathshead upon every pinnacle of it. Another was a shrunk-down bird of paradise with variegated feathers, though whether the feathers were real or not I am unable to say. There would seem to be problems in finding feathers like bird-of-paradise feathers except that they had to be one-tenth, perhaps, of the size. What I *can* testify is that our wee friend squawked as loud as his full-grown cousin can possibly have done in the forest deep.

How could Ursula afford such treasures? Where did she find her clocks, in any case? Only once, to the best of my belief, did she return after her marriage to Germany. That was when she went with me on our little trip around the region where we had met and had become · such friends. And, as far as I am aware, she did not then range even near to the Black Forest.

The answer to my two questions appears to have been that a seller of clocks visited our house when I was not there; and that his terms were easy, though in one sense only.

I am reasonably sure that these visits went on for a long time before I had any inkling of them. Needless to say, that state of affairs is common enough in any suburb; matter mainly for a laughter session, except for those immediately affected.

I used merely to notice when I came home, that the clocks had been moved around, sometimes almost all of them; and that every now and then there seemed to have been a new acquisition. Once or twice it was my ears that first told me of the newcomer, rather than my eyes. The mixed-up noise made by all the different clocks had odd effects upon me. I felt tensed up immediately I entered the house; but it was not entirely disagreeable. Far from it, in fact. The truth seemed to be that this tensing up brought me nearer to Ursula than at other times, and in a very real and practical way, which many other husbands I am acquainted with would be glad to have the secret of. For example, we were never quite the same together when we were elsewhere, even when we were together in her own homeland. Then it was more like brother and sister, as I have said; though fine in its own way too. What is more, my response to the clocks could vary almost 100 per cent. Sometimes the real din they made could drive me quite crazy, so that I barely knew what I was doing or even thinking. At other times, I hardly noticed anything. It is difficult to say anything more about it.

Then I began to observe that divers small repairs seemed to have been done. For a long while I said nothing. Ursula could not be made to talk about her clocks, and that seemed to be that. One shakes down even to mysteries, when so much else in a relationship is right, as it was in ours. But on a certain, important occasion, there were two things at the same time.

This house offers a completely separate dining-room (as well as a third sitting-room which I tried for a time to use as a kind of sub-office), and in this dining-room Ursula had set up a clock made like a peasant hut, with imitation thatch, from beneath which Clever Kuckuck peeked out every half-hour and whistled at us. (We were spared the other two quarters—with this particular clock.) During a period of time before the evening in question, it had become obvious that something was wrong with Kuckuck. Instead of springing at us with his whistle, he seemed merely to sidle out, quite slowly; to stand there hunched to one side; and rather to croak than to shrill. He was plainly ailing, but I said nothing; and he continued to ail for a period of weeks.

Then on that evening I heard him and I saw him as he spoke up at the very instant I entered the dining-room. He was once more good as in the factory.

I truly believed my comment was spontaneous and involuntary.

"Who's fixed Old Cuckoo?" I asked Ursula.

She said nothing. That was as usual on the particular topic, but this time she did not begin serving the broth either. She just stood there with the ladle in her hand, and I swear she was shaking. Well, of course she was. I know very well now.

I think it was this shaking, combined with her rather insulting silence (accustomed though I was), that made me behave badly, which I had almost never done before. Perhaps never at all. I think so. Never to anyone.

"Well, who?"

I am afraid that I half-shouted at her. It is well known that seeing a woman in a shaky state either softens a man or hardens him.

As she just went on silently shaking, I bawled out something like "You're just going to tell me what's going on for once. Who is it that looks after these clocks of yours?"

And then—at that precise moment—a voice spoke right behind me. It was a new voice, but what it had to say was not new. What it said was "Cuckoo"; but it said it exactly like a human voice, speaking rather low, not at all like one of these infernal machines.

I wheeled round, and there at the centre of the dining-room sideboard, staring at me, stood a small clock in gilt and silver that had not been there even at breakfast that morning, or, as far as I knew, anywhere else in the house. It was covered with filigree which sparkled and winked at me. It was also very fast. I knew that without having to consult my watch or anything else. Ursula, as I have said, never seemed to bother very much about whether her clocks showed the right time or not, but I had become so conscious of time—at least, of "*the* time"—that for most of it I knew what it was as if by a new instinct.

At this point, Ursula spoke. Her words were: "A man comes from Germany. He knows how to handle German clocks." She spoke quietly but distinctly, as if the words had been rehearsed.

I am sure I stared at her; probably even glared at her.

"How often does he come?" I asked.

"As often as he can manage," she replied. She spoke with considerable dignity; which tended of itself to put me in the wrong.

"And what about you?" I asked.

She smiled—in her usual, sweet way. "*What* about me?" she rejoined.

And of course I could not quite answer that. My own question had been too vague, perhaps also too idiomatic for a foreigner; though I knew myself what I meant.

"It is necessary that he should come regularly," Ursula continued. "Necessary for the clocks. He keeps them going." She was still smiling, but still shaking also, possibly more than before. I fancy that what had happened was that she had made a big decision: the decision to disclose something to me for the first time. She was bracing herself, nerving herself, consciously drawing upon her hold over me.

"Oh, of course it would never do," I said, sarcastically taking advantage of her, "it would never do if all the clocks stopped at the same time."

And then came the greatest astonishment of that important evening. As I spoke, Ursula went absolutely white and fainted.

She dropped to the floor with a crash, an extremely loud crash for so small a person. And there is something else to be sworn to, if anyone cares. I swear that the small filigree clock with the soft, human voice said "Cuckoo" again at this point, although two or three minutes only could have passed since it had spoken before.

I looked up the *Homelovers' Encyclopaedia* and did not take long to bring Ursula round again. But it was, naturally, impossible to return to the same subject. And, what is more, Ursula from then on developed a new wariness which was quite obvious to me—perhaps meant to be obvious, though that was hard to tell. But now I am fairly convinced that the evening when I made Ursula faint was the turning point. It was then that I really muffed things; missed my chance—possibly my only chance—of coming frankly to terms with Ursula, and helping her. Of helping myself, also.

As it was, Ursula's rather too obvious wariness had a bad effect on me. I feel that if a wife has to have a big secret in her life, she should at least make a successful job of concealing it from her husband completely. It is generally agreed to be the kind of thing a woman should be good at. But no doubt it is particularly difficult when the husband and wife are of different nationalities.

What I found was that the absence of change in Ursula's behaviour towards me in any other respect (or, at least, of visible change) only made things worse. I could no longer be completely relaxed with her when all the time I was aware of this whole important topic which we never mentioned. I felt myself beginning to shrink. I seemed to detect a faint patronage in her caresses and her affection. I felt they were like the attentions paid to a child before it is of an age to come to grips with the world on its own: sincere, of course; deeply felt, even; but different from the attentions bestowed on an equal.

I believe that Ursula's idea, conscious or otherwise, was to make up for having to shut me out in one direction by redoubling her assurances in others. As time passed, she seemed for the most part not less demonstrative but more; sometimes almost too responsive to be quite convincing. I found myself comparing my situation with that of a man I know whose wife took to religion. "Nothing could be any good with the marriage after that," he said; and, poor fellow, he actually wept over it, in the presence of another man. It was one of those dreadful liberal kinds of religion too, where one never knows where one is. Not, of course, that I am criticizing religion in a general way. There's much to be said for religion in general. It's just that it's no good for a marriage when one of the parties enters a whole world that the other cannot share. With Ursula it was not perhaps a whole world, but it was certainly a secret world, and certainly a terrible one, in so far as I have ever understood it at all.

I began trying to catch her out. I am ashamed of this, and I was ashamed of it at the time. The bare fact was that I could not help myself. I think that other men in similar situations, or in situations that seemed similar, have felt the same. One cannot prevent oneself setting trips and traps. And something else soon struck me. This was that had not Ursula and I been so close to one another, so exclusive, the present situation might have been more manageable, might have caused me less anguish. I saw what a *sensible* case there was for not putting all one's eggs in the same basket. And my seeing the sheer common sense of that—while being totally unable to act upon it—was another thing that was bad for both of us.

By now I had left Rosenberg and Newton and was set up on my own. I called myself a property consultant, but right from the start I was making small investments also, and borrowing the money to do it. I have always been able to keep my head above water, partly because I have never sought to fly up to the stars. If one wants to go up there, and to stay up there of course, one needs to rise from foundations set up by one's father, and preferably one's grandfather also. My father was just not like that, and neither of my grandfathers made much mark either. As a matter of fact, one of them was no more than a small pawnbroker: a very useful trade in those days, none the less.

Being on my own enabled me to watch over Ursula in a way that would otherwise have been impossible. I insisted upon clients and enquirers making an appointment. A local girl named Stevie looked after all that, and did it quite well, until she insisted on marrying one of those Indian students, strongly against my advice, and then going out there. The next local girl was less satisfactory; the great thing about her being that she was always ill, one thing after another, and all of them supported by medical certificates. Still we got by: most people expect little in the way of efficiency nowadays, and especially when, by one's whole existence in their lives, one is supposed to be making money for them. Nowadays that makes them so guilty and uneasy that difficulties and delays pass unnoticed.

So that when there were no appointments in the book, I was usually to be found snooping round my own happy home, spying on Ursula, hoping (or dreading) to catch her clock man by the heels.

I took to arriving home "unexpectedly". Some days, and with equal unexpectedness, I refused, at the very last moment, to depart from home at all.

I could only be touched when Ursula seemed filled with joy to see me back so soon; or sweetly delighted at finding she had a whole, long day in which to do nothing but look after me, perhaps go to an entertainment with me. For I felt that taking her away from the house for hours on end without warning might serve some useful purpose too. If I had an appointments book, surely the clock man must have one also, coming, as he did, from so great a distance?

On several different occasions, and unmistakably, I did hear retreating feet: and each time, or so I thought, the same step, rather quick and, as one might say, sharp on the ground, but never, seemingly, in anything that could properly be called flight. This house offers a completely separate approach to the back door: a path paved with concrete slabs and leading to an access road for the delivery vehicles. But passing round the side of the building from one front to the other is a little troublesome. On one side is a very narrow passage, which, as well as being unevenly paved, is often damp and slippery with dead leaves. On the other, is one of those trellis gates so often seen in the suburbs and which no one ever opens if he can possibly help it. The idea of giving chase, therefore, was hardly even practicable. On the other hand, I was not so far sunk as to tax Ursula with vexing questions as soon as I had entered the house. Nor did I ever hear these steps from *within* the house; always from the little garden in front, or even from the road outside. And I should say at once that the steps of others visiting the back door were often perfectly audible in that way. There was nothing odd in itself about my hearing those particular steps, except that they were particular, or seemed so to me.

And once, but only once, I heard a voice for which I could not account. It was a winter night and there had been a fall of snow. I cannot remember whether I had returned especially early. I took advantage of the muffling snow to creep up the few steps of path from the gate and to bend beneath the lighted living-room window with the tightly drawn curtains. (Ursula was attentive to all details.) It was not a thing I often did. In the first place, it was only practicable when it was pitch dark. In the second place, I disliked having to listen through the window and the wall to those clicking, clacking clocks. None the less, it was the room in which Ursula normally awaited me; a room with a coal fire and big soft sofas. After a while, I straightened up, and set my ear to the icy glass of the window itself. Possibly it was from some kind of intuition or telepathy that I listened that particular night.

I heard a voice, which was certainly a strange one, in more senses than one. It was the voice of a man right enough, and assuredly not of a man I knew. In any case, very few men entered our home as guests. Neither of us wanted them in that way.

It was a rather monotonous, rather grating voice. It said something, there was a silence, and then it said something else. I supposed that during what seemed to me to be silences, Ursula had spoken, and that the man had then replied. I strained and strained, but not a sound from Ursula could I hear, and not a word from the man could I understand. Of course not, I thought: he is speaking in a foreign tongue. As for Ursula, it was true that her voice was always a low one (doesn't Shakespeare say that is a good thing in a woman?); and I had acquired little experience of eavesdropping upon it, because I had seldom before made the attempt.

From the first moment of hearing it, I linked the man's voice with those quick, firm footsteps. It was exactly the voice I should have expected that man to have. I was doubtless almost bound to link the two, but it was really more than a link. I can only state that it was a certainty. And the fact that the man was probably talking in a foreign language further enraged me against all trespassers, all uninvited guests.

I stooped down again as if I might be detected through a crevice between the curtains, even though Ursula's drawing of curtains left no crevices, and then realized that my heart was pounding fit to bust. How preposterous if I were to have one of those attacks that so many men have! The thought did enter my mind, but it availed nothing to stay the whirlwind of fury that was now sweeping through me. I drew myself to my fullest height (I felt it was far more than that) and rapped uncontrollably on the glass with my mother's ruby ring, which I always wear on my right small finger. The noise, I thought, would be audible all the way to the corner down by the church. At last I had made a demonstration of some kind. As I rapped, a few small flakes of snow began once more to descend. Perhaps it would more properly be called sleet.

The front door over to my left opened, and Ursula charged out into the sleety darkness. Her high heels clattered down the crazy paving. She always dressed up to greet my coming home; making a mutual treat of it every evening.

She cried out to me. "Darling!"

In the wide beam of silvery light from the open door, she looked like a fairy in a pantomime.

"Darling, what has *happened?*" she cried.

She stretched her hands up to my shoulders and, even though my shoulders were touched with sleet, kept them there. It occurred to me at once that she was gaining time for someone to make off. I could not bring myself actually to force her away, to push her down into the freezing whiteness.

"Who was talking to you?" I cried. But my voice was caught up in the tightness within me and only made a cackle, completely ridiculous.

"Silly boy!" said Ursula, still holding me in such a way that I could not throw her off without a degree of force that neither of us could forgive.

"Who?" I gurgled out, and then began coughing.

"It was just the bird crying out," she replied, and let go of me altogether. I knew that I had forced her into saying something she had not wished to say. Her ceasing to hold me also: it was true that a visitor would by then have had time to make away, but it was also true that I had behaved in a manner to forfeit her embrace.

Still choking and coughing, quite ludicrous, I dashed into the house; and inside was something which was not ludicrous at all. The hallway and the living-room were less than half-lighted (it would hardly have been possible even to read, I thought subsequently), but, dim though it was, I saw that indeed a bird there seemed to be: not merely squawking but actually flapping round, just under the living-room ceiling, and more than once striking itself with a rap or thud against the fittings.

It was very frightening, and I made a fool of myself. I cried out

"Keep it off! Keep it off!" I covered my eyes with my hands, and should have liked to cover my ears also.

It lasted only a matter of seconds. And then Ursula had entered the room behind me and turned the lights full on from the switchplate at the door. She had a slightly detached expression, as of one reluctantly witnessing the inevitable consequence of a solemn warning disregarded.

"It was just the bird crying out," she said again soberly.

But what I saw, now that the light was on, was the look of the cushion on the sofa opposite to the sofa on which Ursula had been sitting. Someone had been seated opposite to her, and there had been no time to smooth away the evidence of it.

As for the bird, it had simply vanished in the brighter light.

All I could do was drag upstairs in order to deal with my attack of coughing. When, after a considerable time, I came down again, the cushions were all as smooth as in a shop, and Ursula was on her feet offering me a glass of sherry. We maintained these little formalities almost every evening.

That night, as we lay together, it struck me that Ursula herself might have sat, for some reason, first on one sofa then on the other, her usual one.

All the same, Ursula *had* once actually admitted that a man sometimes came to mess about with the clocks; and about six months after the evening I have just described, I was provided with third-party evidence of it. And from what a quarter!

It was young Wally Walters. He is not a man I care for—if you can call him a man. He seems to think the whole suburb has nothing to do but dance to the tune of his flute. He has opinions of his own on everything, and he puts his nose in everywhere—or tries to. He has had a most unfortunate influence on the Parochial Church Council, and the Amateur Dramatic Society has never been the same since he took it over. What is more, I strongly suspect that he is not normal. I saw a certain amount of that during the war, but men who are continually under fire can, I fancy, be excused almost anything. In our suburb, it is still very much objected to, whatever may be the arguments on the other side. Be that as it may, young Walters always greets me when we happen to meet, as he does everyone else, and I have no wish actually to quarrel with him. Besides, it would probably by now be a mistake.

Young Wally Walters never says "Good morning" or "Good evening" in the normal way, but always something more casual and personal, such as "Hello, Joe"—that at the least, and soon he is trying to put his hand on one's arm. He makes a point of behaving as if everyone were his intimate friend.

And so it was that evening—for it was another case of things happening in the evening.

"Hello, Joe," Wally Walters cooed at me as I stepped round the corner of the road into sight of my home. "You're just in time to miss something."

"Evening," I rejoined. Almost always he has something silly to say, and I make a point of refusing ever to rise to it, if only for the simple reason that it is never worth rising to.

"I said you've just got back in time to miss something."

"I heard you say that," I replied, smiling.

But nothing ever stopped him saying his piece, just like the village idiot.

"Great tall bloke with clocks all over him," said Wally Walters. "Man a mile high at least."

I admit that this time it was I who clutched at him. In any case, he was watching me very steadily with his soft eyes, as I have noticed that he seems to watch everyone.

"*Covered* with clocks," he went on. "All up his back and all round his hat. Just as in the song. And pendulums and weights dangling from both hands. He must be as strong in the back and arms as a full-time all-in wrestler. I missed most of his face. Unfortunate. I'd have given a shilling to see all of it. But he was dressed like an old-fashioned undertaker. Wide-brimmed black hat—to carry the clocks, I suppose. And a long black coat—a real, old bedsider, I should call it. Perhaps he *is* a turn of some kind? What do you say? I presume he's a family friend. He came out of your front gate as if he lived there. I say, lay off holding me like an old boa constrictor. I haven't said something out of place, have I?" Of course he said that knowing he had, and knowing that I knew he had.

"Where were *you?*" I asked him, taking my hand off him. I was determined not to over-react.

"Coming out of Doctor Young's. I'm collecting for the Sclerosis, if it interests you, but the doctor's answer was a dusty one."

"Where did the man go?" I asked him, quite calmly and casually; almost, I thought, in his own style.

"You mean, the man with the tickers and tockers?"

Wally Walters was continuing to stare at me in the way I have de-

scribed. I have never been able to decide whether his gaze is as pene-
trating as it seems, or whether it is all somewhat of an act.

I nodded, but concealing all impatience.

"Well," said Wally Walters, "I can tell you this. He didn't go into
any of the other houses that I could see."

"So," I enquired, as offhandedly as I could, "you followed him for
some of the way?"

"Only with my eyes, Joe," he replied with that slightly mocking
earnestness of his. "But my eyes followed him until he vanished. He
wasn't carrying on like the ordinary door-to-door salesman. He
seemed to be making a special call on you. That was why I spoke. Do
you collect fancy clocks, Joe?"

"Yes," I replied, looking clean away from him. "As a matter of fact,
my wife does collect clocks."

"She'll have had the offer of some weird ones this time," responded
Wally Walters. "Bye, Joe." And he sauntered off, looking to right and
left for someone else with whom to pass his special time of day.

I stormed into my house, banging several doors, but failed to find
Ursula all dressed up in the living-room, in accordance with our usual
routine.

I tracked her down in the kitchen, where she was slicing up rhu-
barb, always one of her favourite foodstuffs. "Sorry, darling," she said,
wiping her hands on her apron, and stretching up to kiss me. "I'm late
and you're early."

"No," I replied. "I'm late. I've just missed a visitor."

And, as so often, one of the clocks chose that precise moment to
shout at me. "Cuckoo. Cuckoo." Only I suppose it said it five times, or
six: whichever hour it was.

"Yes," said Ursula, looking away, and not having kissed me after all.
"All the clocks have been adjusted."

I could tell that they had. There was an almost simultaneous clam-
our of booming and screeching from all parts of the house.

"I'm sure that's very useful," I jeered feebly; or I may have said
"helpful".

"It's very *necessary*," Ursula observed calmly, but with more spirit
than usual, at least on this particular subject. It was as if she had
taken a double dose of some quick-acting tonic. That struck me even
at the time. It was as if she were staying herself artificially against my
pryings and probings and general gettings at her. I thought even then
that one could hardly blame her.

And then—a few weeks later, I suppose, or it may have been two or three months—came what the local paper called our "burglary". It was not really a burglary, because, though it happened during the night, virtually nothing was taken. I imagine it was a job by these modern young thugs who just like smashing everything up out of boredom and because they can so easily come by too much money too young; smashing people up too, when the circumstances are right. No one was ever laid by the heels for wrecking our house. It is very seldom that anyone is. The kids cover up for one another against us older people, and especially when we seem to have a bit of property.

Ursula and I were away for the weekend at the time, or of course I should have wakened up and gone after the thugs with a rod and a gun, as our colonel used to put it when urging us on to the slaughter. We had a rule that we went away for one weekend in every four. I thought it was good for Ursula to have a change at regular intervals; a short break away that she knew she could depend on. And I liked to drag her away from her clocks, even though she never seemed quite the same without them. We went to different small hotels in the car— in quiet towns 40 or 50 miles away, or sometimes at the seaside: from the Friday night to the Sunday night. I must acknowledge that often we spent much of the time in bed, paying the extra to have the meals brought up. We never went to stay with friends; partly for that reason, but not only. Staying with friends is seldom much of a relaxation in any direction, I should say.

When I woke that Sunday morning in the hotel, I thought immediately that Ursula looked different. This was even though I could only see her back. I sat up in bed and really peered at her, as she slept with her head turned away from me, and her mouth a little open. Then I realized what I was seeing: there were grey threads in her beautiful blonde hair, and I had never noticed them before because the light had never fallen in quite the right way to show them up. In that very strong early morning sunlight, the grey in Ursula's hair seemed to come even in streaks, rather than merely in threads. The sight made me feel intensely sad and anxious.

Ursula never had trouble with sleeping. It was one of the many, many nice things about her. That morning, as I watched her—for quite a time, I believe—she was deeply sunk; but suddenly, as people do, she not merely woke up, but sat up. She put a hand at each side of her face, as if she saw something horrifying, or maybe just felt it within and around her. Her eyes were staring out of her head, and, what is more, they looked quite different—like the eyes of some other person.

I put my arms round her and drew her down to me, but even while

I did so, I saw that the change in her seemed to go further. The clear, strong, holiday sunshine showed up lines and sags and disfiguring marks that I had never noticed before. I imagine it is a bad moment in any close relationship, however inevitable. I admit that I was quite overcome by it. So sorry did I feel for both of us, and for everybody in the world, that I wept like a raincloud into Ursula's changed hair that would never, could never, be the same again; nor Ursula, therefore, either.

I do not think we should be ashamed to weep at the proper times, or do anything to stop it, provided that we are not in some crowd of people; but that time it did little to make me feel better. Instead, I kept on noticing more and more wrong with Ursula all day; not only with her looks and youthfulness, but with her spirits and behaviour also. She just did not seem the same girl, and I became more and more confused and unsure of myself. I am fairly easily made unsure of myself at the best of times, though almost always I succeed in concealing the fact, apparently to the general satisfaction.

And then, to top it all, when we reached home, we found the scene of ruin I have just referred to. It was quite late, well past eleven o'clock, I am certain; and the very first thing we found was that the lock to the front door had been forced. The young thugs had not even done the usual trick with a piece of plastic. They had simply bashed the lock right through. Of course to do as much damage as possible is always their precise idea—pretty well their only idea, as far as one can see. They had done themselves proud in every room of Ursula's and my home—and done their parents and teachers proud too, and indeed their entire generation. In particular, they had stopped all the clocks— *all* of them (Ursula soon made sure of that); and smashed several of them into pieces that could never be humpty-dumptied again and had to constitute the first clock burial in our garden. Early the next morning I looked after that. The thugs proved to have ripped down the different electric meters—something that is not always too easy to do. I can still hear—and, in a manner, even see—Ursula pitter-pattering in her high heels from room to room in the darkness, and uttering little gasps and screams as she discovered what had been done to her precious clocks, one by one. I doubt whether I shall ever forget it. In fact, I am sure I never shall, as it gave me the first clear and conscious inkling of what was afoot in my home and married life.

After that, the funny man, the expert, was in and out the whole time —trying to make good, to replace. I was hardly in any position to demur, and I am sure his visits were many, but I never saw him once,

nor have I ever tracked down anyone who did at that particular time—
or who will admit to it.

I even sank so low as to *ask* Wally Walters.

I stopped him one bright afternoon as he sauntered along the road
which goes past the new bus sheds. I had even taken trouble to put
myself in his way. He was wearing pale mauve trousers, and a crimson silk shirt, open almost to his navel, showing the smooth skin of his
chest, the colour of peanut butter. I had crossed the road to him.

"Wally," I said, though I have always avoided calling him by that
name. "That funny fellow. You remember?"

He nodded with a slowness that was obviously affected. Already his
soft gaze was on me.

"With all those clocks?" I went on.

"Of course," said Wally Walters.

"Well," I continued with too much of a gasp. "Have you seen him
again?"

"Not I, said the fly. With my little eye I see nothing again. Never
the same thing twice. I should remember that for yourself, Joe. It's
useful."

He paused, very calm, while I fumed. The weather was hot and I
was perspiring in any case. I felt a fool, and that was too plainly what
I was meant to feel.

"Anything else, Joe? Just while the two of us are alone together?"

"No, thank you."

And he strolled off, to nowhere very much, one knew; but cool as an
entire old-fashioned milk dairy.

It was not an encouraging conversation, and it played its part in
further damping down a curiosity that I did not wholly want satisfied
in any case. I continued enquiring as opportunity seemed to offer, but
in most cases the response suggested only that the other party was
embarrassed by my attitude. I failed to find any outside trace of the
man who was now visiting my home so frequently; just as the police
had failed to find a trace of the young thugs.

Not that there was the very slightest doubt about the man being
constantly there. Once, for example, he did an extraordinary thing. I
came home to find that he had allowed one of the clocks to drop its
heavy weight on to the floor so sharply that it had made a hole right
through the boards. Somehow the weight itself had been extricated
before I arrived, and re-suspended; but the hole inevitably remained,
and as poor Ursula was desperately insistent upon its being repaired
as soon as possible, I had to spend most of the next morning standing

over Chivers, our local jobbing builder's man, while he worked, and exercising all of my authority over him.

"Aren't the clocks rather getting out of control?" I asked Ursula sarcastically.

She made no answer, and did not seem to like what I had said.

In general, by now I was avoiding all sarcasm, indeed all comment of any kind. It had become fairly obvious that Ursula was not at all herself.

She had completely failed to recapture her former brightness—and despite the attentions of our curious visitor, as I could not help thinking to myself. And despite the fact too that his ministrations would appear to have gone well, in that what could be repaired had been, and that replacements were all too numerous and clamorous everywhere, assuredly for me. None the less, Ursula looked like a rag, and when it came to her behaviour, that seemed to consist largely in her wringing her hands—literally, wringing her hands. She seemed able to walk from room to room by the hour just wringing her hands. I had never before in my life knowingly seen it done at all, and I found it frightful to watch. And, what was more, when the time came round for our next regular weekend in a country hotel, Ursula refused to go. More accurately, she said, very sadly, that "it would be no use her going".

Naturally, I talked and talked and talked to her. It was a moment of crisis, a point of no return, if ever there was one; but I knew all the time that this was nothing, nothing at all, by comparison with what inescapably and most mysteriously lay ahead for me.

Ursula and I never went away together again. Indeed, we never did anything much, except have odd, low-toned disagreements, seldom about anything that could be defined. I had heard often of a home never being the same again once the burglars have been through it; and that replacements can never equal the originals. But Ursula seemed so wan and ill the whole time, so totally unlike what she had been since I first met her, that I began to suspect there was something else.

It was hard not to suppose there had been some sort of quarrel with the other man, though not so easy to guess what about. Indeed, there seemed to me to be some slight, independent evidence of a row. Previously I was always noticing changes in the positioning and the spit-and-polish of the different clocks; to say nothing of the completely new ones that materialized from time to time. Now, for months, I noticed no changes among the clocks at all, only a universal, stagnant droopiness; and certainly there were no arrivals. I wondered whether the tall fellow had not been peeved about our recent mishap, and perhaps indicated that while he was prepared to put all to rights that once, yet he must make it clear that he could not so do again. He might have taken a critical view of our being away from the house at the time (and, in any case, had we not spent much of that time merely sprawling about in bed?). That might well be why we had never since been out of the house for a single night, nor looked like being ever again out of it. But of course Ursula and I never said one word to each other about any aspect of all this.

That allowed me the more scope for surmise, and I knew quite well that I had more or less accurately assessed much of what was up. I have often noticed in life that we never really *learn* anything—learn for the first time, I mean. We know everything already, everything that we, as individuals, are capable of knowing, or fit to know; all that other people do for us, at the best, is to remind us, to give our brains a little twist from one set of preoccupations to a slightly different set.

In the end, Ursula seemed so run down that I felt she should see a doctor, though my opinion of doctors is low. I know what goes on in my own profession, and see no reason why the medical profession should be any different, by and large. All the same, something had to be done; and in circumstances such as I now found myself in, one clutches. But Ursula positively refused to visit our Doctor Tweed, even though I begged her.

Our little talk on the subject came at the end of a week—at least a week—when we had hardly spoken together at all, let alone done anything else. Ursula was all a dirty white colour; her hair was now so streaked and flecked that everyone would notice it at once; and she was plainly losing weight. She had given up any attempt to look pretty, about which previously she had been so careful, so that I loved her for it. And, as I say, she hardly let fall a word, do what I would. Evening after evening, we just sat hopelessly together listening to the clocks striking all over the house.

Ursula had always had much the same attitude to doctors as mine, which was yet another reason why I loved her. But now that made it difficult to press her on the subject.

She simply said "No," smiled a little, and shook her pretty head. Yes, a pretty head it still was for me, despite changes.

I put my arms round her and kissed her. I knelt at her feet, wept in her lap, and implored her. She still said "No, no," but no longer smiling, no longer moving at all.

So I thought the best thing—the only thing—was to visit Tweed myself.

Of course, it did no good. Tweed simply took his stand upon the official line that he could say nothing without first "examining the patient" herself. When I repeated that she refused to be "examined" (and, truly, I found it hard to criticize her attitude), he actually said with a smile, "Then, Joe, I suspect that she's not really very ill." Tweed calls me Joe, though I call him Doctor Tweed. Of course he is considerably older than I am, and I've known him since I was a boy. I should find it difficult to speak the same language as these new young doctors. I come between the generations, as it were.

I tried to remonstrate. "After all, I am her husband," I cried, "and I'm very worried about her."

"I could examine *you*," said Tweed, fixing me with his eye, only half-humorously.

Obviously it was out of the question even to attempt a description of the strange and oppressive background to it all.

"She's in the grip of some outside power, and it's nearly killing her," I cried. It was all I could get out, and of course it sounded ludicrous.

"Now, Joe," said Tweed, professionally conciliating, but firmly silencing me all the same. "Now, Joe. You make me think that I *ought* to examine you. But I've a better idea. Suppose I make a joint appointment for the two of you, so that I can examine you both? I'm sure your wife will agree to that."

"She won't," I said, like a stubborn schoolboy.

"Oh, you husbands! Have you no authority left? Joe, I'm ashamed of you."

And I think there was a bit more between the two of us along the same lines, but I know that Tweed ended by saying: "Now, of course, I'll see your wife. Indeed, I'd *like* to, Joe. You might tell her that. Then just ring for an appointment almost any day, except Tuesday or Friday."

As I drove away, the idea occurred to me of consulting a quack, a proper quack—one of those people who are not on the medical register, and of whom in every company there are always some who speak so highly.

Then I thought that a consultation with a priest might be another possibility.

So as I wove my way home in the car, I was meditating—though fretting might be a better word—upon which priest or parson I could consult. The difficulty was, of course, that Ursula and I belonged to different faiths, Pope John or no Pope John; and that I had always been excluded from Ursula's creed as fully as from her life with the clocks and their overseer. Moreover, as far as I could see, she had largely allowed the matter to lapse for some considerable time. Ursula's official faith was probably most incompatible with that other preoccupation of hers. And, what is more, I myself was on little more than affable nodding terms with our Church of England vicar. I subscribed to things, and I had a regular classified advertisement in the monthly parish magazine, but that was about all. A home where the religions are mixed always presents problems. And, finally, I could not see an appeal to Ursula to confide in her confessor as likely to achieve more than my appeal to her to confide in Tweed. Ursula was locked up within herself, and the key had either been thrown away or entrusted to one who no longer seemed to be visiting us.

Far from easing my mind in any way, my interview with Tweed had applied a new twist to my torture, and soon my last and desperate expedient of resorting to a priest had begun to seem hopeless. I had so little knowledge of what a priest could be *expected* to do, even, as it were, at the best. By the time I reached home, I was so wrought up as to be quite unfit for driving. Though I never, if I can help it, go more than steadily, I had by then no right, properly speaking, to be on the road at all.

I noticed as I chugged past the clock outside the new multiple store (it is a polygonal clock with letters making a slogan instead of figures), that it was past three o'clock, even though I had not stopped for any kind of lunch. My idea was that I would look in on Ursula fairly quickly, and then make tracks for my neglected office. Ursula knew that I had been to see Tweed, so that something would have to be invented.

Ursula no longer seemed to appreciate the little ceremony of opening the front door to me, so nowadays I used my own key. As soon as I had opened the door that afternoon, the first indication of chaos lay spread before me.

In the hallway had stood, since Ursula and her friend put it there, a tall clock so bedizened and twisted with carved brown woodwork as to have lost all definable outline or shape. Now this object had been toppled, so that its parts and guts were strewn across the hallway floor. I hurriedly shut the outer door, but then stood for several moments taking in the details of the ruin. The entire head of the clock, containing the main part of the mechanism and the dial, had almost broken away from the rest, so that the effect was as if the clock had been strangled. And all over the hallway mat were disgusting pink and yellow pieces from its inside that I knew nothing of.

It was a revolting sight as well as an alarming one and, tense as I had been before even entering the house, I was very nearly sick. But I took a final pull on myself and plunged into the living-room, of which the door from the hallway was already open.

This time there was devastation of another kind: all the clocks had disappeared.

That morning, the last time I had been in the room, there had been no fewer than six of them, and had I not often counted them—in that particular room, at least? Now there were only marks on the wallpaper, faint shadows of all the different heights and breadths—except that, even more mysteriously, there were a few mechanical parts, quite obviously clock parts, scattered across the roses in the carpet. I think they are roses, but I am no botanist.

I gingerly picked up one or two of the scattered bits, small springs and plates and ratchets, and I stood there examining them as they lay in my hand. Then I shouted out "Ursula, Ursula, Ursula," at the top of my bawl.

There was no response from Ursula, nor in my heart had I expected one. But my shouting instantly brought into action Mrs Webber, Mrs Brightside, and Mrs Delft, who had undoubtedly been keenly awaiting some such development. They are three of our neighbours: one each from the houses on either side, and the third from the house immediately opposite. I had been grimly aware for a long time that events in our home must have given them much to talk about and think about. Now they were all three at my front door.

I cannot hope to separate out their mingled narratives.

During the dinner time hour that day, a black van had stopped at our gate. All the ladies were most emphatic about the size of the van: "bigger than an ordinary pantechnicon," one of them went so far as to claim, and the other two agreed with her on the instant. But into this vast vehicle went from my abode only clocks—as far as the ladies could observe; but clock after clock after clock; until the ladies could only disbelieve their eyes. Ursula had done most of the carrying, they said, and "a great struggle" it had been; while the man who came with the van merely stood by, to the growing indignation of my three informants. But then came the heavier pieces, the grandfathers and chiming colossi, and at that point the man did deign to lend a hand, indeed seemed perfectly capable of mastering the huge objects all by himself, entirely alone, without noticeable effort. "He was a great big fellow," said one of the ladies. "As big as his van," agreed another, more awed than facetious.

"How long did it go on?" I put in.

"It seemed like hours and hours, with poor Mrs Richardson doing so much of the work, and having such a struggle."

"Perhaps the man had to look after the stowing?"

"No," they all agreed. "Until near the end he just stood there, twiddling his thumbs." Then two of them added separately, "Just twiddling his thumbs."

At which a silence fell.

I was forced to put the next question into words. "What happened in the end?" I enquired.

In the end, Ursula had mounted the big black van beside the driver and been driven away.

"In which direction?" I asked quite feebly.

They pointed one of the ways the road went.

"We all thought it so strange that we dashed in to one another at once."

I nodded.

"It was as if Mrs Richardson had to fight with the clocks. As if they just didn't want to go. And all the time the man just stood there watching her struggle."

"What do you mean by struggle?" I asked. "You mean that some of the clocks were very heavy and angular?"

"Not *only* that," the same lady replied, perhaps bolder with her words than the others. "No, it was just as if the clocks—or some of the clocks—were fighting back." She stopped, but then looked up at the other two. "Wasn't it?" she said in appeal to them. "Didn't you think it was like that?"

"I must say it looked like it," said one of the others. The third lady expressed no view.

"And did you get the same impression with the big clocks?" I asked the lady who had taken the initiative.

But this time they all replied at once: No, the man having weighed in at that stage, the big clocks had been "mastered" at once, and single-handed.

"What are you going to do?" asked a lady. One can never believe that such a question will be put, but always it is.

I am practised in social situations and after a moment's thought, I produced a fairly good response. "My wife must have decided to sell her collection of clocks. I am not altogether surprised. I myself have been thinking for some time that we had rather too many for the size of the house."

That made the ladies hesitate for a moment in their turn.

Then one of them said, "You'll find it quieter now." She was obviously meaning to be pleasant and sympathetic.

"Yes," I said, smiling, as one does in the office, and when with clients generally. "Quieter for all of us, I suspect." I knew perfectly well how far the din from Ursula's clocks had carried.

"Not that those clocks wanted to leave," repeated the lady who had just now taken the initiative. "You and Mrs Richardson must have given them a good home," she smiled sentimentally.

The other ladies plainly thought this was a point in no need of repetition, and the slight embarrassment engendered facilitated our farewells.

I closed the front door, shot the bolts, and returned to the living-room. Presumably, the spare parts which nestled among the roses on the carpet, had fallen off during Ursula's "struggle". And, presumably, the hideous monster I had just stepped across and through in the hallway had successfully defied even Ursula's thumb-twiddling friend; had defeated him, though at the cost of its own life.

I traversed the entire house, step by step. Every one of the clocks had gone, apart from a scrap or section here and there on the floor; all the clocks but three. Three clocks survived, two of them intact. As well as the monster in the hallway, there remained Ursula's small travelling clock that had accompanied us on our honeymoon. She appeared to have delved it out from its hiding place—and then done no more with it. I found it on our dressing-table, going but not exactly ticking. It never had exactly ticked, of course. But I wondered if it had ever stopped going, even when hidden away for years. There was also the clock that had been left to my mother in old Mr Rosenberg's will: a foursquare, no nonsense, British Midlands model that had always gained at least five minutes in every two hours, so that it was as good as useless for actually telling the time. My mother had fiddled endlessly with the so-called regulator, and I too in my late adolescence, but I have never found the regulators of clocks to give one any more control than do those press-buttons at pedestrian crossings.

I stumped wearily round from room to room and up and down the stairs, assembling all the clock parts into a compact heap on the rosy living-room carpet. I went about it carefully, taking my time; and then I placed the two surviving and intact clocks on top of the heap. Next I unlocked a drawer in my little dressing-room or sanctum and got out my club.

My club was a largely home-made object that had come in remarkably useful for a variety of purposes, including self-protection, during my schooldays. A number of the chaps had things somewhat like it. Since then, I had never had occasion to use my club, though I had always thought that there might again be moments for which it would be exactly the thing—moments, for example, where my home might be invaded from outside at a time when I was within to defend it.

I staggered downstairs once more, worn through to the bone; but not so worn, even then, that I lacked the force to club the heap on the living-room carpet to smithereens, whatever—exactly—they may be. I included the two intact clocks in the carnage. Indeed, I set them in the forefront of the battle. There are no beautiful clocks. Everything to do with time is hideous.

Then I edged the shattered bits into dustsheets and, while the neighbours were possibly taking a rest from watching me, I carried through my second clock burial in the back garden.

When, for three days, there was no sign of or word from my wife, I thought it wise to notify the police.

And now whole weeks have passed.

O Ursula, Ursula.